CW00958161

With love,
Mom & Dad.
XX.

Ed Reardon's
Week

Ed Reardon's Week

CHRISTOPHER DOUGLAS
&
ANDREW NICKOLDS

Scribner

First published in Great Britain by Scribner, 2005
An imprint of Simon & Schuster UK Ltd
A Viacom Company

Copyright © Andrew Nickolds & Christopher Douglas, 2005

This book is copyright under the Berne Convention.
No reproduction without permission.
® and © 1997 Simon & Schuster Inc. All rights reserved.

Scribner and design are trademarks of Macmillan Library Reference USA, Inc.,
used under licence by Simon & Schuster, the publisher of this work.

The rights of Andrew Nickolds & Christopher Douglas to be identified as
authors of this work have been asserted in accordance with sections 77 and
78 of the Copyright, Designs and Patents Act, 1988.

1 3 5 7 9 10 8 6 4 2

Simon & Schuster UK Ltd
Africa House
64–78 Kingsway
London WC2B 6AH

www.simonsays.co.uk

Simon & Schuster Australia
Sydney

A CIP catalogue record for this book is available from the British Library.

If the author has inadvertently quoted from any text or verse in copyright, the
publisher will be pleased to credit the copyright holder in all future editions.

This book is a work of fiction. Names, characters, places and incidents are either a
product of the author's imagination or are used fictitiously. Any resemblance to
actual people living or dead, events or locales is entirely coincidental.

ISBN 0-7432-7633-7
EAN 9780743276337

Typeset in Horley OS by M Rules
Printed and bound in Great Britain by
Mackays of Chatham plc

Threshers, without whose three-for-two Chilean Merlot offer the writing of this book would not have been possible.

Acknowledgements

I would like to thank the editorial staff at Simon & Schuster, but after the sheer thoroughgoing asininity of their suggestions it would not be appropriate.

1

The Swim

Monday

It is the morning of my fifty-second birthday. An age when I no
longer care to receive cards reminding me of it; nonetheless I
am unable to prevent a sudden pang when the postman delivers
nothing but another wheedling appeal for money from a charity.
To compound the felony, the letter claims that the envelope
contains a pen, to facilitate my signing a deed of covenant. It
palpably contains no such thing, even when I check the landing
outside my flat to see if it has fallen out in transit. What way is
that to treat a writer?

No one could deduce that Ed Reardon is fifty-two from scanning the Today's Birthdays column of the *Guardian* or the

The Swim

Telegraph, or the *Independent* in either its vacuous broadsheet or its pocket-sized version for pocket-sized brains. It comes as some small consolation to discover that my brother scribblers, Nick Hornby and Tony Parsons, have been omitted, too, though I have to admit the possibility that it may not be their birthdays.

Being left off the list of the *soi-disant* 'great and good' is an error first perpetrated twenty years ago, and repeated annually since then despite repeated phone messages from 1985 to the relevant newspaper departments, followed by faxes from 1989, e-mails from 1998, a text message with a decidedly unsmiley face last year, and, as of today, a Jiffy Bag filled with the contents of Elgar's litter tray. Never let it be said that Ed Reardon does not keep himself abreast of the latest technology. Although now resident in the Home Counties rather than north London, I like to think I live at the cutting edge, as well as – the felicitous thought occurs to me – above it. The Cutting Edge is the typically asinine punning name of the hairdressing emporium directly below my studio flat, one of many such in this placid Hertfordshire backwater, which according to a sign that greets one upon entering the town has earned Berkhamsted the title of 'Grooming Capital of the South-East'.

I would have checked *The Times*, the *Express* and the *Mail* to see if my humiliating non-appearance in the birthdays' list was complete but for the intervention of my friendly local newsagent.

Let me set the scene for this nasty, brutish and short encounter. As a writer I need to keep *au fait* with the news, be it a bad review accorded a book, play, TV series or film written by one of my temporarily more successful peers, or – an increasing occurrence these days – one of said contemporaries' obituaries, sad to say. Sad by and large, that is. Clearly it is impossible to buy all the newspapers every morning, not that one would want to read them all anyway with their cacophony of 12-year-old columnists putting the world to rights, so I tend to sneak a peep at the newsagent's when his attention is diverted by some sad pensioner fumbling in her purse for the means to purchase fifty scratch cards.

Not that Ed Reardon is a snob about the Lottery, by any means. If there happens to be a rollover on a Saturday and the racing on Channel 4 has yielded even meagre fruits, I am sporting enough to plough my profits back into the gaming industry, happy in the knowledge that my £1 will go some way towards providing a new park for those not fortunate enough to live in the leafy and canal-girt environs of Berkhamsted. I tend to pick the same numbers each time, which have relevance to my current and past life: 3, the number of my former house in Camden Town; 9 (technically 9a), the number of my new domicile; 12, the age of my cat, Elgar; 15, the number of years I have been banned from driving (though when Elgar reaches 15 himself the overlap will necessitate a rethink); 20 and 27, the ages of my children, Jake and Ellie; and 49, my age when I first went in for the Lottery. I am, of course, aware from checking the Lotto and Thunderball numbers on Ceefax twice a week that I could enter the Spanish or US lotteries whose range of numbers would include my present age, but that way gambling fever if not madness lies.

Time was I could lurk outside the newsagent's waiting for the right moment to nip in and browse. But that was before the damnable rise in popularity of the 'phonecard', much patronized by African students, nurses and neurosurgeons who need to ring home cheaply. The garish advertisements for 'Freedom', 'Go Bananas' and 'Yes!' card tariffs are now plastered over every inch of the window where once there were merely innocent postcards for violin and French lessons, making it impossible to see in. Accordingly I had to take a chance and hope that the newsagent was occupied helping an old dear manoeuvre her tartan shopping trolley among the stacks of pre-viewed Chuck Norris DVDs.

My optimism was short-lived, as I heard the dread sound behind me.

'Are you going to buy any of those papers?'

'No, I'll just take a copy of the local freesheet. *Suburbo* – honestly, what 12-year-old genius came up with that?' I added witheringly, hoping to elicit a smile from a man who after all was self-employed like myself and had time to watch life passing by and remark upon its vicissitudes.

Chummy wasn't biting. 'That's "35p Where Sold", mate.'

Now being called 'mate', especially as part of a reprimand from somebody who doesn't even know me, is something to which I take particular exception. I didn't accept it from London cabbies in the days when I could afford taxis, rounding my tip downwards accordingly, and I don't accept it now from the likes of the infant assistant in Threshers, when I find myself a few pence short of the wherewithal for a bottle of barley wine. Especially now they seem to have discontinued that excellent 'Help yourself to small change' scheme whereby spare coppers would be left in an ashtray on the counter; another example of so-called progress.

Happily, satisfaction presented itself almost immediately after I asked for a tin of Beef and Heart Whiskas, then made the nylon-jacketed churl reach up to the shelf again to get the 'In Jelly' tin because, as I correctly pointed out, the 'In Gravy' one goes everywhere. The pencil perched behind his ear fell satisfyingly to the floor, which gave me the chance to glance at the main story in the pile of 'freesheets' (*sic*) on the counter. 'I see from the new *Suburbo* that "Giant Asda Plan Spells Death Knell Threat for Local Shops". A mixed metaphor, but quite effective. Oh dear.'

'Forty-seven p, mate.'

'Thank you, *mate*. Good morning – or is it goodbye!'

Energized by this encounter, I was ready for my daily fifty-length pre-lunch swim. Some take their 'lifestyle lessons' from the politburo of inanity otherwise known as daytime television. I take mine from the Greeks – those from fourth-century BC Athens, that is, not Nick and Chris who run The Cutting Edge underneath me. You would not want to take a lesson from those two in anything, apart perhaps from where to buy faded, framed colour photos of Cyprus. Like the ancients, I find that daily vigorous exercise keeps the physique within its allotted waistband and the writing-muscle toned. Moreover, I am on something of a roll with the lockers at the Berkhamsted Sports Centre, it being now more than three weeks since I last encountered a faulty door-lock and was obliged to unload everything all over again and wander around the changing room in search of a safe haven shedding items from my bundle of shoes, cords, underpants, loose change, etc. like some latter day Mother Courage.

I have also been basking in the glory of victory after getting one back at the sickeningly genial one-legged swimmer with his infuriating catchphrase 'Dropped something there, mate.' After Smiler shuffled away from the row of clothes hooks last Thursday, I waited till he got to the exit before saying in a voice loud enough to carry – yet soft enough to convey complete lack of concern – 'I think you've left your towel behind.' Being able to ignore his 'Cheers mate' was one of the most satisfying moments in my athletic career, and one I think Phidipides himself might have envied.

But the laurels of victory soon lose their lustre and locker-room triumphs, however glorious, do not get one mentioned in the Today's Birthdays columns of the broadsheets. My mind, therefore, was troubled as I checked my rucksack for clean socks, trunks, shampoo and Bic razor (to do the neck below the beard line). If Ed Reardon's fifty-third birthday is to feature in twelve months' time then bull's horns must be grabbed, bullets bitten and bestsellers written.

So I sat down on the sofa, sparked up the meerschaum and, in order to aid my concentration further, switched on the cricket from Auckland. During a forty-five minute rain break, which I used to put the post-dated Egg and Barclaycard cheques in the wrong envelopes, it occurred to me that only in the world of cricket are so many household names provided with so many free meals in return for so little effort. The thought was father to the strategy but, after being told by both Middlesex and

Northamptonshire County Cricket Clubs that they were sorry but they had no plans to take on any new players at present, I put in a call to my agent to try to sting him for lunch. And possibly tea.

'My dear fellow! How lovely to talk to you! How's life up in the Faeroe Islands or wherever it is you've moved to?'

Felix Jeffrey, my sole representative on this earth, continues the proud tradition of literary agents in that he has never knowingly read beyond the first page of a book and rarely strays outside SW1 for anything other than adulterous purposes. He is tirelessly vague about his clients' current circumstances and finds it hard to accept that anything of significance occurs beyond the confines of the congestion zone. It is true that one does not have to fork out £8 to drive through Berkhamsted (and over its 7,500 speed bumps) but the town is, as its relentlessly upbeat newspapers are forever boasting, the fastest growing property market in Europe. This is, of course, a euphemism for 'the fastest growing chip on its shoulder about anything to do with London'.

Nevertheless Berko's range of writers' conveniences is mighty impressive, as I pointed out to Felix perhaps a little defensively. There is the aforementioned Threshers perfectly positioned between here and the station, the pool, of course, which means I am hardly likely ever to fall sick (except perhaps as a consequence of a superbug picked up at the pool), the Blockbuster in the High Street, etc. And I live less than four hundred yards from a bus that whisks me in twenty minutes to the Asda in Watford, with its fastest falling pipe-tobacco and Bulgarian Cab-Sauv prices in Europe.

'Well, there you are you see, you've stolen a march on us again,' said Felix. 'I wish I had the courage to uproot, instead of being stuck in Knightsbridge.'

The ill-concealed slight says much about the murderous envy that middle-aged men feel when one of their contemporaries manages to cut loose from the domestic yoke and set himself up in bachelor splendour – even though, strictly speaking, it was my wife Janet who did most of the unyoking. And the cutting too, come to think of it, as I don't think there was a tie unslashed in the wardrobe after the bill for a five-bottle lunch with my old friend, Ted Cartwright, unfortunately showed up on her credit card statement. Then came the discovery of the barley wine supply in the Wendy house and that was pretty much closing time for our marriage. No matter, I'm a free man – and they hate me for it.

'Well, it's been wonderful to talk to you, Ed. Love to the family.'

'Thing is Felix, I've got a lot of ideas to run past you – idea number one, it's nearly thirty years since *Who Would Fardels Bear?* was published—'

'Who would what?'

'*Fardels Bear*. My first novel. Published in 1976 – "Like a cold bucket of water in this hot summer" as the *Sunday Times*—'

'Good lord – have we been together that long? How dreadful!'

'God, isn't it. Anyway I was thinking about an anniversary reissue. Then there's the *Tenko* film idea and I don't think we've yet done full justice to the matter of Ted Cartwright's liver transplant.'

'I can see the way your mind's working, Ed, and I like it. We must have lunch. Why aren't we having lunch now for heaven's sake? I must fire my secretary – in fact, I'll fire all my secretaries, idle clutch of floozies. Now tell me, how's that lovely wife of yours?'

Tuesday

A lunch with Felix booked in for tomorrow meant it was vital to get in a hundred lengths at the pool, as a prophylactic measure against the orgy of excess that he insists on inflicting on his favoured clients. However, by the time I'd scrubbed the mud off my best cords with a wire brush, sewn a button on to the Tattersall check shirt and given the oxbloods a polish it was three o'clock in the afternoon, and bang on time the post came through the letterbox.

I was overwhelmed to receive, amongst the pizza vouchers and a small sachet of dishwasher powder, birthday presents from my ex-wife and children, only a day late – a display of affection rivalling the book token that arrived three weeks after my heart attack.

The gift list was as follows:
1. From She Who Would Slash my Neckwear: one copy of *Eats, Shoots & Leaves* by Lynne Truss.

2. From my daughter, Ellie, who has apparently experienced a similar breakdown of communication with her mother to the one I did: *Eats, Shoots & Leaves* by Lynne Truss.

3. From my son Jake, currently studying 'Literary Theory' (but apparently not the practice) at East Northumberland University (formerly Cleveland College of Sheep-Rogering): a Post-it note saying 'Hapy Birthday Dad' attached to a copy of . . . well, it wearies me even to press the 'copy' and 'paste' buttons on the keyboard. Suffice it to say it was also by Madame Truss.

Shooing Elgar off the calculator, it was the work of a moment to reckon that, at current rates of royalty, la rebarbative Truss was some £3.75 better off as a result of the outbreak of sentiment among my family. Whose bloody birthday is it, hers or mine? I asked myself before hurling the punctuator's bible (the one that Janet gave me as a matter of fact) across the room on to the dining table and thence by a sort of Barnes Wallis process through a pane in the front window, necessitating an emergency visit from my friendly local glazier's. Or is it glazierses'? Wherever he places his apostrophe, his late arrival meant I had to forgo the swim.

'Lot of books here, mate.'

'Yes.'

'Did you write 'em all?'

'No.' (I could have gone on, as my study alone must have contained upwards of 4000 books, and not even 'Lord' Jeffrey Archer could have turned out that many in his career, pretend to have done so though he no doubt would. But I didn't.)

'Bet you wish you'd written this one though!' he said, brushing shards of glass off the defenestrated Truss. 'Changed my life, I'll tell you that. Turned out I'd been using the semicolon incorrectly for years!'

For that he was given a cup of tea with only one sugar in it. Full stop.

Wednesday

While searching for my Berkhamsted Sports Centre Over-50s pass in the pockets of my yellow cords prior to the morning swim, I discovered as well as the 'Berk Card', the unstamped return half of a train ticket to London, valid at peak times. Heartened by this good omen I decided I could skip the swim for once and set off at 8.32 for lunch with my agent. This, however, turned out to be a misnomer on both counts.

I was unaware of the events to come as I entered the pub chosen for our rendezvous, a crowded central London establishment that could only be described as loathsome. Or non-smoking to be more specific. Stowing my pipe with some reluctance, I made my way in search of Felix among hordes of loud 12-year-old office workers secure for the time being in their salaries, all of them risking heart disease by gorging themselves on very long sausages on very small plates, lasagne sporting a deep perma tan from the hot bar lights or ploughman's lunches – though needless to say the nearest any of them had been to a plough was the one in outer space.

Standing out from this grey-suited miasma was a very tooth-some young thing indeed. Though she drew admiring glances from the stubbled youths who stood aside to let her pass, it was clear she had eyes for only one man in the room. A moment to savour.

'Mr Reardon? Hi – I'm Ping.'

Though her name might have suggested otherwise, there was nothing remotely Chinese about Ping, although as some small talk established while we were waiting to be served with our 'Buy 2 glasses of Shiraz and get the bottle free before 12.30' offer, she had visited that country while backpacking after what she called Yooni and what I would call Balliol, Oxford. It was clear that Ping possessed brains as well as beauty, though as is the convention among youngsters today, she did her best to conceal it behind an unlovely array of slang, half-words and glottal stops.

'That's very clever of you – how did you recognize me?'

'You're carrying a copy of your nov. We handled the publishing deal, yeah? It must be quite valuable – there can't be many left in circ now.'

'This is true,' I said, putting the slight down to the unwitting cruelty of youth. 'But as I said to Felix, this year is the thirtieth anniversary of *Who Would Fardels Bear?*, so we might be able to persuade the publishers to reissue—'

'Right, yeah, I'm not sure they still do fiction,' said Ping. 'Those guys are more Second World War and erotic massage books these days.' A small smear of deep crimson Shiraz had appeared beneath her lower lip and I had to resist the strong temptation to dab it gently away for her. Such a moment of familiarity would no doubt coincide with the arrival of Felix and be greeted with a laughing cry of 'Leave my PA alone you dirty old pervert!'

'Oh oh oh – Felix says sorry by the way.'

'What for?'

'Not being able to make it. Actually what he said was "Je suis désolé", but he'd just come off the phone yeah, talking to Thierry Henry about his new thriller.'

'How's that going?' I said. What I was thinking was, I have this lissom creature to myself for the next four hours. And possibly longer if I play my cards right. Always assuming I can first get the cellophane off the pack.

'It's going to be a monster. I wrote the proposal, yeah?'

It was time to deal. 'I wish they'd put you on the cover. I'd buy it. I'd buy a dozen copies. Better than that ruddy punctuation woman.'

'Um – that's a compliment, right?'

Emboldened, I took a tissue that I had saved from the purchase of my tall (i.e. small) latte on the train and dabbed away the mark from that divine lower lip. The burst of sunshine that was Ping's grateful smile lit up the room, and my heart was lost.

'Well now – should we have a couple more drinks here or head straight for a martini or three at the Caprice?'

Ping frowned, and the sun from the paragraph before last went straight back in again. 'Actually, Mr Reardon, would you mind if we ate here? You see, I've only been allocated £17.50 for this lunch. Though we could always share a starter.'

So there it was. I had been downsized or outsourced or

13

whatever non-word the twelve-year-olds are using these days for being thrown on the scrapheap. Unceremoniously, and without even a black bin liner to protect me from rats and scavenging seagulls pecking away at my rotting entrails. As far as my agent was concerned, henceforth Ed Reardon's career journey would be made on board a no-frills airline.

Naturally enough, being a professional I made the best of it. Though I can't remember trying to make myself comfortable on a barrel since my old school production of *Treasure Island*. 'E. F. Reardon's Squire Trelawney effortlessly achieves an aristocratic disdain' – *The Salopian*, 1968. It was my first review, which I still have somewhere.

Even though the third glass of Shiraz was beginning to take its insidious and soporific effect, I was still sufficiently in control of my senses to persevere with the real reason behind this meeting, viz. getting my name back in the Today's Birthdays list between Paul Reaney, retired soccer player, and Merlyn Rees, retired Home Secretary. Ed Reardon on the other hand was very much an active volcano as Ping, toying with her half of the terrine, was about to realize.

'I see from my newspaper that the film that was based on *Who Would Fardels Bear?* is coming out on – DDV, is it?'

I had opened an unwelcome floodgate. 'Oh yeah – *Sister Mom*! I saw it last night! And I'm like "Wow – what a great movie this is!" Because I wasn't even born when it first came out! And I'd always heard *Sister Mom* was one of Jaz Milvane's seminal early works – he's just so brilliant! He's one of our clients, did you know that, Ed?'

'Yes.'

The ubiquitous Jaz Milvane. My nemesis, a constant thorn in the Reardon side and, of course, while he's in a position to offer me work, one of my oldest and dearest friends. I tried to put the girl right without sounding in any way bitter about what in my opinion had been a thorough botch-up, a sensitive novel in the tradition of Arnold Bennett turned into a Sally Field weep-fest.

'Well yes, I suppose he did a reasonable job – it was his first film not made for television, and really he only got it because somebody dropped out and I suggested Jaz – he was a good mate, still is, talk a couple of times a week, we still play in a band together for God's sake. You should come and hear us—'

Ping, however would not be deterred from her paean of praise to Los Angeles' current favourite schmaltzmeister.

''Cos my ex-partner, yeah, did his PhD thesis on Milvane's Hollywood oeuvre – it's being published this autumn, "All That Jaz", I'll send you a copy . . . and he was like "You *must see this movie*" . . .'

'Well, now you have. So anyway, Ping, I was thinking that in view of all the brouhaha about Jaz in the weekend magazines and so forth, now might be the time to talk to Felix about a new edition of *Who Would Fardels Bear?*, with a picture of Sally Field and – why not – the 6-month-old Scarlett Johansson on the cover—'

'Or Ricky Gervais,' said Ping thoughtfully. 'We put him on a lot of books.' What she said next floored me completely and I fell in love with the girl all over again.

15

'I hope you don't mind me saying this, Ed – but I love your work . . .'

'You're very kind. I'll admit I wasn't totally displeased with *Who Would Fardels Bear?*.'

'No – *Jane Seymour's Household Hints*. I really thought you got Jane there.'

As before my infatuation lasted for about five seconds, which I suppose is all a man of my age can realistically expect. At times like this I imagine what my illustrious predecessors might have said in the same situation. Graham Greene, of course, formerly a resident of Berkhamsted himself, would merely have laughed it off, describing a previous hack job as 'an entertainment'. Ed Reardon had no such excuse. *Jane Seymour's Household Hints* had rescued me from a tricky domestic problem, providing the deposit on my new flat when the alternative was sleeping rough in the shed at the bottom of the garden of my ex-house.

I thought it wise not to convey any of this just yet, at least until Ping and I knew each other better.

'Well – it's all writing isn't it, if you're a true professional. I like to think some of Jane rubbed off on the novel I had to put aside at the time.'

'Sadly I didn't see your episode of *Tenko*,' said Ping, and give the girl her due, she sounded as if she meant it. 'But *The Brands Hatch Story* – whoa, that book was so real it was like actually being in the pits with Damon Hill.' This was possibly because I had copied most of it out of Damon Hill's *History of Formula One*, but again I chose not to disabuse Ping when she was in such flattering mode.

Wednesday

'So when it came to restructuring the clients list I'm like, can I have Ed Reardon please?'

This called for another bottle and further exploration of Ping's promising phrase '*ex*-partner'. Since the benighted pot-house was next door to Felix's agency I guessed that he would not only be a regular but that he would also, crucially for my purposes, have a tab. I challenged the barman to scour his cellars for something that wasn't 'oak-aged' to the consistency of Vegemite and charged it to Mr Jeffrey's account. I could tell by the way Ping pretended to check her text messages while all this was going on that she was impressed by an act of freeloading that would have been creditable in a writer half my age. It seemed a suitable moment to capitalize on the advantage gained by outlining my views on the decline in public service broadcasting – a trenchant credo which, though I says it as shouldn't, improves with every outing, and it duly left her temporarily speechless.

Television may, as I said, be dumbed down to the point of imbecility but one has to eat. So I outlined my most commercial idea of the moment – or 'product' as they call it in their charmingly philistine way. Essentially, *Bouquet of Bamboo* would be a mini-series developed from *Tenko* and exploring the burgeoning sexual attraction between a group of Englishwomen and their Japanese prison guards after the war. Erotic, good to look at and offering ample opportunity for fusion cookery (tofu turnovers, etc.) – all the things that British TV does best. However, I could tell that my pitch was not going well. Ping took a sip of wine and changed the subject.

'I preferred the Shiraz, actually. Thing is, there's something come in that we think has Ed Reardon written all over it.'

'Right,' I said, looking non-committal while clinging on to the hope that it might be a repeat fee.

'*Pet Peeves.*'

Pet Peeves indeed! Are there no depths of alliterative asininity to which the Morlocks of Television Centre will not stoop? Another vet series for heaven's sake. Just what we all need with the earth, the environment, politics, religion, manners, indeed the whole shooting match, heading rapidly for oblivion!

'All right, Ping. We're both realists. How many episodes do they want?'

'It's a book. Silk Purse want to do it. They're really good people, Ed. We worked with them on the Thierry Henry thriller and the *Little Book of Big Willies* which was mega for them. Basically the brief is: celeb cats and dogs grumbling about their owners. What does the Downing Street moggy really think about Cherie Blair?'

'Just cats and dogs?' I asked, out of politeness.

'No – rabbits, hamsters, whatever. You're the author. Could even be a fun chapter by an Aussie insect about what it's like to be eaten by Janet Street-Porter. It's so you.'

Fortunately the prospect of spending six months in this anthropomorphic hellhole was so deeply repugnant that it wasn't difficult to turn down. It doesn't always happen like that. Sometimes – as was the case when I couldn't decide whether to accept the £1,450 commission fee for *The Brands*

Wednesday

Hatch Story – one lies awake at nights on a mate's floor in an agony of uncertainty. *Pet Peeves* was not such an instance.

'Sorry, Ping. I'm afraid I'm not your man.'

'We need someone who can turn it round in six weeks.'

'I'm sure you'll find that someone.'

'For two grand.'

Among the many benefits of maturity is an understanding that compromise doesn't necessarily mean a total surrender of dignity and manhood, so bowing to the inevitable I asked the barman to bring us a bottle of Shiraz.

'Actually, Ed, I better get back to the office.'

'But I've ordered now. It's your favourite. Can't drink it on my own, now can I?'

I cleave to the heretical belief that Shiraz is not a wine – it's a syrup designed for twelve-year-olds looking to move on from the glue-sniffing stage but who aren't quite ready for the restrained sophistication of cranberry and banana alcopops. However, a job is a job and a book is a book – or rather a 'berk' as the new received pronunciation has it. So we toasted the success of *Pet Peeves*, an assuredly 'gerd berk' and sure-fire winner – though probably not of the Whitbread.

One bottle led to another. Life stories were exchanged, confidences breached, a hotel room booked for the afternoon, lips locked in the taxi, and we made love in a feverish yet strangely detached author–agent relationship way . . . or so I was in the process of imagining when the ironclad cleaning lady of Caribbean provenance woke me up by poking me with her mop.

'You gotta wake up darlin'. Euston Station facilities closin' now.'

A humiliating, perhaps, but not entirely hopeless end to a seventeen-hour visit to the capital. After all, in the plus column I had a commissioned book to write, I hadn't had to pay for my lunch and the policeman who escorted me from the station lavatory at 2 a.m. – after an admittedly overharsh exchange with Momma Mop – was far from the uniformed thug of popular myth. He restored my baguette, my miniature of barley wine and with them my faith in human kindness which had been somewhat shaken by Ping's indifference to her client's urgent biological needs. I explained that I was in the process of writing a book so commercial it could knock the *Little Book of Big Willies* from its lofty position next to the checkouts, and into the remainder bin where it deserved to rot, detumesce and moulder.

'Looking forward to it, Sir,' said the kindly officer. 'Don't forget your shoe.'

Thursday

No contract for *Pet Peeves* yet. The thoroughgoing inefficiency of these people really takes the breath away. I imagine it's just the same for Thierry Henry, and that even now he's at the training ground, running backwards and fuming about what it would be like if he took a leaf out of his agent's book and only made an appearance in the Tottenham Hotspurs defence (or whatever it is) as and when he chose! But in a charitable spirit of onwards and upwards I decided to swim off my mood of frustration, not to mention the aftereffects of last night's excess and the circuitous minicab ride home from Watford, which took care of most of the £30 I was obliged to borrow from Ping. Matey with the A to Z did, however, leave me with enough for both a swim and a sauna provided I hit the Over-50s 10–11 a.m. window, otherwise patronizingly known as the Grey Sharks Zone.

Shooing Elgar off the bathers I reflected on how my attitude has changed towards finding cat hairs all over my clothes. Like my previous feline companions – Gorbachev, Pasolini, dating back to Pete and Dud in the 1960s – Elgar unerringly makes for the pile of laundered clothes on the bed or chair and settles down for the day thereon. This used to be an irritant, a 'pet peeve' indeed, but I have now come to look on it as both an economy and an efficiency measure, harnessing nature to provide a handy way of getting the ironing done and freeing me up for work or exercise.

I was on my way out of the flat with my swimming togs in a Selfridges carrier bag (to show that I have a life outside Berkhamsted) when the telephone rang.

I think it is worth putting on record my method of dealing with subsequent events to demonstrate that it is possible for the resourceful if temporarily impecunious author to turn a potentially sticky situation, if not to advantage, then at least to buffing up his self-esteem.

'Oh how stupid of me,' I said to the offensively polite Asian voice on the other end of the line. 'I know what's happened – I must have put the Barclaycard cheque in your envelope and your cheque in theirs – all my baskets in one Egg eh?!' (a touch of humour which was greeted with silence). 'I do apologize – so what shall I do, wait till you send me another bill in a month or so, or . . . What do you mean you've paid it in? So you and Barclaycard are in the habit of paying in each other's cheques are you, just like that? Well that's all very cosy I must say!'

This was a bit of a facer, I had to admit. I am by now well past the jejune stage of 'forgetting' to sign my name on cheques or putting last year's date on cheques posted in January, February or even March, and I like to think that any half-intelligent accounts department coming across a cheque in the wrong envelope will conclude that this was an inadvertent mis-take brought about by my impossibly busy schedule. But apparently not, and I now had the prospect of the next few days' mail bringing not one but two notifications of bounced cheques with their concomitant £27.50 fines. Lynne Truss would have to sell a mere twenty or so books to cover that, a slow royalties day in other words, but Ed Reardon had no such comfortable back-up. The unfairness of it all suddenly hit me and I turned the verbal temperature up a notch, secure in the knowledge that my interlocutor in his Pacific Rim call centre was unlikely to come round and get me.

'So you gang of usurers all get together to decide whether or not I eat next week, is that the way it works? Well, it just serves you right if it has bounced! Good morning to you, or whatever time it is there in Bangalore!'

Mindful as I was that at the pool the Grey Sharks 'window' was rapidly closing, it was nevertheless time for the worm to turn, before Barclaycard's call centre rang with their own all-too-predictable complaint. It was the work of a few moments to find a suitable piece of music – Stockhausen's Concerto for Helicopter just getting the vote over the free Harrison Birtwistle CD that fell out of the *Guardian* a few Saturdays back. Then, with the help of a small piece of sellotape placed over the gap on the back of the Naxos cassette I was able to record my own voice before the start of the (it must be said) industrial cacophony.

'Thank you for calling Ed Reardon. All our operators have gone for a swim, but your call is important to us, so please continue to hold . . . beep!'

Honour satisfied, I went out whistling. And a damn sight more tunefully than anything my creditors would have to put up with on my answering machine. I arrived at the pool with a good two minutes to spare after breaking into a trot for the last half-mile. What's more I had brought with me the exact change to facilitate fast entry. Not that this cut any ice whatsoever with the 12-year-old receptionist behind the counter, who demanded of me another 30p.

'But it's not eleven o'clock – I'm still in the Grey Sharks Zone,' I said, resenting wasting valuable not to say short breath on the idiotic slogan, only to be informed that the price band for Grey Sharks was now £2.50, that the facility was under something called 'the ow-spiss-ees' of AquaSplashLeisure and that the tariffs had risen that morning in accordance with the upgrade in customer care. To which end she handed me a laminated safety notice, which I was invited to read.

'"Due to the nature and use of the changing rooms, the floor may be wet." What, you carry out blood transfusions in there now, do you? Or maybe make some dangerously wayward soup?'

The irony, and the raised eyebrow and scratching of the beard just under the chin that accompanied it, were of course lost on her. 'No, it's to ensure that our customers realize that they enter the changing village entirely at their own risk. So that's another 30p please.'

My plea that I only had with me the previously correct money was met with the advice that I could always wait till 'Turtle Time' at 8.30 that evening. There was nothing else for it but to surrender my 50p for the locker to make up the shortfall, knowing that I risked running the gauntlet of Douglas Bader swimming his wretched one-legged lengths as I carried my clothes and shoes out of the 'village' and along the side of the pool.

'I'm really sorry, but you've missed the Grey Sharks Zone now and it's Mid-Morning Mellow Out. That'll be another 75p.'

I bade the girl good day and, ignoring her invitation to fill in a Customer Satisfaction Questionnaire, turned on my heel and made a dignified exit. Or I would have done but for taking a bit of a purler on the wet floor.

Never one to let the creative juices stagnate, I was able to put the extra hour at my disposal to good use, embellishing and updating my lecture notes. The rewarding thing about teaching is that you get paid. Unlike the world of publishing where they dole out the writer's groats as and when it suits them, teach an evening class and you get £15, in your hand, at the end of three hours. I believe that when one has reached a certain stage in one's profession it's important to put something back, so I regularly run a creative writing course at the University of the Third Age, in the same sports centre as it happens as the swimming 'facility'. The girl on the desk had long since gone home (or had, I rather hoped, been fired for sheer asininity) and thus missed my professorial entrance as I swept through the security barrier with my staff pass and went up to the fourth floor where my class was panting with enthusiasm – and exhaustion, as once again the lift was out of order, which always takes a useful ten minutes out of the teaching schedule.

'. . . And if I've learned one thing during my long career, be it in movies, television or the bitch goddess radio it's this – and I want you all to write this down – Write What You Know, and Nobody Knows Anything.'

'That doesn't make sense, dear,' came a voice from the back.

Every teacher knows the feeling, be it in one of our higher halls of learning or in a noisome comprehensive school on one of the sink estates that feature every evening in the local news bulletins, that his or her words are falling on deaf ears. Perhaps not quite as deaf as the pupils in my class, consisting as it does of three (five when the course started) pensioners who yet retain all the characteristics of naughty schoolchildren, sitting at the back where the table-tennis tables have been stacked and barracking at every opportunity. Tonight's lesson – 'Sell that Screenplay!' – as usual proved to be no easy ride.

'So the phone rings again and it's the producer. In tears.

"Ed – the Fardels movie's gone tits up" – jugs up as they say over there—'

'Does he have to swear so much?'

'Yes, he does – that's part of it.'

Presumably these same senior citizens would be going home after the class to turn on their TV sets and have their oh-so-sensitive ears assaulted by some foul-mouthed celebrity chef, without even turning a hair. But I let it pass. '"The director's dropped out, Lindsay Anderson's playing silly buggers . . . can you help us out Ed, we're desperate?" Well, who should happen to be on my floor, passed out drunk I might add, but a certain young TV director called Jaz Milvane. That's right – Jaz Milvane. You may have heard of him. Anyway, big friend, still talk· two or three times a day *at least*. I said, "Wake up, matey, do you want to direct a movie?" So. Moral of story?'

'Are you saying you have to get drunk and lie on the floor?'

This came from Stan, the one man in the group. He'd once confided to me during the coffee break that he hoped to be the next Arthur Miller. Nothing at all wrong with that, I'd replied, a model writer to emulate – without realizing that what Stan really wanted was to be thirty-five years younger, over six feet tall and married to Marilyn Monroe, without it seemed being prepared to put in the hours that had produced *Death of a Salesman*, a play to which I had also lent my presence at school ('E. F. Reardon's Biff is an only too plausible portrait of futility and wasted effort').

'Yes, but more importantly – be in the right place at the right time.'

'What, drunk on the floor?'

This produced an easy laugh from 'the girls' as Stan liked to call them.

'I don't know, 75p for this?' said Pearl. 'And look at these biscuits. I'd rather have a swim.'

My extensive knowledge of literature, for which I make no apology despite its deep unfashionability these days among supposedly clever people, has taught me that there is always a troublemaker in any educational establishment – the names Flashman, Billy Bunter and William Brown spring to mind. My own particular bugbear was Pearl, a woman who gave every indication of only coming to my class because it was warmer inside than out. Luckily there tends also to be a shining-eyed counterbalance to the awkward squad, a pupil whose thirst for knowledge is undiminished by the rabble around them. Such an eager learner was Olive, who seemed genuinely keen to absorb everything she could from my years of experience, in her touching quest to become a writer.

'But I don't begrudge Jaz one penny of his success, and you know why?'

'No,' said Olive, pencil poised.

'Because your Hollywood directors might have their flash cars and their personal assistants, and their speedboats and their houses in Notting Hill and Malibu and their use of Johnny Depp's place in St Moritz or wherever the bloody hell it is—'

'Gstaad,' said Stan.

'No, that's Beyoncé you're thinking of,' said Pearl, the mental *Hello* magazine Rolodex flicking over behind her bovine eyes. 'It's Chamonix.'

I arrived at my peroration undeterred. 'But you, me – we're the lucky ones. Because writers are the genuinely rich people in this business.'

'Why are you stood there in your tracksuit then? Can't you afford a tie?'

Ignoring Pearl, I walked across to the VCR machine, a moment I looked forward to every week almost as much as collecting my brown envelope containing £15.

'Well we've still got an hour left, so bearing in mind all I've taught you this evening, let's just have another look at my episode of *Tenko*.'

The usual chorus of disapproval from Pearl and Stan, which I half-believed they rehearsed in the tea-bar before the class:

'We know it by heart by now, dear! Plink clink bong bong!'

'Why couldn't he write *Minder*? Or *Heartbeat*?'

'I like *Monarch of the Glen*.'

Olive, I noted, merely put on her other glasses, intelligently awaiting what repeated viewings convince me is a modern television classic.

'So while I'm trying to get this thing to work, does anybody have any more questions?'

'Have you ever met Lynne Truss?'

Et tu, Olive.

'Yeah, she's good,' said Stan. 'And she's got a bob or two.'

'And she didn't get it by resorting to foul language either,' said Pearl, putting her hat on. 'I think I'll get the earlier bus.'

Friday

Bending down at the front door to put on my shoes en route to the pool, I am hit quite hard on the back of the head, not by the contract for *Pet Peeves* coming through the letter box, which would have made the blood from the cut sufferable, but by a returned manuscript. *Ed Reardon's Little Book of Publishers' Rejections* has been turned down on the grounds that 800 pages is too long for that last-minute impulse buy, and supposedly would make it 'difficult for customers to get to the till' as it says on what I will now have to call page 801.

Being obliged to apply a plaster to a publisher-inflicted flesh wound in an inaccessible place was irritating in the extreme – and as I was forced to admit as I attended to myself in the bathroom mirror and tried to make my hands move the other way, it was probably the first time I'd missed having my ex-wife, Janet, around in two years. But that was nothing compared to the annoyance which was to come.

'My castaway this week is probably Britain's most successful export and arguably the best film director of all time. The irony being that if he hadn't turned his talents to the big screen I'd probably have been introducing the world's greatest trumpeter—'

'You promised you wouldn't say that, Sue.'

Oh the nauseating flirtatiousness of it! It was bad enough that Jaz Milvane had conned his way on to *Desert Island Discs* by virtue of a clutch of saccharine uplifting films, I'm sorry, *feel-good movies*. Far worse was the simpering giggly tone of his interviewer, a sure sign that Jaz had soft-soaped himself into the affections of a woman whom I confess I had admired from afar since her days reporting traction engine rallies in the West Country on *Nationwide*.

I doubt I am the first person to compile a list of eight favourite records for an imaginary appearance on *Desert Island Discs*. Though I am equally sure few could match the sheer eclectic breadth of my selections. After many years of honing said list, also my combined book and luxury (wine boxes disguised as a set of Dickens), I was on the point of committing it to my journal for future generations to enjoy, in the event of these *pensées* being published. But then a casual look at the new offering by Nick Hornby at Luton Airport – my flight to Norway for the prestigious Trondheim Literary Festival being delayed by an unforgivable fourteen hours – revealed that this self-professed writer had dared to produce a book consisting of nothing *but* lists of favourite music. Ed Reardon is by no means a plagiarist, much less a bald one, and so the secret of my eight selections must die with me because (as will soon be made clear) after the way today's events developed I am unlikely ever to be invited on to the programme itself.

'But then came the movie that put you on the international map, *Sister Mom*.'

'God bless it.'

'How did that come about, Jaz?'

Oh yes, Jaz, do tell. And don't forget to mention how you had the original author barred from the set (and even more cruelly, the catering wagon) out of sheer embarrassment at the mangling the thick-eared American cast was giving his words.

'Well, it started out as a novel that hardly anyone remembers now, written by an old drinking buddy of mine called Ed R—'

'But when did Sally Field come on board?' breathed Sue, the sound of her knickers struggling to stay on clearly audible through the bathroom radio.

'Oh, Sally's wonderful. And we were both absolutely determined to take on the studio and tell the story we wanted to tell—'

A traduced writer can only take so much. 'My story! It was my story! I remember it! Here it is!' I roared at the radio, brandishing the copy of *Who Would Fardels Bear?* that I keep on the shelf by the toilet for moments of contemplation of past glories. Without in any way descending into Hornby-style list-making, the book stands between a signed card of thanks from Jane Seymour pictured in her *Dr. Quinn, Medicine Woman* costume, and a framed page of the *Radio Times* from the day my episode of *Tenko* was broadcast.

The damnable *Desert Island Discs* continued its offensive way unabated.

'. . . Which at the time must have been very brave, Jaz.'

'I suppose it was, Sue.'

At this I simply had to get out of the bathroom and into the kitchen for a drink, reckoning I was entitled to finish the half-bottle of Scotch that the chip shop next door had given me last Christmas for being their best customer. What I hadn't bargained for was the digital radio also being tuned to Radio 4, with its 7-second time delay . . .

'. . . a novel that hardly anyone remembers now, written by an old drinking buddy of mine called Ed R—'

'But when did Sally Field come on board?'

'Oh, Sally's wonderful—'

There was nothing for it but to compose an e-mail to the 12-year-old ignoramus of a producer responsible for producing this travesty of literary history. I sat down at the computer, filled my pipe and set about an Ed Reardon special, Toxicity Level 6 – forgetting however that I'd tuned the computer to Radio 4 online . . . time delay 24 seconds . . .

'. . . a novel that hardly anyone remembers now, written by an old drinking buddy of mine called Ed R—'

'But when did Sally Field come on board?'

'Oh, Sally's wonderful—'

The secret of the successful abusive letter or e-mail, I submit, is to offer an innocent-looking velvet glove of disinterested comment before unleashing the iron fist to the unwitting recipient's solar plexus. I have used this tactic effectively on such bureaucratic behemoths as Dacorum Borough Council (for refusing to take last year's discarded *Yellow Pages* in my recycling box) and the General Synod (for persisting with the dumbed-down Series 3 prayerbook). Now it was the turn of the British Broadcasting Corporation to have an artery severed by the sword of common sense. (I should say that I rarely send these letters, once spleen is satisfactorily vented. The thrill is in the hunt for the right offensive epithets.)

'Slipshod journalism for which the BBC deserves to lose its charter . . .' No, far too kind. 'The producer deserves disembowelling it gives me no pleasure to say . . .' This was more like it and would undoubtedly get *Feedback* taken off the air. 'And as for Ms Sue Lobotomy . . .'

The telephone rang just as I was hitting my stride, and saved the jumped-up local news presenter from a well-merited punishment popular in the Dark Ages.

It was Jaz Milvane himself, whose unctuous falsehoods I had just turned off with an oath. Three times. I adopted a policy of dishonesty which I thought appropriate in the circumstances.

'Yes?'

'It's Jaz.'

'Jaz who?'

'It's me, you pillock.'

'Oh, that Jaz! How the bloody hell are you? Are we still on for the gig on Sunday?'

'Yes. Look I'm sorry about that just now.'

'What?'

'On the radio.'

'Wasn't listening, mate. Too busy working to have the radio on.'

'Oh. Doesn't matter then. I had to do *Desert Island Discs*, that's all.'

'Oh you didn't. You old whore! Y'know, I still think Roy Plomley was the only one who could really do it. So, what did you say about me then? No mention at all, I bet.'

'No I did. I said . . . well—'

'Might as well tell me. I'm never going to hear it – we'll be busy gigging when the repeat goes out.'

I had paid out enough rope by now, and Jaz duly hanged himself with it.

'Um. I said you . . . helped me get started and I just hoped I'd done justice to, er, your book.'

'Did you? Did you really say all that? About *Who Would Fardels Bear?*'

'Well, something like that.'

'I'm sorry I missed it now – but there was no need to go overboard. I'm just happy to bask in your reflected glory, mate.'

'Piss off, Reardon.'

'Right. See you Sunday – first sharpener at twelve? Cheers, Jaz. And thanks again!'

Elgar leapt up on the computer table and gave me a basilisk stare of which the Egyptian cat goddess, Bast, would not have been ashamed.

But Master was in no mood for truth and reconciliation. 'What are you looking at? Have you never pretended you haven't been fed?'

Stepping disdainfully over the keyboard, Elgar's paw brushed against the mouse, pressing the 'Send' button, committing my e-mail to cyberspace and thence to Broadcasting House . . . and as I said, in all probability disqualifying me from a future appearance on the programme.

Life is so much simpler on that desert island, where communication is via messages in bottles.

Saturday

I'm woken up at 3 a.m. by what passes for a dawn chorus in this godforsaken corner of Hertfordshire . . . or is it Buckinghamshire? At this hour I neither know nor care. From outside comes the merry sound of scavenging winos sorting through the large, wheeled refuse bins outside the charity shops across the road, bestrewing the pavement with stuff scorned by Oxfam and its next door rival, whose proprietress is yet another member of the monstrous sistren of Sues (Ryder of that ilk).

'You've been told before, you're not supposed to do that! Now clear off and make someone else's life a misery!'

The justified rebuke, delivered clearly and firmly from the opened window, appeared to have zero effect. Since I am an accomplished mimic and master of accents, including the argot of the down-and-out, I added by way of a final flourish, 'Or as you say in your language, gnarrr-gnyaarr-garrrrh-argh-bleurgh.' But the irony was lost on the unfortunate dullard.

'Sorry, what'd you say, mate?'

The pavement began to clear of destitutes but I was still obliged to take my slippers off, put my shoes on and go across the road to lock the bin, a public-spirited act for which I never get any thanks or acknowledgement, however loudly I slam the lid down. To do this I use my triangular Gas Board key, an essential tool of the wordsmith's trade which I also use to bleed the radiators, adjust the volume on the bathroom radio and, if there's nobody about, open the chocolate machine on Berkhamsted station.

The Swim

Amid the unlovely detritus of rejected trainers, jigsaws and children's encyclopedias I spotted a not-bad-looking hardback copy of *The Moon's a Balloon*. I remember noticing when I was selling my treasured copy of *Executioner* by Albert Pierrepoint on eBay the other week that a first edition of Niven's memoirs currently fetches upwards of £29, so here was a God-given chance to recoup some of the losses sustained by the *Little Book of Publishers' Rejections'* rejection, as well as to put one over on Ms Ryder and her toffee-nosed crew. I was within inches of fishing David Niven out of the bin with a misshapen leg of a gold tea trolley but the celebrated charmer remained maddeningly out of reach, debonair smile flickering in the glow of the faulty streetlight. So I clambered in.

'Excuse me sir, I shall have to ask you to vacate that rubbish bin.'

It is a truth universally acknowledged that policemen only show up when there is nothing for them to do, but this was time-wasting of a heroic order.

'Oh it's him, guv, the one who rings up all the time – lives above the hairdresser's – always complaining about noisy scissors. Got a file that thick.'

'Come on sir, out you get.'

'It's a pity you couldn't have arrived ten minutes ago when there was a serious breach of the peace in progress, but I imagine you were both busily parked in a lay-by, deaf to everything but the sound of masticated crisps.'

'There's no need to use obscene language, Sir.'

The Queen's English is obviously not on the curriculum at

the Hendon College of Bribe-Taking and Thuggery, an omission I felt bound to mention to its two alumni. The armlock of the 12-year-old PC was not unduly painful but that changed when his superior ordered him to 'Do that thing with his head, Green.' I think I lost consciousness for a few moments and it was not until I heard a loud pop of bursting plastic bag that I realized I had been bundled on to the back seat of their patrol car.

'He's sat on the Kettle Chips. That's £2.20 up the Swanee.'

With that level of police expenditure, it's no wonder the council tax is sixteen hundred quid. Just as well I don't pay it.

I haven't actually been inside a police station in the middle of the night since my children were growing up. I say police station – my local in north London used to be more of a Job Centre. It was a regular media rendezvous in the early hours of Sunday morning – you'd find many an influential producer or director there at 4 a.m. picking up his or her delinquent offspring. Some of the most important deals in broadcasting were thrashed out on screwed-down, orange plastic chairs and toasted in powdered tea from the vending machine. I got two radio play commissions one night when the entire BBC Drama Department seemed to be there – as well as Alan Bennett, who'd just come along for the crack. It was as good as having an agent, and, of course, it was how *Z Cars* started. But that was the golden age of TV drama, and this is Berkhamsted 2005, where the pickings are thinner on the ground. Or so I thought.

After an hour in the cooler I was escorted by the duty officer back out to the reception area, a free man once more.

'Now get off home. You're a very lucky writer.'

As I turned away to ignore his patronizing admonishment my eye was caught by a poster on the wall.

ID PARADES. VOLUNTEERS NEEDED.
EARN TEN POUNDS AN HOUR

Recent experience had led to a certain cynicism in the Reardon psyche with regard to money-making opportunities. Furthermore, I wondered just how much credence to give to the bottom line of the poster: 'If you get picked out by mistake – NOTHING HAPPENS.'

'Fancy a crack at it do you?' asked the officer, and if he was enjoying this he did at least have the decency not to show it and directed his attention towards *The Hoobs* on his CCTV monitor. I admitted that the proposition did intrigue me.

'What it entails, Sir, is standing in line with a number of other self-employed people such as yourself and one genuine suspect. Can be a bit hard on the legs if we don't get a result first time but then there's a chance of overtime, so it's swings and roundabouts.'

'And does one come just as one is?'

'Well, perhaps not the pyjamas, but the beard would be a decided advantage – for accusations of gross indecency, say.'

How often does the chance come to strut one's stuff as a suspect, I wondered. Monthly? Quarterly? Anything less and it would hardly be worth narrowing the eyes and moistening the lips. But I was determined to make the most of this opening. If my acting days at Shrewsbury taught me one thing it was that the

key to being in demand as a live performer is versatility ('Reardon
(IVa) invests Titania with a near-perfect Irish brogue which is as
charming as last term's Glaswegian Macduff was menacing'). I
was keen to impress on the officer my willingness to 'play as cast'
and said I'd be perfectly happy to shave the beard off if they
wanted a smooth-chinned suspect such as a drug dealer. Fixing
him with a lazy stare, I slipped easily into a lilting Jamaican
patois, 'Hello man – you want to score?' I rumbled. So astonished
was he that all he could say was 'Pardon?' I know when I've got
my audience held and I teased him with a protean shift to the
accent of our own urban underclass, or that section of it which
places an imaginary question mark at the end of every phrase.

'Or maybe I could be a younger criminal? Whose voice goes
up at the end? Because they all do that for some reason.'

'Spoilt for choice, aren't we, Sir.'

Having displayed my wares it was time to come to terms.
'Any chance of getting paid in cash?'

'We couldn't really do that, Sir, could we?'

But there was something trustworthy about these people – a
sense that if they said they would pay you £10 then £10 it
would be. It's a feeling one never gets, for example, within the
portals of the BBC. Moreover, the experience might furnish me
with useful research material, grist for a taut new drama –
Twelve Bearded Men, perhaps. *The Dirty Filthy Dozen*? I offered
to write down my contact details but before I could unscrew the
Waterman the officer held up the charge sheet to show they
knew how to get hold of me. A case then of 'Don't call 999,
we'll call you!' But that, too, was met with a blank stare.

By now it was 7 a.m. The pool was just opening and invitingly empty. Time to make up the deficit of lengths that had built up over the last five swimless days. But I didn't have my bathing things with me, and besides if I was to bring a clear head to bear on *Channel 4 Racing* I needed to get some proper rest.

Sunday

And the time-honoured ritual of finding out what taboo they were determined to break in *The Archers* this week. The predictable, sun-dried, Radio 4 brand of iconoclasm-lite began with the all-too-familiar sound of Jack Woolley's dull Midlands whine – an accent, I might say, I can do far better than the wooden-larynxed mummer the BBC lavishes my licence fee upon, or would lavish it upon if I hadn't witheld it in protest. No one would be more willing than Reardon to part with the required £121 if only the quality of BBC programmes was to rise to a level that merited it – say somewhere just above 'surpassing idiocy' and a notch below 'brain-damaged banality'.

Jack Woolley's urgently whispered 'Ooh Dolly, we mustn't! I'm married to Peggy' was followed by the equally unconvincing 'baa' of a sheep reared and fattened on the pastures of the BBC sound effects library. Woolley moaned once more. Could this really be what I thought it was? Had I so underestimated the writers' yearning for notoriety? The answer apparently was yes – or even 'Ow yes. Ow yes! Ow yes!!' as Jack increased the tempo of his manly thrusts fit to shake the foundations of Grey Gables if not the skyscrapers of far-off Felpersham.

'Baa.'

'No, I can't stop myself either, Dolly. To hell with society's traditional values! We can have a same sex marriage, we're both *woolly*.'

Dum-dee-dum, Dee-dum, Dee-dum . . .

The bedside alarm, which now went off, read 12.05 p.m. – proof that even in the fretful sleep that afflicts all victims of police injustice, I had still conceived a much more entertaining story line than anything offered up by the sanctimonious, smug, puritan housewives who write (evacuate would be a better word) the real *Archers* scripts. My morning, nevertheless, had to go down as a wasted one.

Still, anything is preferable to that loathsome Family Fun Day at the pool. The men's changing room seethes with divorced dads and their various offspring hurtling about, shrieking and upsetting the dressing and undressing routines of the regular swimmers. Furthermore, I don't see why I should have to put up with having my private parts scrutinized by 6-year-old girls just because their parents can't hold their marriages together.

So, a week *sans* swim, but no matter, I have a gig to play, and there's no better workout for the mind and body than music: Bach for the austere demands of structure, Shostakovich for the giddy pain of love and loss . . . However, for catching the sheer joy of life on the wing I find nothing comes close to blowing a jug in a Dixieland jazz band while wearing a striped blazer and a straw boater.

The Swim

The Bayou Boys have been together for twenty-five years – 'together' is perhaps not quite the word as Cliff has a tendency to veer off into 'Sweet Georgia Brown' during the lyrics of 'My Very Good Friend The Milkman', while Frank is apt to forsake his drum kit and carry his stool over to one of the Lock-keeper's Arms' tables as soon as he sees his laden plate of Sunday lunch emerging from the kitchens. Ray, the trombone player, has recently remarried, so his punctuality depends on the length of the checkout queues at IKEA. Our trumpeter – the egregious, the very egregious Jaz Milvane – exists in a world of his own self-importance, tootling off into flights of fancy so indulgent that time seems to stand still, after which he'll often modestly reflect, 'I don't know, guys, I just seem to get better and better.'

Despite his great wealth and fame, Jaz's face is seldom if ever recognized in this mundane setting, rather in the way that Harold Pinter becomes utterly nondescript when tucking into a slice of teatime Battenburg at one of the fourth eleven cricket grounds his team frequents. Jaz enjoys these tourist visits to the real world and even relishes the amiable shouts from the Lock-keeper's Arms' patrons along the lines of 'Fuck off and die you old wanker, you're crap.'

My own musicianship has evolved over the years – what one lacks in lung power one makes up for in richness of tone. I began my concert career by blowing an empty cider jug before graduating to a two-handled, glass demijohn; there was a brief flirtation in the eighties with a Victorian, stone hot-water bottle followed by another loveless decade with the cider jug, essentially because neither of us could be bothered to find anything better, but a couple of years ago I mated for life with my current instrument and we shall be together till death, or droppage on the Lock-keeper's Arms' flagstone floor, do us part. The meeting happened by chance when my son, Jake, returned from a visit to the Baltic states and presented me with this oddly shaped jug of spirits – the young take these weekend trips abroad in the same way as I used to take a Saturday bus to Carwardine's in Bristol, there to make a cup of coffee and a buttered roll last for five hours, long enough for Celia King to realize I was reading Proust but not long enough, alas, for her to be compelled to strip off and ravish me at the formica table. *Eheu fugaces!*

Anyway, the jug of Estonian hooch turned out not to be a liqueur but a balsam for the relief of rheumatic pain. Nevertheless it was drunk within the week by Ted Cartwright and myself one night after the pubs had shut and the last of the ouzo from Jake's summer holiday had gone. The balsam jug proved, when empty, to have a sublime acoustic with a sweetness of timbre that made the unpalatable eucalyptus blowback more than worth the trouble. I imagine Rostropovich loves his cello in much the same way.

Today's gig at the Lock-keeper's Arms began like any other, half an hour late with an argument about petrol money. The fine weather meant that the landlord asked us to play outside on the towpath – to attract more Sunday walkers, he said, though I suspect his real reason was that with us out of the way he could cram more underage drinkers into the bar.

We got through the first set, rising above opposition in the form of a car alarm and a child with purple hair throwing pitta bread at us (to the evident delight of its doting, pink-haired parent). Jaz received enthusiastic applause from some mad woman in a frock at the end of his solo while my riff on the jug was met with – silence, admittedly, but a silence with more than a hint of respectful appreciation.

For the Bayou Boys the buying of drinks in between sets is a process that redefines the meaning of brinkmanship. It's not unusual to see five or even ten minutes of stalemate pass before the thirstiest man cracks. I have seen Ray order and eat an entire second lunch so as not to be close to the bar at the critical moment. Cliff went through a period of deliberately buying us drinks he knew we didn't want, like whisky mac and brandy and peppermint if memory serves, so that in time we were forced to get our own. In recent months, Jaz has been getting the first round in so he can then complain about being taken advantage of. The ploy has consistently failed to shame the rest of us into action and he has been forced to make ever more extravagant claims about what he's had to give up in order to be with us: award ceremonies, honorary American professorships, pool parties with people the rest of us pretend never to have heard of even if we have. It is, as I say, an intricate and elegant quadrille.

'What are you drinking, Frank, Guinness? Cliff, Stella yes? Ed?'

'Didn't you get the last round, Jaz?'

'Who's counting? It cost me twelve grand to get a flight over here so what's another couple of quid? Sue – you made it!'

Sunday

Believe it or not, there behind me, wearing a summer frock and a smile so broad she could have swallowed Lynne Truss whole, was the lickspittle Lawley.

'I told you I'd come, Jaz,' she said, eyeing him in a manner which might actually have contravened the laws of public decency. In fact, had we been outside a pub in Watford town centre on a Saturday night she would have been a virtual ASBO certainty.

'You hear any of that rubbish? Bet we wouldn't be one of your *Desert Island Discs* – you'd drown yourself!'

'Well . . . not if I could have you as my luxury, Jaz.'

It was time to put a spanner in the works. I introduced myself with a cheery smile and a firm handshake.

'Sue, settle an argument,' I began, and I could see Jaz's eyes flicker with suspicion. 'In the unlikely event of my being invited on to your show – which is great, by the way – would I be allowed to take my own book, as my book?'

'What book is that?'

'Oh you know, *Who Would Fardels Bear?* The novel that was the inspiration for *Sister Mom*. Jaz mentioned it on your programme this week.'

Jaz's features slackened in a way that showed he was prepared to slug it out.

'You said you didn't hear it.'

'I didn't, but you told me you said you owed your entire career to me. You just hoped you'd done justice to such a wonderful book . . . was what you said you said.'

'Oh yes, I did. That's right.' Jaz took a sip of beer as he considered his next move.

The Swim

'I don't remember you saying that, Jaz,' said Lawley.

'Maybe it ended up on the cutting-room floor,' I said. 'I always think your show should be longer, Sue. I could listen to it all day.'

'That's not what you told me on the phone,' said Jaz, a weaselly smile playing about his fat collagen-enriched film director's lips. 'You said Plomley was the only one who was any good and it's gone down the khazi since then. No offence, Sue.'

The discomfort and slight embarrassment at being exposed in no way diminished the warm glow of satisfaction I felt at what now lay before my eyes: the magnificent spectacle of a scorned Lawley.

'To be honest,' she said with a flick of the head, 'I've never liked Sally Field much. Or treacly Hollywood endings where everyone hugs each other.'

'Rules out a fair chunk of your oeuvre, Jaz mate,' I said with a philosophical tug on the pipe. 'Come on, time for another blow.'

La Lawley left at the precise point in the next set where Jaz began his solo. We played on through our popular repertoire, including Cliff's unique conflation of 'Ain't She Sweet' and 'Your Feet's Too Big', while I set about planning my strategy for the next drinks break. The Bayou Boys, I reflected, are a tightly knit group in all but the musical sense and outsiders interfere at their peril. Accordingly it was a thirsty but grudgingly contented five who convened at the water's edge for the post-gig gargle.

'Right-ho, my round,' I said, placing my jug carefully on the ground. 'Cliff, Jaz, Frank, Ray? Same again.' I aimed for the gap between the table and the canalside, and the balsam jug did her work beautifully, bless her Estonian earthenware heart. I caught my foot, executed a clean trip and plummeted with an oath into the chilly depths of the lock. Thrashing and gasping I surreptitiously removed the empty wallet from my back pocket and allowed it to fall to the bottom. The ploy backfired somewhat when, containing only air, it bobbed up to the surface immediately. However, in the melee of churning water and discarded crisp packets it wasn't noticed, and I struck out for the steps on the other side of the lock.

Cold it may have been, smelly certainly and perhaps a little undignified, but it saved me from financial embarrassment and meant that I did at long last get my swim. Needless to say it was cut short by a showy and completely unnecessary rescue act staged by Jaz Milvane, or 'Hollywood's Have-a-Go Hero' as it said on the local news. And in the next day's *Times*. And the *Guardian* and the *Telegraph* and the *Independent*, in both its vacuous broadsheet and its pocket-sized version for pocket-sized brains.

On my return to the flat in dry clothes borrowed from the pub and with a ten pound note from Jaz (which he had been snapped handing over to me), I was nevertheless cheered to find a contract for *Pet Peeves* on the doormat – it had been misdelivered to the chip shop next door judging by the layer of rancid fat on the envelope. And winking on the answering machine was yet further evidence that Ed Reardon is the must-hire writer of the moment.

'So if you could come down to the station between the hours

of five and six and report to our Identity Parade Liaison Officer? And if you wouldn't mind keeping the beard, Sir, that'd be lovely.'

Jaz's loan meant I was able to take advantage of Threshers' three bottles for a tenner offer – hard to resist as long as you don't mind Shiraz, which isn't so bad I suppose, especially after the second bottle's gone down. I fired up the PC in preparation for a good night's work.

'What's it like to be Lynne Truss's cat, people often ask. "Very nice" I purr contentedly. "I especially like the balanced diet she gives me – Eats Fishes and Leaves" . . .'

2

Pulp Non-Fiction

Monday

All but the meanest intelligence (earning a large salary in television, probably) would have gleaned from the foregoing that the writing profession is among the more precarious around. What is not so well known is that it is also one of the most potentially injurious to the mind and body. Consider, for example, the psychological damage inflicted when a friend's book is favourably reviewed by Fatty on Radio 4's *Front Row*. Follow that up with a thumbs-up from Fatty in the next day's *Guardian* and then to cap it all a rave from the magistracy of wild silk shirts and outsize earrings that goes by the name of BBC2's *Late Review* (regular presenter: Fatso).

Actually, 'review' is hardly an accurate description of a process that involves Lardypants regurgitating a publisher's press release while his mind, or what passes for it, remains clearly focused on the subject of cakes, pies, toffees, baps and buns. 'Ooh look Germaine, a super hamper from my rich uncle. Let's scoff the lot.' Obesity must addle the brain. Or how else to explain the verdict that Nick Hornby's latest so-called novel is 'essential reading'. It might be essential if you've had the misfortune to run out of toilet paper but otherwise not.

So the psychological dangers faced by the working writer are very real indeed. What of the physical perils? To take one example, only last week I suffered a bout of sunstroke after falling asleep on a park bench while trying to unblock a narrative line. And now, of course, there is a new affliction sweeping through the ranks of scribblers – repetitive strain injury. Some of our younger novelists are especially prone to it, sitting all day at the keyboard and continually pressing the function key for 'Insert Reference to 1970s TV Show or Pop Song Here'.

My own condition, which necessitates the frequent insertion of index finger into ice bucket, is a consequence of clicking the mouse to check my sales ranking on the Amazon website. An act of melancholy masochism to be sure, especially as previous titles in the Reardon canon have long since disappeared off the radar. Although *The Brand's Hatch Story* did occupy a challenging position in the low 150,000ths for a heady week, prompting wild thoughts of new trousers and unmetered electricity, before those too spun off into the straw bales of obscurity.

However, this morning's ritual revealed an unexpected departure from the norm so pronounced that I had to repeat the process three more times to check it was right – and suffer the resulting sharp shooting pain up the right arm. But it was worth it.

'Hello, Felix, it's Ed. I've had some astonishingly good news about sales of my book.'

It was, perhaps, overoptimistic of me to expect my agent to share my excitement, but so rarely do I have the chance to pass on glad tidings – the last being the early closure on Broadway of a play by Michael Frayn, and that was months ago – that I was in a state of near-euphoria.

'You've written a book? Jolly well done, clever old you. What's it called?'

'It's *Pet Peeves*, Felix. You did the deal.'

'Did I? Clever old me. What's it about?'

'Well, it says here it's "A sideways look at life with the famous as told by their adorable but not always mildly spoken pets." But the thing is—'

'Ah, so it's a play.'

'No, it's a book.'

'I saw an awfully good play the other night. Marvellous actress in it. What's her name? You should do a play, you know. She had the most corking pair of legs . . . started at her shoulders.'

'Good. The thing is Felix, *Pet Peeves'* Amazon sales ranking has gone up to—'

'Just a minute.'

Felix's attention-span works on a need-to-know basis. If the matter under discussion cannot be pan-fried, poured or paid into the agency's account at Coutts then he doesn't feel the need to know about it. His mind can flit around like a butterfly with 'commitment issues', as the current jargon has it, until it lights on something that engages his interest. In this instance, a dispatch rider coming into his office with a consignment of Burgundy.

'I'm sorry, Ed, but an extraordinary-looking spaceman has just brought me a case of Gevrey Chambertin.'

I waited while the helmeted visitor from the far-flung galaxy of Bottoms Up painstakingly coaxed Felix through each step of the process of signing for it: take pen; locate space for signature; try again, this time clicking the pen so that it writes, and so on. All this to an accompanying soundtrack of amazed exclamations from Felix.

'Oh! Ah! Ha! I see. It's all terribly confusing. Right, there you are, now off you go back to Mars. Hello? Hello, who is this?'

'It's me. Ed Reardon. I was trying to tell you about my Amazon sales ranking.'

'Oh, were you? Well, look here, I hate to take up your time like this.'

I could sense I was losing him again and calculated I had about fifteen seconds to get to the point.

'It's an online indicator of how quickly and how many copies of your book are selling. And *Pet Peeves* has just gone up to 197th! It's astonishing. I think you should try to get me on to

Front Row at least,' I added, swallowing my pride like one of
Fatty's éclairs.

'Absolutely. We need to bring Ping in on this. Ping's your
man for novels. Now then, let me see if I can transfer you.'

There was the agonizing sound of Felix fumbling with the
buttons on his phone and just enough time to hear his answering machine telling him that he had 'ONE. HUNDRED.
And. TWENTY. THREE. Messages' before the line went
dead.

Thus one may add to the list of physical dangers faced by the
freelance writer massive cardiac arrest brought on by a conversation with one's agent. A mere four hours elapsed before Ping
returned my call and I was able to pass on the news about *Pet
Peeves'* consolidation (I had checked several times) of the 197th
spot.

'Aaahh, never mind – I'm sure sales will pick up nearer to
Christmas. It's no tradge.'

'No, you don't understand Ping. It was 123,000th yester-
day. That means – I've just worked it out – I've sold 122,803 *Pet
Peeves* in twenty-four hours. At this rate I'll go past Lynne
Truss on Thursday.'

'No, Ed, all it means is that you've sold more copies than
122,803 other authors.'

'But that's fantastic, isn't it?'

'It's good, but those authors probably haven't sold any books
at all since yesterday. So, you see, if you sell just one book you
jump ahead of them.'

The news was disappointing certainly, but it was

compensated by the knowledge that 122,803 of my colleagues were currently having to face the stark reality of no sales at all, and I allowed myself to entertain the delicious possibility that one of them might conceivably be Nick Hornby. And on a more practical level it was at least proof that I had actually sold a book.

'Not necessarily, Ed,' said Ping, her voice taking on the tone of one humouring a senile uncle. 'You see it might be just an order for a book. How it works, right, it's called exponentially exaggerated sensitivity, yeah? This guy explained it. He's like a professor of robots or something? And I mean, okay, he was really sweet and bought me dinner and a rose and shit, but I hate that thing when they text you after a date, you know. I like to get a proper voice mail.'

Fixated though I was upon the Ed Reardon page of the Amazon website, which now announced brutally and without warning that *Pet Peeves* had plummeted to 453,276th, I couldn't help but be affected by Ping's touchingly old-fashioned lament for the lost art of courtship. An art which I, too, mourned – and, indeed, would have been only too happy to start practising again in as long a time as it would take me to get from my flat to Euston, and thence up to the fourth floor of Ping's block in Thurloe Place.

'It changes all the time, Ed. Look, you see, it's gone down to 453,276th now.'

'Thank you, yes, I had noted the sudden lurch.'

'Aaahh bless. Thing is, Ed, these figures aren't that reliable and you'll just make yourself really sad getting your hopes up.'

'I imagine that's close to last place.'

'Oh, I shouldn't think so. Not by a long way.'

'Really? Can you find out who I'm ahead of? Get their names and e-mail them to me, maybe?'

'Well, I'm kinda really busy this morning.'

'How about lunch then? I can jump on a train from Berkhamsted and be inside you within the hour . . . erm, I mean be with you inside the hour . . . Hello? . . . Hello?'

So with collateral damage sustained to mind, body, manhood, self-esteem, *amour propre*, professional reputation and hopes of a winter coat, I reflected on a day in which I had sipped from the Amazon cup of success only to have it dashed from my bruised lips. I had flown too close to the *Sunday Times* bestseller list and crashed in a molten heap below. Half a million points below, as it happened, Amazon's chart-topping, number 1 darling of the day being *Enough Is Enough*, the latest 'sparkling satire' by Mark Lawson (£11.89).

'Lawson's eye for political humbug is unpitying and his mastery of dialogue, both comic and serious, suggests a formidable writer' (*Sunday Telegraph*).

As I clicked the cross in the top right-hand corner of the window to rid my screen of this orgy of bum-kissing, a searing pain convulsed the nerve ends and sinews of my mouse hand. Time, I concluded, for a restorative quarter bottle of Bells. Or maybe two, in case I should happen to wake up with *Front Row* on.

Tuesday

Another day of mental and physical punishment. I had pre-viously encountered the Saga phenomenon shortly after my fiftieth birthday. A thick glossy brochure was handed to me by the postman, who was apparently under instructions not to let the package fall on the mat in case the recipient was too infirm to bend to pick it up. Besides welcoming me to the Saga fold and informing me that my 'membership profile' entitled me to substantial savings on Stairmasters and bath handrails, the brochure nevertheless promoted various ener-getic holidays ranging from kayaking in Vancouver to candlelit cruises in the Aegean, all guaranteed to cause a shudder in someone whose idea of relaxation is quite frankly to be left alone.

But a clause in my contract for *Pet Peeves* stipulated that I would be available for publicity purposes, and so it was that I prepared to 'strut my not inconsiderable stuff', as the twelve-year olds say, on Saga Digital Radio. The author, if he is any good that is, finds himself engaged in an unending struggle over how best to maintain his popularity without compromising his seriousness or, perish the thought, dumbing down. Nowhere is this conflict more intensely contested than on the bloody battle grounds of the promotional tour. I doubt even Olympic athletes have it as tough as this.

For a start they have someone to drive them to the stadium. My journey to Saga's broadcasting basement was made first on a commuter train to London, then on a Northern Line service so crowded it would have been regarded as inhumane even by Tokyo underground staff wielding cattle prods, and finally on a squalid suburban train, which with the addition of a bit of filthy straw on the floor could have come straight out of *Doctor Zhivago*. Or at any rate the film version thereof, which I saw at my local Essoldo three times in one weekend. As a teenager I was, in common with most of my generation smitten with Julie Christie, and – speaking for myself – with Tom Courtenay too, one of whose celebrated performances I attempted to emulate in my school's courageous adaptation of *The Loneliness of the Long Distance Runne*r ('E. F. Reardon's understanding of the mind of a Borstal boy will surely stand him in good stead in later life').

At least Strelnikov's train kept moving across the steppes. Mine came to a rest somewhere in south London at a signal half-buried in nettles, while the other side of the train afforded a view of rioting cow parsley as far as the eye could see (about two feet given the amount of grime on the window). No doubt some would have found this scene, complete with deafening birdsong, quite lyrical, but they weren't in danger of arriving late for Saga Radio's 'Easy Reading' slot. I dare say even that poet of the permanent way Edward Thomas would have burst through the studio door both addled and in a strop.

I was shown in while a record was playing by an assistant who was clearly a beneficiary of the station's policy of positive discrimination, being at least three generations younger than the Saga membership profile. He offered me a 'Refreshing Towelette' in a sachet to mop my brow and reassured me that Don Wade the disc jockey had a copy of my book.

'Did he like it?'

'Oh yes – he always likes them.'

This was a promising start. But I was still determined not to take any personal responsibility for my being late, while at the same time wishing to strike a jovial note and not sour the atmosphere of what was the first of only two stops on my promotional tour.

'Effingham Junction? Effing and Blinding Junction would be closer to the mark,' I said, sucking my breath in to indicate irony.

'You won't say that on air will you, Ed,' said Don Wade, whose preternaturally black hair suggested that he was either Irish, or the regular user of a catering-sized tin of Cherry Blossom boot polish. Sitting on my side of the console was a plump woman with spectacles on a chain round her neck who I took to be Jasmine Davies, as this was the author of a garish paperback about speed-dating that she had in front of her, bookmarked with about twenty Post-it notes. I did have a momentary flash of anxiety that perhaps I should have come similarly prepared, instead of rereading *Jude the Obscure* on the journey down – but it passed, as I was keen not to let the matter of my vile journey rest.

'I'm sorry I'm late, it's just that the train literally came to a complete standst—'

'Sshhh!' hissed Don Wade, putting on his headphones, which also being black became immediately invisible in the ebony forest of his hair. The Val Doonican record that had been playing (evoking memories of snazzily patterned cardigans that my ex-wife and I used to think were interference on the television in our basement kitchen in Camden) reached its jaunty conclusion and the red studio light came on.

'Well,' said Don, the laugh in his voice turning it into a four-syllable word. 'I don't know whether Paddy McGinty – the owner of that there goat – was as famous as some of the celebrities in a lovely new book written by my next guest, Mr Ed Reardon, who's finally here, a bit red in the face, but it's great to have him with us.'

'Thanks, Don – it's great to be here. No thanks I might say to our wonderful transport system . . . I mean it must be the worst in the world, it must be! Surely it's not beyond the wit of man to design something in the twenty-first century that actually works and gets you from A to—'

Don Wade had the seasoned broadcaster's gift of being able to turn conversational dross into gold, and vice versa.

'Well, something that very definitely does work is this smashing book of yours,' said Don, opening *Pet Peeves* at a picture of Jennifer Aniston cuddling a chihuahua. "I used to be best *friends* with my celebrity owner till Brad came on the scene. He's the *Pitts*! Grrrrr!" Lovely stuff!'

'Thank you.'

'So, Ed . . .'

'Of course, the book went to press before Jennifer and Brad split up,' I said. 'But I think the central argument of the piece still works.'

'Right. So, Ed, tell us a little bit about *Pet Peeves*. How did you come to put it together?'

This was my opportunity to sound a clarion call to writers everywhere, rallying the downtrodden and hard-done-by behind the flag of freelance rebellion. For Maid of Orleans read Bard of Berkhamsted. I realized I was thinking this through live on air, as Don Wade and now Jasmine Davies were staring at me and Don was reaching hastily for a Matt Monro CD.

'The way it works is that the publishers generously encourage you to write a thirty-page treatment for nothing. Then they make you rewrite it to accommodate their own surpassing inanities before giving you an advance so tiny it's barely visible to the human eye, and requiring you to deliver a completed manuscript within six weeks.'

'Right. But it's well worth it in the end,' said Don, clearly keen that nothing should cloud the sunny disposition of *Wake Up With Wade* (which out of deference to its listeners' habits, stretched through to midday). I, however, was not prepared to let the point go, remembering the dozens of unanswered e-mails and letters – many of them posted abroad, at my own expense – to alleged celebrities requesting an anecdote and if possible a photograph of their furry, feathered or scaly friend.

'I sincerely hope it is worth it,' I said. 'I'm a novelist really, I'm just doing it for the money, such as it is. Two grand.'

Mentioning an actual sum of money was clearly a taboo, as Don Wade's eyes glazed over and he went into autopilot presenter mode as he cued up a CD.

'Can't be bad! For anybody just joining us, the answer to the earlier quiz was "raspberries", and with me in the studio are Ed

Reardon, author of *Pet Peeves*, and speed-dating guru, Jasmine Davies. So Jasmine, how would you go about getting a speed-date with a celebrity's pet?'

'Er – oh, I don't know,' said Jasmine, caught out while checking for messages on her mobile phone. I quickly came to the rescue.

'That's bestiality, isn't it?' I said.

'Marvellous stuff,' said Don. 'And while we're all pondering that, here's Mr Matt Monro . . .'

'Absolutely fantastic, guys,' said Don, turning down the volume on 'Born Free' and studying his own mobile phone. Not wanting to be marginalized, I looked at the mini-timetable I had picked up at Waterloo to plan my journey home.

'You really think so?' said Jasmine, pulling a face for my benefit. 'How's the book doing, Ed?'

'Can't grumble,' I said. 'It was 197 on Amazon this morning.'

'Wow!' said Jasmine.

Don's headphones reappeared like lightning from their camouflaged thicket as he whipped them off.

'Goes up and down though, doesn't it,' he said, in a tone which would have dismayed those loyal listeners who saw Don Wade as the natural son and heir to Cheerful Charlie Chester. 'You can be 197th in the morning, 400,000th by lunchtime. That's what happened to my *Little Book of Weather Links*. One way or another you always get clobbered in the end. I'd be better off cockle-picking than sitting here doing this.'

'But that's so great, Ed,' said Jasmine, ignoring Don who was now breaking a finger off a KitKat and not offering it round. 'You can do both things – the serious novels and the popular stuff as well.'

'Yes, I suppose it's not a bad way to earn a living,' I said. Now that I looked at Jasmine Davies properly I saw that I had been a little harsh in my judgement of plumpness. 'Comely' was nearer the mark. 'There's television, too, of course,' I said, wondering what she'd look like without her fawn trouser suit. 'Movies—'

'If you'd just like to sign this copy of *Pet Peeves*, Ed?' said Don, brusquely thrusting it at me.

'Sure – is it "To Don"?'

'No, it's a prize for the person who got "raspberries" right.'

I signed with as much of a flourish as I could muster, given that I had left the flat in haste to catch my train, and the only pen I found I had on me was a tiny blue one from Joe Coral's.

'By the way Don, is it you I see about getting my travel expenses?'

'Oh – *between* movies at the moment are you?' said Don, the headphones vanishing again as Matt Monro's soaring voice reassured Saga listeners that they were 'as free as the roaring tide, so there's no need to hide'.

'Can I give you a lift anywhere, Ed?' said Jasmine. This was palpable progress – time now to see if Reardon could maintain the pace.

'Yes, if you're going near Maidstone – I'm doing Medway Towns Hospital Radio. All five at once.'

'Oh, that's a pity – I'm going to do *Woman's Hour*. It's the other direction. Actually, Don, can you check if my car's arrived yet?'

'Your *what?*' I shouted, not able to contain my outrage at the double whammy of unfairness and cruelty that these words conjured up. I hadn't had a car come to collect me in thirty years, in fact since the premiere in Leicester Square of *Sister Mom*, the film that was allegedly based on my novel *Who Would Fardels Bear?* And then I had been sent a bill afterwards, for instructing the driver to take me and my party in the opposite direction, to a greyhound meeting at Walthamstow Stadium – an entirely justifiable protest at the travesty that was about to unfold on the big screen. We for our part enjoyed an evening's honest and unpretentious entertainment, even if my wife and her sister and brother-in-law never did quite forgive me.

'People – please!' said Don urgently as the record finished and the red light came back on. 'Well – you may be "Born Free" but the cost of dying is no joke these days, is it? So now's the time, if you haven't already, to start planning for that cremation . . .'

Mortality was to cross my mind more than once later in the day, as I sat staring out again at the acres of cow parsley at Effingham Junction.

Wednesday a.m.

Waiting for the reviews is, as any writer will tell you, an exquisite uncertainty. Noël Coward would sit up all night in Sardi's restaurant in New York until the first editions came in, concealing his nervousness behind an urbane carapace and the curling smoke of a Du Maurier. I, for my part, continue the tradition by thumbing through the newspapers for a mention of *Pet Peeves* at my local public library. At least it calls itself a library. In the brave new cappuccino world books have been relegated to the bottom of a pile of user-friendly infotainment artefacts such as videos, DVDs, cassettes of the top ten, Christmas cards, Nintendo numbskullery and the ubiquitous Internet.

Café Da Vinci occupies the corner of the library which was once the proud realm of the reference section. Where formerly resided neat rows of gazetteers, ready reckoners, Hebridean steamer timetables and the perennially useful *Whitaker's Almanack* there now stands a serving counter in the shape of a fish. The rightful home of the eleventh edition *Britannica* (its last lofty hurrah before the dunderheaded Americans got hold of it and turned it into 'a treasury of knowledge', God help us) now houses a machine for producing overpriced coffee froth. It is pleasing to reflect that the words latte and espresso would have merited not so much as a mention in the 1911 index of the onliest encyclopaedia.

As for the writing table where the massively bearded tramp once slumbered peacefully, his head resting on the blotter that absorbed the drool from his mouth with such discreet efficiency, this has been replaced by a tall round zinc table and high stool on which the same gentleman of the road is now forced to perch awkwardly.

'Oi, Antonio! Where's ma toast?' he shouted this morning, frustration with this so-called progress evident in his voice.

Wednesday a.m.

The dull-witted infant behind the counter, his head bowed under a weight of metal studs and rivets that pierced his features, turned his blank pincushion face to the tramp and uttered the standard interrogative of unlettered youth – 'Ha?'

I was at pains not to risk eye contact with either protagonist and was only too glad to be occupied in scanning the day's papers for reaction to my latest published work. The *Sun*, the *Mirror* and the *Star* were full of peeves about the state of the country, to be sure, but none of them came from the mouths of my celebrity-owned pets. The *Daily Telegraph* and *The Times* simply reproduced what was in yesterday's editions of the red tops but at greater length, as did the *Guardian* and *Independent* except they claimed somewhat unconvincingly to be in disagreement with the others. It is true that there were a great many pictures of small furry animals in the *Mail* and the *Express* but nary a one was being quoted from the pages of the new Reardon. The *Spectator, New Statesman, TLS* and *New York Review of Books* were similarly disinclined to venture an opinion.

''Scuse me pal, finished with that *Express?*'

I was suddenly in near darkness, the natural light shut out by a looming mass of Scottish beard.

'Not yet.'

'Give us the page that says "Free cup of tea for every reader".'

Either I could give McBeard what he wanted sharpish or argue my right to hold on to the *Express* until I'd looked at everything including the ads for wide-fitting shoes, and risk more of his noisome breath in my face. I located the tea coupon and tore urgently.

'Hey careful, it's Void if Defaced.'

He released a long and almost lascivious moan of satisfaction as he grasped the token and shuffled away to his perch at the table, there to smooth it tenderly with the back of his hand on the zinc surface.

It took an hour or two to get through all the newspapers, but I was at last rewarded on turning to the magazine racks with a rare nugget of praise. In this month's *Caravan and Camper* – a publication, I might say, with ten times the circulation of the *Spectator* and *New Statesman* combined – *Pet Peeves* is described as 'a nice little read'. The reviewer is the anonymous but highly respected Wayfarer, himself the author of the successful *Pubs that Like Kids*, and the even more successful runaway bestseller *Pubs that Don't Like Kids*. Respect from one's peers is always to be treasured, if not attached to the fridge. And it merited a visit to the reception desk to get change for the photocopier.

'Can I just direct your attention to the notice at this time,' said the functionary who must have begun the lengthy librarian's qualification process shortly after his seventh birthday.

'Yes, I know it says "No Change Given" but you see I've only got a two pound coin, and the photocopier doesn't give change either.'

'Well, if you were to purchase a beverage or muffin from Café Da Vinci – we have Blueberry or Famous Regular at this time.'

'I don't want a muffin I want a 20p,' I shouted, banging my fist on the issue desk.

'I'm afraid we're not allowed to give change, Sir. Now is there anything else I can help you with at this time?'

'What do you mean "anything else"? You haven't helped me with anything at all, simply parroted platitudes from some half-remembered customer relations training seminar. And since relations between us are, I sense, rapidly deteriorating beyond the point of repair, I should also like to mention that helping people is a matter of what one does rather than what one says, in the same way that, say, sporting a "stop tuna fishing with nets" badge does considerably less for the unfortunate fish than it does for the smug self-satisfaction of the wearer.'

I paused for breath, and realized gratifyingly that I had the full attention of the whole room. But before I could move on to some equally trenchant observations about the green and pink ribbon pinned to the lapel of the librarian's Hertfordshire Libraries denim jacket, McBeard came shuffling over on the cadge again.

'You got a pair of scissors there, chief?'

With a pleasant 'Certainly, Sir' the tuna's friend slithered off to an inner office. As he did so, McBeard took the opportunity to reach across the librarian's desk and steal the plastic card that made the photocopier work without any money having to be inserted.

I, too, opted to take the law into my own hands 'at this time'. I slipped *Caravan and Camper* inside my jacket, along with a copy of the new *Oldie* containing a completely gratuitous attack on Nick Hornby, which besides being vitriolic was also highly pin-uppable – 'I Can't Believe It's Not Fiction' ran the headline, at which I was still guiltily smiling as I made my way through the turnstile exit.

Unfortunately I activated the alarm system, bringing the librarian hurrying back, ribbon a-flutter as he crested the wind.

'Excuse me, Sir, I don't think you've had your books stamped.'

I should have realized that the magazines would have bar code labels attached, but it was too late. Nothing for it but to brazen it out.

'I'm afraid your system must have gone haywire. I haven't got any books.'

'Would you mind opening your jacket? The way you're holding your arm by your side suggests, Sir, that you're concealing something in there.'

I tried to pass it off as a writing injury – which wasn't a complete lie – but he merely repeated his request more loudly for me to open my jacket, and this time threatened to involve the police if I didn't.

I told him I had no intention of taking my clothes off for him or anybody and I certainly wasn't about to do it in an atmosphere so polluted with illiterate lowlife that I'd be sure to catch some other obscure disease that he'd have to wear a ribbon for. I was quite pleased with this sally, but realized as I surveyed the faces all staring at me that I'd now lost the sympathy of my audience.

'If you want to apprehend a real criminal,' I said quickly, 'I suggest you do something about that tramp.'

McBeard was in the process of photocopying the *Daily Express* free cup of tea coupon for about the twentieth time, singing 'Tea fer Two' in a surprisingly tuneful Glaswegian.

As the librarian – I'm sorry, as the 'Customer Assistant' – turned to look I ran for the exit and was into the High Street and out of sight among the stalls of the Wednesday market before he could say 'Stop the Bypass.' It was heartening to know that the turn of pace which earned an approving mention in the athletics section of the 1967 *Salopian* was still there ('E. F. Reardon (4a) once again dominated the sack race although jostling and biting is unlikely to be permitted in next year's event').

I got away with my freedom and the two magazines but I couldn't shake off the voice of that tramp singing 'Tea fer Two' and it stayed with me infuriatingly for the rest of the day. I even caught myself whistling it as I underlined the salient bits of the Nick Hornby review before pinning it up.

p.m.

Home. And a comforting check on the sales ranking showed *Peeves* had risen a modest but acceptable 38,000 places. Moreover the Ed Reardon page had now been expanded by whoever edits these things to include the legend 'If you enjoyed *Pet Peeves* by Ed Reardon you might also enjoy *The Highway Code* and the Bible.' August company indeed, though a click to see the Bible's sales ranking revealed that it had been a distinctly

bad day for the good book. The modernizers have only themselves to blame: they sowed the wind when they did away with
the King James version and now, as the prophet Amazon.co.uk
hath spake, they are reaping the whirlwind.

Researching further by typing 'literary failures' into Google,
I came across a most interesting article about the fate of what
the publishing industry is pleased to pass off under the politely
coy title of 'remaindered books'. Remaindered that is in the
sense that a cargo of depleted uranium, or a 10-month-old
sausage found in the back of the fridge, is remaindered. It used
to be the case that prisoners spent their days sewing mailbags
and taking degrees at the Open University. Now, it seems, they
are given the job of putting unsold and frankly unwanted works
of literature out of their misery by drilling holes in them prior
to their being sent to the pulping machine. The holes soften up
the hapless volumes apparently, putting less strain on the blades
and extending the life of the machine. It is a salutary thought
that countless thousands of my colleagues sweat and agonize for
months, if not years, of their lives only for the fruits of their
labours to be reduced to a substance resembling instant mashed
potato.

Evening

Emboldened by the day's positive developments, I decided to
try to get some return on the £8.50 I'd foolishly paid that
Jasmine Davies woman for a copy of her speed-dating book. I

had made the offer out of a vague sense of guilt for declining a lift in her car, but hadn't expected her to accept. Clearly a tyro author, she had no idea about our happy freemasonry, where signed complimentary copies and e-mail addresses are exchanged over a drink after the gig. So that evening found me dipping a speculative toe into the dating pool at Zoltan's in Station Approach, Watford, where I hopped from table to table in search of kindred spirits, soul mates, wealthy and desperate heiresses – call them what you will. Should the outing prove romantically unrewarding, I reasoned, I could always put it down as a research trip, and claim back the cost of the book and my travel expenses.

My first speed date was with a pleasant-enough-looking woman with no obvious signs of self-harm, who listened to the story of my day with polite interest.

'I really like your DSOH,' she said.

'My what?'

'Your dry sense of humour,' she said, presumably a veteran of this type of encounter with its somewhat cynical shorthand. I thanked her anyway and stayed with the theme of book pulping, which had served me well throughout the first ninety seconds of our life together. 'What must it have been like for Jeffrey Archer when he was at Her Majesty's pleasure,' I wondered teasingly, 'being obliged to take the Black and Decker to one of his own sorry efforts!'

'Yes,' she said.

'Surely there were enough holes in the plot already! Dear God, have you ever read one of those things?'

71

'All of them, actually. They were a great comfort to me after I lost my husband. Helped take me out of myself.'

'Well, yes. Er . . .'

'And if it hadn't been for Jeffrey's short stories, I don't think I could have got through being made redundant,' she said, wiping a tear from the corner of her eye. I would have come to her aid, but discovered that all I had in my pocket was yesterday's towelette from the adventure at Saga Digital, now dried up like a dead leaf.

'No, indeed,' I said.

Time hangs heavily on a relationship that has run its course, and the remaining minutes passed awkwardly like so many loveless anniversary dinners in increasingly bleak restaurants. Eventually a bell rang and the cheery voice on the PA said, 'This is your Datemaster. Ten minutes up, so all change please boys and girls!'

I moved to Table Four as it said on the card to meet Alice, who I confess made such an immediate and profound impression on me that I hardly minded not smoking my pipe for ten minutes.

'Well,' I began, 'I'm a writer and—'

The noise of her chair scraping backwards across the floor of Zoltan's cut me short.

'Sorry Datemaster,' she said. 'Is it too late to change?'

Well then, third time lucky. 'Table Twelve. Mary.' But it was going to take me a good forty-five seconds to get over my break-up with Alice – perhaps even longer – and as Mary made the early running, my feelings were still too raw to be able to pay much attention to her. But in time I came to realize that life is for living and after we had been seeing each other for maybe a minute I suddenly thought, the hell with it, why *not* Mary?

'And I like theatre, red wine – and smoking I'm afraid. Is that a problem, Ed?'

'Not at all, my dear.'

'Oh good. I really like cinema – specially 1950s' cinema.'

'Oh yes, me too,' I said, warming quite appreciably to the woman.

'Um, and I like driving out to country pubs, having a laugh, Dixieland jazz, cheap lunches . . .'

'Oh, that's great, yes – yes! – me too.' And she had a car. This was beginning to look very much like a match made in heaven.

'And what I don't like is bad manners, aluminium and the worm.'

'The what?'

'The white worm in my head that keeps making me do these awful, awful things.'

My own chair now scraped back with a panicky screech. 'Datemaster! Excuse me, Datemaster! She's barking M, this one, I'm afraid.'

Thursday

A day, I suppose, I am lucky to be able to greet with my cus-tomary 8 a.m. pipe and pint of caffeine. Who knows what might have happened if I had brought White Worm Woman home? It is an aluminium coffee pot for a start, purchased many years ago on a British Council writers' trip to Leningrad. The time-honoured invitation 'Would you like to come in for coffee?' would probably have ended not in bed, but on the floor in a pool of blood, the stain spreading over the cerise ceiling in the hairdresser's below like the death of Alec in *Tess of the D'Urbervilles*. The £10 that the speed-dating experience had cost me – plus the extravagant fiver I'd blown on an A1-size colour photocopy of the Nick Hornby review – now presented a problem. Elgar's piteous miaow of hunger was anything but satisfied by the reassurance that a £30 royalty cheque from the BBC for a screening of my episode of *Tenko* on Polish Airlines (a 'trapped audience' as it is called, appropriately enough) was due three weeks ago. In fact by mid-morning we were both ravenous, leading to the desperation of what I call Plan B.

But a search round the cycle racks at the railway station for loose change fallen from the pockets of late and harassed commuters proved fruitless. Likewise the returned coins trays in the payphones at the station – all empty, and another consequence of the damnable rise in popularity of the mobile phone.

I contemplated something that had come to the rescue once before: feigning a trip and a fall into the water feature in the Hemel Hempstead shopping mall. This often contains coins thrown in by shoppers in the hope of bringing them good luck, no doubt finding something with the wrong price tag on it in Littlewoods; however, that was a good an hour-and-a-half walk away, it was starting to rain and in any case even a starving writer has his dignity.

Consequently the coffee (and biscuit) break of my writing class – this week's topic, 'Sell that Blockbuster! – was awaited with unusual keenness and not a little noise from the old tum. When it was in danger of drowning out my lecture, I informed my students that we would continue deconstructing *Wild Swans* by Jung Chang after taking a half-hour break for refreshments. There was a chorus of protest, which under normal circumstances would have been gratifying, but not when a man's gastric juices are running riot.

'But we've only done five minutes,' said Stan. 'She's not even got married yet.'

'I wouldn't have bothered with the lav if I'd known,' grumbled Pearl.

'I think he's hungry. Didn't you hear his tummy rumbling?' said Olive, as ever the one member of the class alert to the nuances of my teaching. 'You should have said, love. I'd have made you a sandwich.'

'That's very kind of you – what have you got?'

'Rolled pork with pickle, but I've only brought the one.'

'And you can stop looking at my crisps,' said Pearl.

Berkhamsted Sports Centre's tea-bar may have lacked the lavishness of Yu-fang's wedding feast, but I fell upon the cellophane-wrapped custard creams with all the vigour of one of General Xue's guests. However, like the aristocratic warlords of pre-revolutionary China I little knew what ferocity was about to be visited upon me after I had resumed my seminar, pausing only to brush the biscuit crumbs off my beard, to which Pearl had drawn unnecessary attention.

'One of the side effects of writing a blockbuster is being thrust into the glare of the media. It's a very similar experience to being a goldfish in a bowl,' I said. 'I've had some recent experience of this with something I've got out at the moment,' I added quickly, to pre-empt the next redundant question from Pearl, whose mouth was itself opening and closing in a piscine manner.

'I heard him on digital radio,' said Stan. 'He wasn't very good. And he was late – had to apologize to Don Wade.'

'Yes, Don and I had a laugh about that afterwards,' I said.

'I was going to ring in about the competition,' said Stan, 'because I knew straight off that the answer was "raspberries". But to be honest with you I didn't much like the sound of your book as the prize.'

'Fair comment,' I said. 'And this is really what I'm getting at – as an author you have to be thick-skinned. You're going to get reviewed, you're out there in the open to be shot at, and, of course, not everybody's going to like it that you're selling shed-loads of books.'

'Did you get off with that woman?' asked Stan. 'You were trying hard enough.'

'What woman?' asked Pearl, suddenly all ears.

'Jasmine Davies,' said Stan. 'He sounded like his tongue was practically hanging out. 'Course you might not have picked that up if you don't have digital.'

'She's the speed-dating one,' said Olive. 'She's good. I heard her on *Woman's Hour*. What's your book about, love?'

'Well, Olive,' I said, '*Pet Peeves* is something of a *jeu d'esprit*, an unashamedly populist piece about talking animals I turned my hand to.'

'Is that why we're doing *Wild Swans*, then?' asked Pearl.

'So is it a bit like *Doctor Dolittle?*' asked Olive.

'They showed that again at the weekend,' said Stan.

'The one with Sexy Rexy?' asked Pearl.

'No, the coloured feller.'

Not for the first time I felt that the class really weren't taking full advantage of the years of experience I was prepared to share with them. 'The point I'm trying to make – if you'll let me – is that whatever kind of writer you are, you are a writer. And if you're a writer it's you against the world. You've got to be prepared to stand up and say, "This is me – this is who I am." It doesn't matter how old you are. One of you could be the next Catherine Cookson or the new Mary Wesley.'

'They're both dead, dear,' said Olive.

'Can I be the new Harold Robbins?' said Stan.

'You can be anyone you like!' I said emphatically. 'Provided – and this should be emblazoned on every writer's very soul – provided you are true to yourself.'

'Excuse me, Sir,' came a voice from the doorway. 'Are you Mr Reardon?'

I turned to see a uniformed policeman – or uniformed police-12-year-old boy to be more accurate.

'No,' I replied automatically.

'Very true to himself,' murmured Pearl.

The interruption was to bring a mercifully early conclusion

to my writing class. What was less welcome was the announcement that I was being charged with anti-social behaviour, to wit, stealing two magazines from a public library. I strenuously protested my innocence, though on reflection I probably didn't do my cause any good by throwing in 'Who reads *Caravan and Camper* anyway?' I most certainly wasn't given any help by the chorus of ungrateful narks and turncoats behind me as I was eventually led away from the classroom in handcuffs.

'And he didn't pay for the biscuits either,' said Pearl. 'He's got form.'

'You're supposed to put 50p in the cup,' said Stan. 'I reckon he took some out. Check your CCTV footage, I would, officer.'

'I thought he was looking shifty when I saw him in the library – I should have said something, I might have got a reward.'

This, cruelly, from Olive. Well, she was welcome to her thirty pieces of silver. Though I rather doubt whether the library would have given it to her in change.

Friday

Any writer expecting to be worth his or her salt, and not just a sodium-free substitute, must be prepared to experience everything, with absolutely no exceptions. My only previous encounter with the judicial system – unless one counts an appearance before the Prefects' Court at my old school for the hanging offence of wearing non-regulation socks, a travesty of natural justice that left me with a lifelong sympathy for the underdog – was the briefing notes for the episodes I wrote for the television series, *Crown Court*, in the 1970s. And they mainly consisted of advice to avoid American courtroom jargon such as 'Objection, Your Honor', 'This is your last warning, Counsellor' and 'Now Perry, how about that steak?'

So it was in a mood of considerable intellectual curiosity that I found myself 'up before the beak'. I was most certainly *born* before the beak. The presiding magistrate at Berkhamsted was probably the first member of the judiciary to be too young to have heard of the Beatles. Something to which she promptly drew unnecessary attention.

'You're much too old to be wasting the court's time like this.'

'Right. Point taken,' I said. 'Shall I make my closing speech now?'

'No,' said the magistrate in a tone uncannily reminiscent of my ex-wife refusing me entry to my own house at 4 a.m. 'You can start by addressing me as "Madam", then you can pay a £20 fine, plus costs which comes to . . . how much?' she asked an usher.

'Three pounds. I beg your pardon, Ma'am, £5.'

'What?'

'It was a summer special double issue of *Caravan and Camping*.'

I have to admit I found this exchange, conducted in its austere wood (or at any rate melamine) panelled surroundings, somewhat risible, and could not forbear to smile. Just as before though, when I failed to stifle a snigger during the prefects' stumbling deliberations – future MPs and captains of industry trying to calculate the number of lines I should write out in direct proportion to the number of clocks on my socks – my air of amused disinterest only served to increase my punishment. Two hundred extra lines of Ovid at Shrewsbury; another fiver on my fine here.

'Thirty pounds to be paid into the court, and I don't want to see you again,' said the magistrate, getting to her feet and making a swift exit, probably to her chambers to watch *Balamory*. Thirty pounds is no doubt a trifling sum for most people – not least the miscreants appearing on the bill before me. A gang of children had roughed up Berkhamsted's floral clock, leaving it with half a little hand and only one number (8). They paid their fines with crisp fifty pound notes – or 'red ladies' as they called them – while arranging on their mobiles to convene the following night for more of the same in Leighton Buzzard, an area not yet covered by their ASBOs.

It is customary to blame parents for the problems besetting society today. Personally, I find agents just as culpable. Had Felix Jeffrey Associates delivered my *Tenko* repeat fee on time, I would have been able to pay my fine – maybe not all of it, after agency deductions for commission and VAT, but at least enough to show willing, and avoid being forced to rub shoulders with genuine ne'er-do-wells and the temptation to join them in a life of crime on the outside.

But no. Instead of the wherewithal to pay my debt to society, my pockets contained only the following: one bunch keys, one pipe, one box matches with burnt ones saved inside. One half-packet Orbit chewing gum, one Sony Walkman containing one Billie Holiday cassette, one half of a return train ticket to London. Valid only until Tuesday unfortunately.

I know this because it was the inventory written down on a clipboard and then read back to me, after I handed over my belongings to a fat man in a short-sleeved white shirt (with a spot of dried blood on the collar from inaccurate shaving), as I prepared to spend the first of ten nights in a minimum-security prison.

Thursday

There is a long and honourable tradition of writers being incarcerated. One thinks immediately of Alexander Solzhenitsyn, Oscar Wilde, Mad Frankie Fraser – all have known what it is like to have only their thoughts for company, a glimpsed patch of sky the desperately poignant connection with the outside world. I can also glimpse Carphone Warehouse which gives me a head start on Solzhenitsyn's gulag, so the pressure is now on to produce a substantial piece of work – prose or verse, at this stage I haven't decided which. Oscar Wilde composed *The Ballad of Reading Gaol* there and I gather from my forays into the Amazon jungle that Reggie Kray's *Poems for Mum* also sold pretty well.

But as the gap in this diary indicates, I have been cruelly denied the tools of my trade for almost a week now. No pipe, no baccy or whisky – only a pen and a ream of A4 paper. But I suppose I will have to make do.

Insult was added to injury this morning when a warder, or rather a 'Customer Security Operative' as it announced on his T-shirt (which was the extent of his uniform, apart from the ubiquitous trainers), came in to deliver my mail.

'Here you go, Reardon,' he said holding up a postcard displaying the Manhattan skyline, while reading the back. 'It's from – ooh! Salman Rushdie refusing to help pay your fine. Oh dear – you must have offended him as well as society.'

'He's a mate, but he has a lot of family commitments now,' I said, reaching for the postcard.

'Still, you'd think he'd be more generous,' said the warder. 'We looked after him during all that ayatollah palaver, didn't we.' He tucked the card into his back pocket.

'Aren't you going to leave it for me?' I asked. 'The picture of New York would brighten the wall up a bit.'

'Couldn't do that,' he said. 'It's got a scalloped edge – you could slit your throat with that as soon as my back was turned. And where would that leave us, pray? Down the khazi watching Group 4 pick up our contract, that's where.'

'I'll write a note,' I offered. 'Absolving you but blaming Salman Rushdie. That'd teach him.'

'Nice try,' said the warder. 'Anyway, I haven't seen you write a word yet. You haven't got long now you know – Lord Archer would have got two volumes of prison diaries done by this time. Some of it true.'

Saturday

The sounds of raucous laughter coming from the television room, as my fellow inmates watched one 12-year-old presenter on a six-figure salary covering another with a bucket of green slime, could only depress anybody whose idea of prison entertainment was formed by Johnny Cash appearing at San Quentin. Doubtless these days that Boy Named Sue would be shipped posthaste to the Special Needs Wing for psychotherapy, and the Man in Black himself kept in solitary confinement on charges of child abuse. But these ruminations were soon interrupted by another, more joyous noise, a voice which when loudly ordering another bottle in the Caprice has been known to set waiters a-scurrying in the Ivy on the other side of town.

'Is he through here?'

Felix! His accounts department may not always have been on the qui vive, but when it came to offering his clients moral support there was clearly nobody faster out of the traps. I wasn't too sure how he knew of my predicament, as I certainly hadn't told anybody close to me – not that there was anyone fitting that description, in truth – and for once I was glad that the *Berkhamsted Gazette* had buried the story about my court appearance ('Shame of Local "Author"', the quotation marks being the most unkindest cut of all) at the bottom of page 4, below the news that a 102-year-old pensioner still enjoyed fruit.

'My dear fellow, how absolutely wonderful to see you!' said Felix. 'I hope I'm not stopping you tunnelling.'

'No no – there is something called "Creative Digging" in

the Performance Art Module which may mean tunnelling, but I haven't signed up for it so I don't know.'

'So there isn't a chap underneath your chair with a fork and spoon and his trousers full of sand? Hagh hagh!' guffawed Felix, drawing looks from some of the longer-term prisoners who were now filing into the television room ready for their weekly fix of *The Saturday Brunch Bunch*.

'No. Let's get out of here,' I said. 'Some of these chaps never miss a teenage show if they can help it. Felix, I can't tell you what this means, I thought everybody had forgotten about me . . .'

'Certainly not,' said Felix.

'I'm just through here,' I said, leading him down the corridor. Felix was making great play of keeping his feet exactly congruent with the yellow line on the floor.

'This is just like finding your way round the Barbican,' said Felix. 'Well, it's been lovely to talk to you, Ed . . .'

'Anyway Felix, the thing is that we need to look at diaries and plan the rest of the year, because there's a whole slew of projects I've been inspired to take on since I came in here—'

'A slew, eh?' said Felix. 'Jolly good.'

'Yes – there's the poetry, there's the prison memoirs, there's a table-tennis play I want to do—'

'A two-hander is it? That's very commercial!' said Felix, producing a small diary from his waistcoat pocket and making a note with the little pencil.

'And I'm in the middle of a letter to *The Times* about conditions in here – it's so angry, well, they'll have to go back to being broadsheet to fit it all in. Anyway,' I said, opening the door and standing aside for Felix to duck in, 'this is me.'

'Very smart indeed!' said Felix, sitting down on the bed. 'Terribly grand. Just like school, isn't it. Have you got a fag?'

'They call them bitches here.'

'A fag *and* a bitch – lucky old you!' said Felix. 'We must be paying you too much.'

'Not enough actually, Felix,' I said. 'That's kind of why I'm here.'

Felix's laugh might have sounded automatic, but I'm fairly sure I detected a hint of nervousness as he acknowledged the bittersweet truth of my observation.

'Ah – now what's this?' he cried, scrutinizing my food bowl with the same gimlet eye I hoped he applied to the electronic rights subsidiary clause in my *Pet Peeves* contract.

'I have to eat out of that,' I said.

'What and you just put it through that little hatch do you and they fill it up? I say, I could do with one of those.'

'Yes, just rattle it at Fiona and hey presto, spotted dick,' I said, recalling the gruesome school dinner I had been invited to *chez* Jeffrey as a consolation for being left off *Granta*'s Hot Novelists list of 1982, along with Pam Erdington and Martin Brainsford – now apparently married to each other and restoring furniture near Newton Abbot.

'This has been a real eye-opener,' said Felix, getting to his feet and brushing lint from the blanket off his twills. 'But look, I'll let you get on because I've got to go now to see another very clever fellow across the way . . .'

The truth dawned like the overhead light coming on at 5.30 a.m. 'So you haven't really come to see me at all?'

'Not primarily,' said Felix. 'I'm hoping to sign him up for a book. He's a cannibal, and he advertised in the *Sunday Times* for volunteers to come and be eaten, by him d'you see. Received a surprising number of replies, too, before the forces of political correctness descended and put him in here. But if he hasn't got a recipe book in him I'm a Dutchman. Anyway Ed,' he said, turning at the door to sign off with the phrase that had never let him down in any social situation, be it a divorce, a raid from the Inland Revenue or even on one occasion being taken hostage by an armed and resentful client, 'we must have lunch.'

'Well, it's nearly quarter past ten, they'll be serving it in a minute,' I said, the day stretching before me.

'Yes, I can see you've put on a few pounds, you lucky devil. Call this a prison? You're living the life of bloody Riley here!'

The door opened at Felix's touch, again causing him to shake his head in wonderment as he set off down the corridor in search of Delia with a Difference, his new author who clearly had the secret of life. And death, come to think of it.

Sunday

Another day without putting pen to actual paper as the Reardon spirits sink further into Stygian gloom. Once again I have been persecuted for being brighter than those in authority. The latest bone of contention was the prison newsletter, or *The Wrong 'Un*, to give it its nauseatingly matey title. Page 3, alongside the selection of semi-saucy polaroids smuggled out of Holloway, contained an editorial from the Governor which perpetrated so many crimes against the English language that I was obliged to take him to task over his crass misuse of the word 'hopefully' in front of 200 inmates at this morning's roll call.

For this crime against humanity I was put on a prison bus and taken with half-a-dozen other 'gobby bastards' as the warder commandeering the front seat called us – prompting a muttered 'I shall be seeking compensation for that' from the tattooed man sitting behind me – to an industrial estate of such unloveliness as to make my current place of residence look like Blenheim Palace. There we were introduced to a machine not totally dissimilar to the Integrated Mail Processor, with which I was familiar from my regular stints working in the sorting office at Berkhamsted during the Christmas period. Five pounds sixty an hour was not to be sniffed at or be snobbish about, and paid not only my mortgage for two months but also furnished Elgar with a present and myself with enough barley wine to tide me over the holidays.

Indeed, I was more than familiar with the 'IMP' as I fondly thought of it. After two years I was officially a skilled operator, and entitled to show the ropes to other Christmas temporaries whose aborted careers ranged from industrial designers to bank managers discarded in their early forties. Altogether a satisfying experience, the Post Office, with a cheap canteen and a noble literary history dating back to Trollope who introduced the pillar box as well as Barchester to the world.

Although it may have resembled the IMP, the machine on which I was now set to work had a more melancholy *raison d'être*. Its conveyor belt contained not 'letters for the rich, letters for the poor' as Auden summed it up in 'Night Mail' – not to mention Christmas cards from people who know each other so well that they're obliged to add their surnames in brackets to the greeting, I seem to receive more than my fair share of those – but hundreds of books which on reaching the end of the belt suffered the indignity of having holes drilled through them prior to the final stage of their journey, the pulping machine.

This, of course, was the very incarnation of the story I had happened upon and which I had used not altogether successfully during my speed-dating experiment. And now here I was, standing where Jeffrey Archer and Jonathan Aitken had possibly also stood, stacking books on the belt (three deep for paperback, two for hardback) so that a lethal drill could puncture their very lungs.

The irony was bitterly complete when I saw coming in my direction a large wheeled basket containing several hundred copies of *Pet Peeves*. My life, or at any rate the six weeks that I had spent compiling the wretched toilet book, flashed before me.

'Come on, put your backs into it! Call yourself a work detail?' shouted a guard above the din of the drill, its whine rising in pitch as it coped with a hundred indigestible Nick Hornby lists of pop songs and old girlfriends.

'This isn't a holiday camp, it's a recycling unit. Prisoner 5672 – Reardon! What are you playing at? Get on with it!'

'But what you're making me do is absolutely inhuman! I don't mind putting holes in the *Schott's Miscellanies*, but some of these are mine!'

'What's this – *Pet Peeves* by Ed Reardon?' said the guard, roughly grabbing a copy of what let us not forget had been described as 'a nice little read' and scowling at it with a rheumy eye. 'All right, autograph it, *then* drill a hole in it.'

'I've done those 20,000 Stella Rimingtons, Sir,' said the ingratiating young man next to me. I had spotted him before in the games room, putting the snooker cues neatly back in their racks and sucking the kinks out of the table-tennis balls while a warder looked on approvingly. In for selling soft drugs, I surmised.

'Well done, your lordship,' said the guard. 'Just do a few baskets of Jon Snows and Rageh Omars, then you can take a break. Come on the rest of you – there's privileges to be earned here.'

'Privileges?' I said. 'Nobody told me about them.'

'Well, you should have read the newsletter instead of just criticizing it, shouldn't you?' said the guard. 'Get half a ton into the drill before lunch and there's a phonecard in it for you. Any more than that you're into Nectar points.'

I needed no further encouragement, and started stacking up the *Pet Peeves*es hand over fist. 'Come on, keep them coming!' I called to the basket-pusher. 'I can do four in a pile at once here – thank God I delivered it fifty pages too short!'

Monday

It is a sad but also in its way a felicitous fact of life that I was eventually able to make more out of destroying *Pet Peeves* than I was ever likely to earn from selling it. But as I remind my students at the University of the Third Age – or I will as soon as my mandatory suspension period is over – these are the commercial realities of the life literary. Pain and its saturnine cohort humiliation are forever lurking in the shadows, though a ray of sunny good fortune can keep them at least temporarily at bay. The well-merited £3 phonecard meant I was able to update my CV with the dating agency and also collect the encouraging number of replies that followed, as I discovered when I accessed my answering machine from the telephone in the prison corridor.

'Hello – it's Bubbly, Blonde and Caring here. "BBC", yeah? I'm assuming "CR" means you've got a criminal record, and I was just wondering when we could meet?'

The second caller was equally impressed by the sound of my CR, but her message – 'I need to know first just how many people you've murdered before I marry you' – put me alarmingly in mind of White Worm Woman. I did, however, write the next number on the back of my hand. 'Hello, am I speaking to Clyde? I think I'd like to be your Bonnie!' promised at least a night at the pictures, with a negotiable raid on a convenience store or petrol station to follow.

Three messages and so far none of them from Barclaycard. Could my luck hold? It could.

'Hello Ed? It's Jasmine Davies – we met at Saga Radio, I don't know if you remember. Ed, I was so sorry to hear about what happened to you, and I just wondered if you needed anyone to feed your cat?'

Ed Reardon had hit pay dirt as they say here, sitting round the Trivial Pursuit table.

3

Holby City

Friday

Water drips relentlessly through the ceiling, the council tax is now three months overdue and today's evening meal was assembled from five Ryvitas and a jar of pickled herring juice with a few bits of onion floating about therein. Substitute Berkhamsted for the stews of St Petersburg and Ed Reardon's life and Dostoevsky's are virtually the same. My work unrecognized, except by *Caravan and Camper*, and the progress of my love life hobbled by grinding poverty.

A more worldly amorist would, perhaps, not have brought Jasmine Davies back here on Wednesday last after a seduction lunch at the Lock-keeper's Arms, but with her husband suddenly deciding to work at home and the price of rooms at the Hemel Hempstead Travelodge being far beyond my means there was no alternative. It was not a success. Had not the sodden wallpaper and dripping ceiling light dampened her lust and sent her scurrying for the London train even before the obligatory cup of coffee was drained, then disappointment would I suspect have been made complete in the bedroom where my own ardour would have shown itself thoroughly extinguished by four pints of Lock-keeper's Arms' Wadsworth's 6X and a cheese 'steakwich' with 'farm-fresh' garnish and fries, the apostrophe inevitably misplaced before the 's'.

That was two days ago. The nourishing effects (beg pardon, 'effect's') of that lunch soon wore off along with any remaining attachment I had to Jasmine Davies, and to complete the bleak picture the wallpaper has now parted company with the section of wall behind the filing cabinet. But like Dostoevsky I can just about find a purpose for living. I, Ed Reardon, may too be in the gutter but I can still look at the sky – Sky 1, Sky 2 and Sky Sports 3 digital interactive, to be precise, which have another ten glorious days to run before they cut me off. For an extra £9.50 I could have had the Playboy Channel as well but like a blind fool I failed to invest in the future during the days of plenty that followed the *Pet Peeves* publication fee. No matter: work must come first.

The writer's knowledge of his subject needs to be so utterly comprehensive that the reader sees but the tip of a vast iceberg of research and scholarship. So for the past week I have been

watching nothing but football, garnering background material
for a new television piece set in the world of the Premiership.
I have watched all levels of the beautiful game from the hot-
house that is the Screwfix Direct Western League to several
episodes of *Footballers' Wives*. Naturally, I have been appalled
by the dismal literacy levels shown by the television commentators and the army of yclept 'experts', but perhaps the most
striking characteristic of these flat-vowelled Steves and Garys
is the unaccountably tortuous conversational routes they take
in order to be able to say the word 'Galataserai'. Money must
be riding on it, and to be sure there appear to be many oceans
of the stuff sloshing around the country's magnificent all-seat
stadia. How things have changed since the day I played in
goal for Shrewsbury against the mighty Corinthian Casuals
('The visitors bulged the onion bag on no fewer than eleven
occasions before the green-jerseyed custodian E.F. Reardon
was sent off before the interval for persistent vileness.' *The
Salopian*, 1970).

I confess to feeling a twinge of sorrow, as I forked out
Elgar's third sachet of Beef with Coley of the morning, that
the chance of earning £80,000 a week as a Premiership footballer has probably passed me by. It is especially regrettable
because just a single afternoon as a professional footballer,
however unsuccessful – 'vile' indeed – would furnish the
means for a seismic alteration to my lifestyle. Elgar could have
a new bowl, I could have some new yellow cords handmade in
Savile Row, a new pipe with a reamer in every room, *furniture*
in every room even – the kind of things that today's

Raymondo of the Rovers with his different daily hairstyle takes for granted.

I imagine young Wayne Rooney could afford a new pipe every game if he chose. I can picture him, sturdy Peterson clenched firmly between his milk teeth, puffing contentedly before delighting the crowd with one of his famous cartwheels. He would, of course, have to be careful when pulling his shirt over his head or he might burn a hole in his sponsor's logo and end up being sued by Vodafone. The effect on Colleen's shopping allowance (Wayne's fiancée at the time of writing, though by tomorrow things might have changed) could be calamitous.

My consoling reverie on the many drawbacks of incalculable wealth was interrupted by the phone ringing – or 'warbling into life' as it says in the clichéd stage directions of soap opera scripts, a language in which I nevertheless hoped to immerse myself over the coming months, if I was to be able to afford a new roof. I decided to see who the caller was before answering, lest it prove to be another woman of a certain age, building herself a forlorn pyre of romantic delusions.

'Hi Ed, it's Ping. You can pick up, I'm not Barclaycard. Oh. Well, anyroad, just to let you know that . . .'

Now here's a suitable subject for a student of today's traits and mores among the twelve-year-olds, on which I would turn my own beady eye were I not hellishly busy preparing a football script. Why must the invariably well-brought-up young ladies who work for agents, publishers, television and radio companies and the like immediately put on a cod northern accent when dealing with one, as if their finishing school was run under the auspices of the late Al Read? I'm sure if I were to call them and parody their own argot, launching into 'Hi Tanya' (or Emma or Tatiana or Georgina or any of the other first vowel-suffixed debs) 'It's like Ed here, ya? Whatever, right?' such a greeting would be regarded as frankly offensive. Since when did Ping use 'anyrord', as she pronounced it, as part of her daily conversation? 'Anymews' would be nearer the mark.

Anyroad up (to give the phrase its correct usage), in my present predicament a call from one's agent has a powerful effect on the central nervous system. After I had trodden on the edge of Elgar's bowl catapulting beef into one trouser turn-up and coley into the other, and by the time I had tripped on the flex for the TV, which I'd had to move out of the drip zone, it took rather longer than usual to cover the twelve feet from one side of the flat to the other.

'Hello Ping, I wasn't filtering, I was just . . . upstairs.'

Now why on earth did I say that? I read somewhere (in *ASDA Shopper*, probably, the freesheet which has perforce replaced my regular newspaper, which costs money) that we tell at least three lies an hour just to get us through the day. I have been innocent for many years of the most commonly uttered untruth, but not having to say 'I love you' leaves one ample scope to practise the many other kinds of deceit that exist beyond the realm of coupledom, 'I was just . . . upstairs' being one of the more asinine. One probably lies to the opposite sex more than to one's own but there's not a lot in it. 'I'm not rich but I've got all the money I need' is possibly the fib most

commonly used by divorcés of my age, closely followed by
'Better get to the gym before it closes', 'Great party' and 'I like
meeting new people.' For the solitary journey home from
London there is the desperate and hardly ever successful 'There
were no ticket machines working at Euston' and 'Certainly,
Officer. My name is Mark Lawson.' (Or Vincent Duggleby or
Bonnie Greer or whoever has recently caused me the most pro-
found irritation.)

And like the football commentators we often take circuitous
routes in our mendacity. Whenever Cliff, the Bayou Boys'
vocalist, cadges a lift to a gig, the first thing he says when he
gets in the car is, 'I need to get to a cashpoint', secure in the
knowledge that the driver won't want to be bothered with the
risk of parking on a double yellow or red line, thereby absolving Cliff of the need to make a petrol money contribution or
buy his chauffeur so much as a half of bitter in thanks. A canny
old fox, is Cliff. So in order to convince my agent that I wasn't
filtering calls to avoid the Barclaycard Gestapo I ended up
saying 'I was just . . . upstairs.'

'But Ed, I thought you lived in a top-floor flat.'

'Yes, I do, but . . . um.'

'Are you having a loft conversion done or something?'

'Yes I am. Now what did you want to talk to me about?'

'Oh just work – but that's *so* brilliant! My parents just had
this roof terrace with a pool put in and they got this Italian guy,
Lorenzo, he works in a cape and uses these special tiles – such
a great roofer. I've got his number here, you must use him.
It's – well you know the code for Rome – then it's 57362-*uno*.'

'Right, thank you very much,' I said, making it sound as if I was noting the number down. 'Anyway, Ping, this work business . . .'

'Just wanted to check you're still on for the *Holby City* meetingy thing at Elstree on Monday. I've made the appointment for before lunch, yeah. I thought that would be sensible.'

'Ah, so they'll be feeding me then?'

'That's not actually what I meant, Ed. And as well as obviously not having a drink, right, it's probably better to let them do most of the talking. And, look, try not to go on too much about the old days on *Tenko*, okay?'

'All right.'

'Because they might not actually agree how everything's all dumbed down these days and that other stuff about spelling that you sometimes say.'

'No. Point taken, Ping.'

'And they might be quite young.'

'Right – so moronic children is what we're dealing with, is it?'

'Ed!'

I assured Ping that I would be a credit to her, to the agency and my profession as a whole. I undertook, moreover, to turn up sober, on time and bursting with ideas, although from what she'd told me about my prospective employers I rather doubted their ability to recognize an idea. A picture of a cow, a car or a dog possibly, but an idea . . . However, an artist must always defer to his patron, and just as Haydn had held himself in check at the Esterhazy Palace and Bach buttoned his lip in the presence of the Margrave of wherever-it-was, Ed Reardon, too, must be on his best behaviour at Elstree Studios on Monday. For whatever insubordinate thoughts the literary bondsman might bandy around below stairs he must be the soul of respectful obedience before his paymasters – pampered, ignorant little squits though they might be. Besides, as I told Ping, I wasn't very likely to lash out for a £12.60 bus fare simply in order to talk myself out of a job.

'Mmm – I suppose I was thinking of what happened when you went to see the *Emmerdale* people.'

'Well, they were just plain rude.'

'Yeah they were but I can see where they were coming from. I mean, I know they'd had a plane crash story line once before but a Japanese kamikaze attack on the Woolpack, Ed, that was a bit far-fetched. Anyway gotta go, yeah. Ten-thirty main reception, okay? And you can't park. Lots of luck darling – bye!'

Sunday

It now needs a bucket, the washing-up bowl and a tankard purloined from the Hat and Feathers to catch the drips. So, like Proust before me, I have been obliged to retire to my bedchamber, the only dry room in the flat, in order to work. The importance of getting this TV job and its attendant five-figure fee to put a dry roof over my head cannot be overstated. However, getting *to* the TV job is the problem as I am currently still £12.45 short of the return bus fare to Elstree.

Sunday

At this point bohemian folklore would have the artist scribble out a poem or sketch a quick still life in charcoal to be hung up on a nearby café wall in exchange for a loan and a hearty cassoulet washed down with a pitcher of *vin rouge*. Picasso and James Joyce were bloody lucky that their local wasn't the Berkhamsted Nando's or they'd have died of starvation and the world would never have heard of them. By Saturday evening I had reached the reluctant conclusion that I would have to offer up for auction my one remaining asset of value, the original typescript of my episode of *Tenko*.

The sale would at least give me some collateral against which to borrow – a highfalutin way of saying persuade my friend, Ted Cartwright, to nick a tenner from his wife's purse. My hopes of salvation rested, therefore, with that marvellous invention called eBay, and I managed to last until 9 a.m. this morning before I logged on to see how the bidding was going. Disappointingly, Episode Five of Series Three ('Escape from the Bamboo Noose') had attracted nary a nibble from the various Japanese libraries and universities that would have been obvious homes for this particular Ed Reardon work. I dared to hope for better things in the afternoon by which time America would be awake and the major collectors starting to trade punches. But by five o'clock the top bid remained at three euros – hardly sufficient to get me as far as Radlett and nothing like enough to service Elgar's expensive Felix Senior habit.

Tempting though the offer was, I resisted. In any case, I hate the thought of my work leaving the country, especially to

101

America, home of the hollow phrase and lachrymose butterball sentimentality. In due course, the Lottery Fund may possibly intervene to save my script for the nation. But for the time being I decided to draw a line under the humiliating episode and opened another sachet for Elgar. Prawn and Vegetable. Not the worst combination of flavours by any means. Forking the brown goo into the dish, I wondered idly if Tom Stoppard had ever been tempted to eat his own cat's food? Indeed, what kind of food would Tom Stoppard's cat eat? No doubt something smart, with an anagram on the tin.

And almost certainly better tasting than Felix Prawn and Vegetable on Ryvita.

Monday

The journey from Berkhamsted to Elstree was scheduled to take three hours, but I could, I suppose, have slashed two hours and forty-five minutes off that when a lorry slowed to offer me a lift on the bypass. Not for me the glum hitchhiker's hand-written destination on a piece of grimy cardboard – I prefer the long piece of meadow grass in the mouth and a stick to swish at dandelions growing on the verge, giving off I like to think the air of Laurie Lee setting out one midsummer morning for a contemplative stroll, albeit on a hard shoulder. The lorry driver, however, wasn't taken in.

'Where you going, pal?'

"Elstree Studios, actually.'

'Oh yeah? Film star, are you? Researching a part?'

'No, I'm a writer.'

'Yeah? Hop in.' The man seemed perfectly friendly and non-threatening given the array of small cuddly toys on his dashboard. Moreover, there was a large Perspex lunch box on the seat beside him, in which I glimpsed crisps, which would have been decidedly welcome even at 7.45 in the morning. What he said next though, as I was poised with my foot on his top step, sent a chill wind through my already weary bones.

'I'll give you something to write about – delivering carpet tiles. Been doing it eleven years. The stories I could tell you – come on, hurry up, I'm on a red route.'

'Thank you – no,' I said, closing the door before he could even contemplate conjuring up the first knock-'em-dead warehousing anecdote. 'The fresh air will do me good.'

'Suit yourself,' he said and drove off, leaving me to find another stick after I had thrown mine in prior to clambering into his warm and dry cab. Because on cue the Pathetic Fallacy kicked in and it began to rain quite hard, on both this gentleman of the road and his defective roof, making it even more essential that I 'got a result' as they say in football.

At the studios I was duly led to the producer's office at 11.15 sharp having been kept waiting for forty-five minutes, which did at least give my trousers and shoes time to dry out, and me time to drink three cups of coffee, which I took black, secreting the little tubs of dairy-style whitener and sachets of sugar about my person for future emergencies. Maddy, a gravelly voiced woman in a shapeless 'LA Lakers' sweatshirt, sat me on a very low orange seat opposite her desk before introducing me to Tim and Horatio, her 12-year-old script editor and dribbling Labrador. I said hi to Tim and tried to pat Horatio.

'No, he's Horatio – this is Tim,' said Maddy, pulling the dog away from me, luckily just before it managed to locate the sugar.

'And what is he – another producer?' I said light-heartedly.

'No, he's my dog,' said Maddy, giving me notice that whatever kind of ride I was in for, it was unlikely to be fun-filled. 'But he's very astute – he's got a PhD in people.'

'I'd better watch what I say then!'

The dog growled, I had to admit, knowingly.

Seeing a dog at a TV production meeting brought back memories of my previous career writing drama for the small screen, when Ted Cartwright would regularly bring his spaniels, Barlow and Watt, along to *Onedin Line* script meetings. I remember them once getting into a scrap in the lift at TV Centre with an Alsatian belonging to John Hawkesworth up for the day for a brainstorming session that eventually became the *Duchess of Duke Street*. Of course, this was a time when I doubt even Horatio the script editor's parents had been born. Clearly the child of a generation that had been fed an exclusive diet of television, Horatio now warbled into life, to coin a phrase.

'Hey, listen, Ed – an actual *Tenko* writer – respect! Y'know Maddy, the guy is just a total grooveball. It was the first piece of eighties retro realism, but it also had a pre-punk innocence.'

'One does one's best,' I said, casting my mind back to try to think where 'pre-punk innocence' might justifiably have described life in a Japanese prison camp. The scenes filmed in Dorset, perhaps.

There was now no stopping Horatio's enthusiasm, though I could see Maddy had one eye on the clock.

'Did you get to meet Burt Kwook?'

'It's spelt Kwouk but pronounced Kwok, actually. Oh yes – I still use his risotto recipe.'

'Wow!' said Horatio. 'Is there a chance you could like e-mail it to me?'

'Anyway,' said Maddy. 'What have you been doing since then, Ed? Because your CV stops after *Tenko* in 1982. Are there some pages missing?'

'Oh, I don't bother with those things,' I said. 'You can either write or you can't, I find. This is the thing that matters. In the room, with the idea – dealing with people face to face.' I was about to add, 'Chewing over the red meat of the drama', but Tim got to his feet and started growling so I gave Maddy the floor.

'So Ed – what's your pitch?'

An odd question I thought, but no doubt dictated by the budget, as I imagined most television was these days.

'My pitch? Well, I thought we could use the standard length, a goal at each end . . .'

Horatio let out a high-pitched giggle and threw his hands up, almost knocking off his square spectacles.

'I tell you, Maddy – this guy!'

'But my *story* is that the entire Holby City team is kidnapped by an unscrupulous oriental property developer, and has to escape before a vital—'

'Let me stop you there, Ed,' said Maddy. 'Which team? The surgical team or the renal unit?'

'No, the football team.'

'Which football team?'

'Holby City.'

'So the hospital's got its own football team?' said Horatio, making a note with a pen which I noticed was shaped like a miniature stethoscope. 'Whoa – serious demographic brownie points!'

'What hospital?' I said.

'The hospital where the series is set, Ed. You do know that, don't you?'

By not telling me that *Holby City* was a medical rather than a football drama my agent surpassed even her own lofty standards of inefficiency. In my own defence I would say that it was broadcast on the same night as I taught my creative writing class (they often cited it in their persistent grumbling, along the lines of 'Are we missing *Holby City* for this?') and that in any case I had completely given up on television drama long ago – anything that has to announce itself as such in programme trailers is patently nothing of the sort – assuming that I would merely be denying myself a lazy procession of mutilated child victims of serial killers, the *Grand Guignol* crimes solved the next evening by forensic pathologists played by the former 'stars' of soap operas.

Putting this point of view would not, however, get me a new roof, and luckily I was able to think on my feet – no mean achievement after a twenty-mile walk from Berkhamsted.

'Right,' I said. 'Okay,' I added. 'So we wouldn't necessarily have to see so much football – which would be good because you'd save on all the exteriors.'

Maddy looked at me with not just pursed lips but pursed everything, which may have been the result of a botched face-lift performed during the hiatus between series.

'We do have an entire hospital set just across there, Ed, which we probably ought to use,' she said, pointing out of the window at a building which, come to think of it, bore a distinct resemblance to the old *Emergency Ward 10* set of nearly fifty years ago.

'Sure,' I said. 'Well, let's think. Er – a Premiership football team gets injured . . . in a motorway pile-up . . .'

One of my words must have had magic properties because Maddy and Horatio caught each other's eyes with a distinct flicker of interest. I couldn't swear to it, but I think Tim pricked his ears up, too.

'The team coach gets stuck on a level crossing. We've got loads of train crash offcuts from *Casualty*,' said Horatio.

'Good, Horatio,' said Maddy. 'Ed, this could be a runner. We haven't done a disaster for three weeks.'

'So . . .' I said, feeling my way gingerly to the moment I could reel them in. 'They're in the hospital, with a vital match coming up – a six-pointer I think they call them – and the doctor who might be Japanese but that's not set in stone – the doctor won't sign them off . . . so they escape. From *Holby City*, as you call it . . . using surgical implements.'

Horatio punched the air in his excitement. 'Yesss! They

could just hack their way out.' He proceeded to mime a machete massacre. 'Total slice-fest. That'd be soooo Tarantinoesque!'

'I beg your pardon?' I said.

'It's all right,' said Maddy. 'He has to use that word every half-hour. And you're forgetting the nine o'clock watershed, Horatio. But carry on, Ed – you're on a bit of a roll . . .'

Being told that you're 'on a roll' by a producer is almost as conducive to the creative juices as 'What are you on, Ed, and can I have some of it please?' This was something once said to me by my editor on *Jane Seymour's Household Hints* when I was able to deliver at least 270 of the contracted 400 hints well ahead of schedule – a feat not altogether unconnected with a ticket to see England versus Australia at the Oval suddenly becoming available when a writer chum had the date of his prostate operation brought forward; it's an ill wind.

By the time I set out again on my homeward trek from Elstree I had persuaded the television people that I could deliver them a memorable fifty minutes of quality drama – or at any rate deliver them a treatment, a medical term with which I had no difficulty. I was also looking forward to my next writing class, and the chance to demonstrate subtly to my grey-rinsed brood that what appeared on their TV screens did not just happen, but was from first to last the brainchild of a writer working at the height of his imaginative powers.

'So how much do you get for that, then?' said Pearl, missing the point with her usual unerring aim.

'Well, I never like to use myself as an example in writing seminars,' I said.

'But you're still wearing your security badge that got you into the BBC,' pointed out Olive.

This was true, and something I hadn't realized – after walking all the way home again the previous afternoon I was in no mood to do anything except flop down in my chair with a bottle of whisky (to purchase which I had been obliged to write a bad cheque at the nearest convenience store) and put my feet up, the better to avoid getting them wet again in the rising waters of the living room. Consequently, I had slept in my clothes and hadn't bothered to check my appearance this morning, reasoning that the only people I would be meeting during the day were a few short-sighted pensioners.

'All I want to do,' I said, unpinning the badge and trying to stand it up in front of me on the table, 'is make the point that in television, of which I have a little bit of experience, the treatment is everything. That three and a half pages – or five if you double-space it – is the wellspring from which everything flows.'

'So how much do you get for it then?' repeated Olive.

'Come on, tell us,' said Stan. 'We've paid good money for this course, we want to know how much we're going to get back.'

'Oh, I forget exactly,' I said, giving up on the badge. 'It's something in the region of 500.'

This caused a sensation. 'Five hundred thousand?' they chorused.

'No no – £500.'

'You mean you've done a whole story for *Holby City* for £500?' said Stan.

'Well no – it's 225 actually, then if they like it they give you the other 275.'

'Is that all?' said Olive. 'For a wellspring?'

'No wonder they let him keep the badge,' said Pearl.

'Yes, but the thing is if you go to the script stage then it's serious money,' I said. 'Tuscany time,' I went on, aware that what had seemed the answer to my prayers yesterday now sounded like something out of the dark days before the minimum wage.

'But you've still only got £225,' pointed out Stan remorselessly. 'And there's no guarantee they'll take it'.

'I wish I'd done the plumbing course now,' said Pearl. 'They get 70,000 a year. And the respect of their peers.'

'What's your story about, love?' said Olive, encouraging as ever. 'I like *Holby City*.'

'Well, originally it was about a football team who get injured in a horrific level-crossing accident . . .'

'They did that one about two years ago – saw it at my niece's,' said Stan.

'As the script editor discovered,' I said. An e-mail from Horatio had arrived that morning, entitled 'Ay caramba! Bit of a cock-up on the story front. Ooh missus', an unlovely conflation of several TV references. 'So now,' I said, 'it's about Dr Kamal and his ex-wife stalking him, possibly at a level crossing but that's not set in stone.'

'Can't you make him get off with that new coloured nurse?' said Olive. 'I like her – she's got a bit about her.'

'No, she's sweet on that driver with ringlets,' said Stan, and I

made a mental note to develop that potentially triangular relationship as my second subplot, or 'C story line' as Horatio had
repeatedly called it.

'Anyway' I said, 'the current thinking is that the ex-wife kid-
naps Dr Kamal and keeps him prisoner until he escapes during
a torrential downpour that floods out the basement where he's
being kept prisoner.'

'Sounds a bit like that *Tenko* story he keeps showing us,' said
Pearl.

'Yes, but they don't know that,' I said. 'And this is normally
the time I would be screening an example of how television
can convey a social message under the guise of popular entertainment in the shape of *Tenko*. But – but . . .' I said, to ward off
the groans as I reached for the remote control, 'instead, why
don't we study the BBC's current output by settling back and
taking an informed look at *Holby City*?'

'Waste of time me taping it at home now,' grumbled Stan.

Tuesday

I lift my eyes from the screen, distracted by Elgar's piteous
mewing, to see him staring at the water leaking from the ceiling,
which is now lapping over the edges of his food bowl, making
his Felix float. Draft three of the *Holby City* treatment has also
taken a turn for the worse. Dr Kamal's ex-wife has been arrested
for shoplifting – or rather the actress who plays her has,
according to all the breakfast-time TV news bulletins, who find

the incident more important than the famine in Africa and the latest dire predictions about global warming. This has necessitated what Horatio, the 12-year-old script editor, is pleased to call 'a tweak'. In plain English this means rewriting the whole plot so that it is now the new black nurse on the cancer ward who is being stalked and kidnapped by Dr Kamal or possibly her babysitter. Who has just discovered that she may be the child's real mother. I think.

I would be happy to give the story an extra-large tweak and make the lot of them succumb to a fatal superbug. Except I really do need this £500 fee to pay for the plumber whose services I have engaged, and who now rings my doorbell, causing me to press 'Save' and steel myself to deal with a morning of inane conversation and requests for tea and toilet facilities with a display of hearty I'm-self-employed-like-you-mate banter.

'Come in, come in,' I said. 'You're just in time, the flood waters are closing inexorably over my head.'

'Oh, I hope not, Sir,' said the man, with a rather refreshing politeness I thought. 'I'm sure we can reach an agreeable settlement,' he went on, rather more strangely. 'If you'd like to look at my ID?'

It was too late. I'd already let the man in, shut the door behind him and was about to offer him a hot drink with two sugars (courtesy of the BBC) without any of the elementary vetting procedures I usually apply to anybody who tries to breach my fortress. I must literally have had water on the brain.

'Bailiffs??'

'That's right, Sir. Bailiffs,' said the man, putting away his official identity card with its municipal crest and bringing out a small, but terrifying-looking, blue receipt book. 'We tried dressing it up with all sorts of other titles and customer-friendly slogans on laminated cards like "Here to serve you – with a writ!" or "Losing your possessions just got easier." But really, that's just an insult to your intelligence.'

'It is, isn't it,' I said, my eyes following his round the room as he surveyed my dripping worldly goods.

'So yes, we're the bailiffs – or rather I am the bailiffs because we're all feeling the pinch these days aren't we – and I'm here about non-payment of council tax, £392.'

One of the first things you learn as a writer is that many have travelled this lonely road before, and that while the scenery may change, the potholes in the road and the blind corners and the unexpected head-on collisions never do. One of my early mentors had been a successful radio scriptwriter, supplying material for among others Jimmy Clitheroe. When that kind of humour went out of fashion he was unable to adapt his style to that demanded by the university-educated wits, and his circumstances were rapidly and drastically reduced. When faced with a visit from the bailiffs, my resourceful friend advised, now with the voice of experience, what you do is put a bag or a box containing items to the value they're demanding just inside the front door, ready to be handed over and thus mitigating the need for any unpleasantness, broken furniture and noses and so forth. He himself was able to appease his unwelcome visitors with a complete set of Jimmy Clitheroe's school uniform, which the star had given him in lieu of payment for an after-dinner speech. For decades the pint-sized humorist insisted on wearing his uniform in public at all times, even during a radio recording. In truth, he had dozens of them and they were much collected by some of the more abstruse fan clubs in the north.

The man must have read my mind, or at least that part of it not relating to the Clitheroe Kid. 'Or goods and chattels in lieu,' he said.

'Well,' I said, 'I can't give you the computer, I need that to work on. But there is quite a rare literary artefact in my possession. An original script of *Tenko*, signed by the author, or it can be if that helps. You may remember it, it was called "Escape from—"'

'Actually, I was more of a *Poldark* man,' said the bailiff. 'In fact it was one of those smuggling yarns that got me into this game. I always admired the excise men's knee-breeches, if the truth be told.'

This developing conversation at least indicated that I was unlikely to be subject to any physical violence.

'They wouldn't be very intimidating now though, probably,' I said, 'especially on some of those rough council estates. Not that there's anything wrong with council estates,' I added quickly, in case my man had pulled himself up from one of them by his bootstraps, or rather shoe-buckles in view of his *Poldark* predilection.

'Just to return to the point, Mr Reardon,' said the bailiff. 'I've got four more self-employed people to see this morning, one of them with a baby dying of leprosy, or so he claims.'

Tuesday

'I suppose my rack of pipes and the tobacco jar are probably worth quite a bit,' I said half-heartedly.

'But they're the tools of your trade, too, by the smell of it. Have you considered cash?' he said. 'It's a form of payment often overlooked in the heat of the moment.'

'D'you know what? You're right, I didn't consider that,' I said. 'I can give you a cheque.'

'Certainly, sir,' said the man with a smile. A trusting smile at that, which I was careful not to wipe from his face by opening the desk drawer and pulling out the chequebook in too guilty a haste.

'So that's £392 payable to Dacorum Borough Council, Sir. And I'll do you a receipt. Afraid it's still got the smiling cash register saying "Ker-ching!" but we're phasing these out.'

'Good,' I said, trying to hide the stub from the other rubber cheque paid to the convenience store with my thumb. 'This is nerve-wracking enough without the gallows humour.'

'Oh the gallows went a long time ago – apart from in the Liverpool area. You have to be cruel to be kind there,' said the bailiff, carefully pocketing my cheque for all the world as if it was worth something. 'That's a nasty leak you got, Mr Reardon.'

'Yes, I thought you were the plumber. That's why I opened the door.'

He looked thoughtfully at the ceiling and put his hands in his pockets. The interview I feared was about to move into an informal phase, the main business having been concluded, or so he thought, to our mutual satisfaction. I dread nothing so much

115

as manly small talk, and when DIY is the topic my throat tightens and beads of sweat appear on my forehead.

'Looks like it's started here,' he said, moving a chair to examine the spot as if he owned the place, which I suppose in a sense he did. 'Then it's ended up ponding over there.'

One could fill a book with handyman's neologisms, and I may well do so if I can find a publisher to subsidize it. When faced with a man who uses words like 'ponding' without a flicker of embarrassment my face flushes with a mixture of contempt and envy. I hoped my nervous cough conveyed some of these feelings, but I could tell that it didn't. When a man is 'sourcing drippage' he is deaf to such nuances.

'It could,' he said, pointing at one of many sodden patches, 'be a mouse.'

'A mouse? A mouse that's incontinent?' I said, but I knew from experience that the disingenuous approach only serves to encourage them.

'No, bitten through the pipe – they're all plastic these days. One chomp and it's through. You want to get yourself a cat.'

'I've already got one,' I said, on sure ground for once.

'Must be feeding it too much, then.'

I coughed again to warn him in no uncertain terms that the powers invested in him by Her Majesty were limited to forced entry and intimidation, but already his mind was racing ahead to the next act of licensed piracy.

'Well, that's all in order,' he said, patting his pocket smugly. 'I'll leave you alone now.'

As soon as I closed the door on him I heard a forlorn miaow

for food as Elgar emerged from his hiding place in the airing cupboard.

'Dream on,' I said, the master once more in my own house. 'Earn your keep for once.' And I may have added a heartless cackle.

The bailiff's intuition about the mouse had a certain folkloric plausibility, expressed though it was in words yet to be announced along with chav, bling and is-my-iPod-too-loud? as brand new entries in the OED. And with the plumber due to arrive at some unspecified point between the hours of eight in the morning and one in the afternoon I gave some thought as to how I might pass the theory on. The less time spent on diagnosis the cheaper the bill. I may even have practised saying 'ponding' out loud.

Wednesday

'A mouse?' said the representative of Kwik-Plumb ('No Kallout Charge') at around 5 p.m. the following day. 'If I had a pound for every time someone said that, I'd be on 250k a year instead of just seventy-five. All that lot'll have to come down.'

He made a terrifying sweep of his hand that started at the ceiling and ended at the floor like some decadent Caesar ordering the disembowelling of a hapless prisoner. There was, though, to be a stay of execution.

'Can't do it now. I'm knocking off. Taking the family to *The Woman in White*. She drowns and all,' he added with a chuckle.

'I don't think she does.'

'Whatever – I'll let you know tomorrow. Be sometime between eight and one. You should be all right till then. I see you've got plenty to read anyway.'

Friday

With three working days having elapsed and the council tax cheque about to be presented it was back to Elstree, where I awaited the discussion of draft five of the treatment with rather more than casual interest. But I was encouraged by a cheery message on my answering machine from Horatio, who with a perceptiveness beyond his years reassured me that the treatment was a 'kazillion times better' than draft four. So encouraged was I in fact, that I threw caution to the winds, wrote another cheque at the bus station and travelled to the studios in some comfort, anticipating a morning of compliments and the promise of lunch.

'But Horatio said it was a ka— quite a lot better.'

'It is, Ed,' said Maddy, and despite this reassurance her use of my name made my blood run cold.

'You just need to look at the beats of Act 3 maybe move some of them to Act One and give the arc of Act Two some grunt and there you are bosh bosh,' said Horatio, or Brutus as I now thought of him. I would like to be able to report that he shamefacedly avoided my eye, but instead I got the full-on beam from his square specs. A boy who had clearly never known a moment of self-doubt.

'It really is all there, Ed,' said Maddy.

'So are you accepting it then?' I asked, pretending to write down 'bosh bosh' at the same time lest my desperation for a couple of hundred quid became too transparent.

'Accepting it? We love it,' said Horatio.

'So that's a yes is it,' I said with a look at Maddy, who clearly controlled the purse strings.

'Just needs a few more tweaks,' said Horatio.

'You mean tweaks of the tweaks I've already done?

'No, those tweaks are great. Just tweak the beats a bit more.'

I sensed Ping, like many other women in my life before her, urging me not to make trouble, providing my own bait at which I could then snap with possibly fatal consequences. I ignored her.

'And add some grunt,' I said.

'Grunt is our DNA, Ed,' said Horatio with a smile and, I could swear, the hint of a wink.

There is an almost enjoyable split second when one knows one is going too far, just after the words have started coming out and it's too late to stop them.

'D'you want to mark in the treatment where you want the grunt?' I said. 'Put "Ug" or something?'

'Come on Ed, you're the writer,' said Maddy, glancing at the clock above the door. 'Look, I've got to pick Tim up from the vet's. Ed, shall we split a cab to the station?'

An offer to share a taxi from a producer is never to be lightly dismissed, as it can often lead to further work and on rare occasions to matters of the heart. To set against this was the fact that

I already had a return bus ticket and, even more compellingly, no money.

'Or d'you want to stay here and go through the story beat by beat with me?' said Horatio. 'I've got till 4.30.'

'If this goes well, you might want to think about doing another one for us,' said Maddy in the cab. 'Because you know Holby's fifty-two weeks a year now. And there aren't that many good writers around.'

'That's very flattering, but I'm not sure I've got the grunt in me,' I said, stealing a look across at Maddy as she took off a large earring, the better to listen to messages on her mobile. It was a gesture strangely reminiscent of – who? Anne Bancroft in *The Graduate*, that's who. And now that the desk was no longer between Maddy and me and we were at the same height, I could see that there was a *jolie laide* quality to her that was by no means totally unattractive. I certainly wouldn't kick her out of a cab, that was for sure – though as the meter inexorably clicked up I was beginning to worry that the boot might be on the other foot.

Maddy snapped the jaws of her phone shut. 'You mustn't take too much notice of Horatio. I don't know how much longer he'll be with us – he's being head-hunted by *Strictly Come Dancing*.'

'Joe Loss and the band had better watch their beats then,' I said, a reference I was confident would mean something to us both.

'Can you stop please?' said Maddy, suddenly leaning forwards to the driver.

Friday

'Sorry, I shouldn't have said that,' I said. The thinness of a fellow-professional's skin is notoriously difficult to judge, in my long experience. Oh well, it was still only half a mile to the bus stop, albeit in a direction which would take me back past the studios, which might necessitate going on all fours for fifty yards or so below the level of the car-park wall, in case Horatio happened to be looking out of the window.

Maddy stared at me. 'What? No, I've got to buy a birthday card for Art Malik. Won't be a sec.'

As the cab waited by the parade of shops, seconds turned to minutes and minutes turned to a gnawing anxiety as the taximeter clicked over into double figures with a rapidity matched only by my escalating heart rate. Normally the correct procedure as laid out in the Writers' Guild guidelines would have been to jump out of the cab and run away. But the prospect of future and, indeed, regular work filled me with optimism which led me instead to a nearby cashpoint to try to secure my half of the fare. The BBC did after all owe me for the first half of my *Holby City* treatment fee and surely it wasn't beyond the bounds of possibility that . . .

It was. It is bad enough seeing the words 'SORRY – THERE ARE INSUFFICIENT FUNDS IN YOUR ACCOUNT' without having to listen to the loud beep that lets everybody in the queue know, too.

Aware that there was someone waiting behind me, I made what I thought was a passable show of having keyed in the wrong number, and tried again. The beep was, if anything, louder the second time.

'Oh, this is absolutely ridiculous,' I said.

'Not a very good actor, are you?' said a voice behind me. 'Not much of a writer either, as I remember.'

It is often said about a face that you can't quite place it. I had the opposite reaction when I turned to look at the man who had delivered this quite unwarranted insult. I had seen him everywhere, or at least that was my impression.

'You're Ed Reardon, aren't you,' he said, in a strange accent that was half Home Counties, half Hong Kong. 'You killed me off in *Tenko*, you git.'

'Did I? Sorry about that,' I said with a friendly smile, though his choice of language made me less confident that he could tell the difference between high-quality popular drama and reality.

'I'm Dave Wang. They told me I was in for another five episodes till you came along, Mr Big Scriptwriter. Then six old biddies in flowery dresses make a break for it and I fall off the bamboo ladder and drown in a swamp. Thank you very much.'

'I thought it was a good story though,' I said. And so it was – at least a third of it was still earning me money almost twenty-five years later, or it would be if Horatio could be persuaded not to tweak it into an early grave.

'Yeah? You know what the ending of that story was?' said Dave Wang. 'We lost the caravan. The wife left me. Then the café went as well with the divorce.'

'Oh, I'm awfully sorry . . .'

'She wouldn't let me see the kids and I ended up in a

hostel. "Ew I'm awfully sorry",' said Dave Wang, fluttering his hands about in what I suppose was meant to be an effeminate impression of the man who, after all, had given him life. 'Now look at me. I'm working as an extra, pushing trolleys on *Holby City* for seventy quid a day.'

He busied himself at the cashpoint, which handed over a sizable wad, no questions asked. Meanwhile, Maddy had come out of Clinton Cards clutching a three-foot square package and a heart-shaped helium balloon and was looking across at us askance.

'Oh, so it all worked out for the best in the end,' I said, edging towards the cab.

'No it did not,' said Dave Wang. 'I was set to break into movies. I was up for a Bond film. *Cannon and Ball Christmas Special. Book at Bedtime.* Then you.'

'Ed, come on,' called Maddy. 'I'm going to miss my train.'

'Look Dave – I'm going to make this up to you,' I said. 'That's the producer over there.'

'I know – I've done seventy-three of these. Same old trolley.'

'How about a speaking part?'

This produced not the expected gratitude, but instead a short dismissive laugh.

'Still writing for a living, are you?' said Dave Wang. 'You could have fooled me – the state of those shoes!'

For some reason I found this more infuriating than anything that had been said to me during the whole *Holby City* adventure, even including Maddy's assumption that the twenty-year gap in my CV had been the fault of a photocopier rather than society. I let Dave Wang have it with both barrels.

'Well, you just try getting money out of this lot. It's five drafts before you even see a penny. I've had to walk here from Berkhamsted twice, and back again. And last time I only got lunch 'cause I half-inched a sausage roll that Madam threw for the dog. It's like a labour camp – no offence.'

'Sorry pal, I didn't realize,' said Dave Wang, who at least had the grace to act contrite.

'Ed!' called Maddy again, who was now sitting half-in and half-out of the cab as she tried to control the balloon.

'Look, I really will make this up to you,' I said to Dave Wang. 'I'll write you a part. It is in my gift, you know – one of the few powers a writer has left.'

'Yeah? How about a ducker and diver type – with an eye for the main chance? I've always fancied playing a real wide boy, Mister Big. Doctor Big even.'

'Lend me a tenner and you can have a gold toothpick and a white cat,' I said.

'Go on then,' said Dave Wang, handing over the money willingly enough – though he couldn't quite disguise the air of a man who's just been fleeced of his betting funds playing Find the Lady on the way to a race meeting.

In the cab Art Malik's card sat between us like a partition, but I could sense Maddy's displeasure.

'Sorry, I was just getting some cash for the fare.'

'It's okay, it's on account,' said Maddy and it was fortunate that she wasn't able to see my emphatically post-watershed reaction. 'But a word to the wise, Ed. Don't talk to the extras.

They never leave you alone. And they're always first to the lunch table.'

So, £70 a day *plus* food. I made a sizable mental note.

Tuesday

A good day. *Now Voyager* on BBC2 followed by racing from Cheltenham on Channel 4. A nap, a bath and a pre-dinner snifter from the bottle of Musketeer gin purchased with Dave Wang's tenner. The leak in the roof is temporarily fixed despite the plumber's deplorable practice of popping out for half an hour then not returning until the following day, leaving one utterly housebound in the interim. The working methods of plumbers, electricians and builders bear a notable resemblance to the behaviour of sheep in that they are never content with the grass on which they stand and are forever seeking a more succulent mouthful elsewhere, however distant and inaccessible. When an artisan's mobile rings alerting him to a kitchen in Hitchin in need of rewiring or a bit of repointing that needs doing in Harpenden, he is off like a startled ewe in the deluded hope of richer pickings for less effort in the next field, only to return disillusioned a day later to resume where he left off. It's a lucky thing authors don't behave like that or no books, scripts or newspaper articles would get written at all, I reflected as I just had a quick look at *Richard & Judy* to see if there were any fellow authors appearing on it whom I could enjoyably berate.

I had received in the morning post a specimen script from the *Holby City* people in order, as they put it, to help me 'get the feel of *Holby* dialogue'. I sat down after dinner with every intention of reading it but, dear God, was ever the occupant of an A&E trolley more cruelly mangled than was the English language in this sorry sixty pages of solecism and infelicity? I gave up and watched the snooker. Until, that is, the start of the latest reality wife-swapping show, but thirty seconds of that was enough, ditto *Newsnight Review* featuring the sage opinions of 'Broadcaster and Playwright' Bonnie Greer. 'Dear BBC,' I began my e-mail to their inevitably 'award-winning' website, 'would you be so kind as to tell me where and when this obscure woman's plays are currently being produced, as I would be interested in buying a ticket to see one?' In fact, the only thing that held my sustained interest was a channel called Red Hot, but that ran out after ten minutes leaving me with the choice of paying a £12 subscription fee ('confidentiality assured') or finding stimulation elsewhere. *The Howitzer Story* on UKTV History fitted the bill admirably – intriguing how a seasoned weapon commands attention and respect in a way that its modern counterpart never can. *The Uzi Story*? One for the twelve-year-olds, I think. Which reminded me to dust off my old Second World War play about the female Russian artillery battalion, *Blam!* Then I did the crossword, and a few notes for a film that's been percolating for a while. It's about a plumber who is called to the house of a distinguished author in his fifties – she is twenty-eight and their love is unexpected, all-consuming and, I think, highly commercial. Also, it's a long time since Dennis Potter cornered that particular market and, anyway, he's dead. As was my companion the Musketeer bottle when I finally retired.

Thursday

A reminder from Ping this morning that Ed Reardon's name on the *Holby City* credits – and hence the life expectancy of his roof – depends on prompt delivery of draft eight of the treatment, beats and tweaks present and correct plus two pages of sample dialogue. Thanks to my innate professionalism it has now been dispatched, complete with telling cameo for Dave Wang, and is ready to be converted into fifty minutes of prime-time popular television – and none the worse for that. Creative artists who disdain the mass market are fools unto themselves. I like to think that if Dickens were writing now he'd be doing *Holby City* and no doubt *Casualty* and *ER* at the same time. Balzac would certainly be turning his hand to *EastEnders*. Jane Austen? They might let her have a crack at *Coronation Street* but probably not *Pride and Prejudice* or *Persuasion* – I imagine they'd still get that shifty-looking type with white hair to adapt those – and inject his trademark 'sexual Semtex' (otherwise known as a quick glimpse of beaver before the break just to make sure you don't go away).

Friday

Another trip to Elstree, this time treating myself to a ride aboard a Shires bus followed by a Centrebus and finally after a two-hour wait at Watford a Red Rose bus, all for roughly the same cost as a taxi and taking about half an hour longer than last week's walk. But what the hell, I'd had the first half of my treatment fee and I could afford a bit of conspicuous consumption, and conspicuous I most certainly was, being the only passenger (sorry 'customer') on all three legs of the journey.

Seated once more on the low orange seat, and feeling like a supplicant at some particularly cruel religious court, I looked up at Maddy and Horatio. In fact, so low was I that I almost had to look up at Tim, who lay wheezing in front of me appraising me coldly with his one open bloodshot eye.

'Did you get the script we sent you?' asked Maddy, and she said it in a way that suggested I had failed to draw lessons from it. Of course, many would say that was greatly to my credit; but hers and Horatio's voices would not have been among them.

'We thought it might help you get your head around, like, twenty-first century dialogue,' he said. 'I mean, I'm not saying you're old-fashioned. Perhaps I *am* saying you're old-fashioned. Is that what I'm saying? I don't know what I'm saying . . .' And he lapsed into silence in order to concentrate on drawing flames in biro on to his baseball boots.

'Maybe what Horatio means,' said Maddy, 'is that young

doctors don't call student nurses "blithering nincompoops" much these days.'

'Well we can tweak that, surely,' I said, showing, I thought, a reassuring grasp of the lingua franca.

'But that's why we sent you the script,' she persisted. 'To show you the way *Holby* characters talk.'

I sensed she was putting on this Nasty Producer act not so much for my edification but to rack up brownie points for the day when Horatio was made Director General of the BBC – sometime next month, probably.

'I mean in a confrontation situation they're more likely to say something like this.' She pointed to a speech on page 12 of the script that I remembered clearly since it was the very point at which I'd hurled the thing aside and turned to the snooker.

'Yes, I noted that exchange,' I said, then read it out loud, in as colourless a voice as I could manage. '"Sort it out Shireen or I'm going to go medieval on your arse." It doesn't seem very twenty-first century to me,' I said. 'It seems more fourteenth. And what does it mean anyway? Is he perhaps intending to inscribe a large illuminated letter on her behind?'

'Now you're being silly, Ed,' said Maddy. 'Look, there's something else, too. Your trolley dialogue.'

'What's wrong with it?'

'There isn't any.'

'Well, they're running down a corridor, pushing a man with a severed jugular, they're out of breath and covered in blood, they're not going to discuss their boyfriends.'

'That's exactly what they *would* be doing,' said Horatio,

springing up into the saddle of what was obviously an especially cherished hobbyhorse. 'Okay, here's the thing, Ed: the
more serious and messy the emergency, the more trivial the
conversation. Dramatic juxtaposition, okay. Cardiac arrest –
they talk about the wedding list. Motorway pile-up – karaoke
night.'

Maddy now held up the dialogue page of my treatment as if
it was a set of singularly unfavourable biopsy results. 'You've
just got Dr Kamal walking away from the trolley saying "I think
he's a gonner." Ed, where are you off to?'

'I think I'm a gonner, too,' I said, having picked up my coat
and headed for the door. Maddy implored me to calm down and
resume my seat while Horatio giggled and pointed at me saying,
'Oh, cool! You've gone completely red. Even under your beard
you can see it.'

'No, you're quite right,' I said to Maddy, 'I'm not going to
storm out without any explanation. Instead,' I said with what I
thought was a dramatic pause but what they would probably
consider dead airtime, 'I'm going to do what my agent told me
not to do – which is to point out that in my entire thirty-five
years as a respected writer . . .'

Tim had woken up by now and was beginning to growl, but
I was beyond fear.

'. . . I have worked in publishing, I've worked in the theatre,
BBC radio, I have even worked in the intellectual black hole that
calls itself Hollywood. But I have never been confronted with
such a display of – well, dumbing down is too charitable – of
sheer surpassing, thoroughgoing asininity!'

I could have done it better if I'd had another go but I probably couldn't have been much louder and I was on the whole satisfied with my performance, especially the neat bit of footwork I pulled off to accidentally tread on Tim's tail. Tim had obviously never had this kind of treatment from a writer before and his dumb, wide-eyed stare was particularly gratifying.

'It's said that society gets the television it deserves,' I said in conclusion, 'but it's hard to believe there's a nation on the planet so indigent, so preternaturally feckless, so irredeemably mired in sin as to deserve this.' I indicated round the office and the studio block outside, then turned the door handle in readiness to deliver a final haughty 'Good morning.'

'You see, there you go again, Ed,' said Horatio, getting in ahead of me. '"This sucks" would have done it in two syllables.'

Monday

There is a basement watering hole in Holborn which for many years has been the haunt of thwarted, disappointed and recently dismissed members of the acting and writing professions. There is sawdust on the floor to soak up the indignation and smoking is encouraged if not compulsory. The bar opened sometime in the late seventies as The Dungeon but when Ted Cartwright got the sack off *Minder* and was sounding off one afternoon about how he'd virtually invented television drama, someone took a marker pen and altered the lettering on the glass door to read Dudgeon's Bar. And Dudgeon's it has been from that day to this, although I believe its official name is O'Halloran's now. And it was here that I arranged to meet Ping for some lunchtime claret and sympathy.

The funny thing about agents is that while pleas for payment, work or even acknowledgement of one's calls generally make little impression on them, a good old-fashioned artistic tantrum – or 'hissy fit' as it's known nowadays – can soften their flinty hearts and turn them into attentive counsellors happy to leave the comfort of their offices and spend an afternoon dispensing tlc by the litre.

'Don't beat yourself up, Ed. You were right,' said Ping. 'I read your treatment. It was too good for them.'

'You read it? All three pages?'

'Yeah.'

'What did you think of the Chinese porter subplot? About him selling the patients' organs?'

'Great. Funny.'

It wasn't meant to be amusing but I was eager to exploit this rare show of enthusiam so I suggested we try to sell the story to *Casualty* or, failing that, to one of the flagship documentary programmes that are always in trouble with Ofcom for making things up.

'No, the second-hand organs story was the bit the producer liked. They want to pay you the balance of the treatment fee so they can use it.'

That one phrase released me from the Japanese water torture of the last couple of weeks. Two hundred and seventy-five pounds might not pay for a new roof but it ought to staunch the flow for a bit. I imagined myself giving the plumber an extra tenner for his trouble, I envisaged carefree walks from the bedroom to the kitchen without having to step over buckets, I even pictured myself working at my desk without a Morrison's plastic bag over my head.

'Right,' I said. 'Another bottle, I think – just a minute, shouldn't we hold out for more money if they like it that much?'

'Too late. The new writer delivered the script this morning.'

'Oh, they've got night staff, have they? Well, bang goes the new roof.'

'I thought you'd had a loft conversion done.'

'Yes but . . .' I said, marvelling at the capacity of the girl's mind to retain trivia while neglecting to tell me *Holby City* was about a hospital. 'Er, I got them to . . . take it away. The thing is, Ping, I wouldn't mind patching things up with the *Holby* people because I've now got a gap in my schedule, which I need to fill quite quickly.'

'You don't want to write another one, do you? Not after those things you said about them in the e-mails. And the fax you wanted me to send them with the letters cut out of different newspapers. And the bag of dogshit.'

'We were never seriously going to go through with that though, were we?' I said. 'No, I want nothing more to do with *Holby City* – as a *writer*. But I thought I could maybe offer my services as a hospital administrator or a surgeon – non-speaking, of course, don't want to have to say the rubbish, just stand in the background.'

'You mean as an extra?'

'Or I could perhaps be a concerned parent of a crack cocaine addict or something – sitting with my head in my hands.' I pulled my chair away from the table and slumped in sleep-deprived despair. 'What d'you think?'

'Yes, that's good.'

'Apparently the going rate is seventy quid a day.'

'I'll make some calls.'

Judging by the alacrity with which Ping scribbled a note on the cover of her Italian property magazine, it seemed that a steady flow of seven pounds a day into the agency's Coutts account would not be at all unwelcome.

But before I could investigate further there was a familiar voice from behind.

'Oi. Beardy. I've been looking for you.'

I was pleased that Dave Wang had come out of the sorry *Holby City* affair a good deal better off than any of us. A speaking role not only brought in more money with the prospect of further work on the back of it but also the use of a dressing room with *en suite* facilities much coveted in his profession.

'Hello matey,' I said. 'I told you I'd make it up to you. You can buy me a drink if you like. We're on claret.'

He stared at me, one would have to say inscrutably.

'Ping, have you met Dave Wang?' I said. 'Or, as he's about to become known, Henry Tan, the hospital porter with a dark secret, and also a hinterland which I think is rare for a character in television drama these days. So Dave, what brings you to Dudgeon's?'

'Can I have a word outside?'

'You can say anything in front of my agent.'

'Hard to put into words really. I s'pose what I'm trying to say is . . .'

And with that he took an almighty swing at me. Fortunately I was able to ride some of the blow, a skill acquired in the boxing ring during my first year at Shrewsbury ('Reardon advanced to the quarterfinals by tiring out his opponents with a strategy of continuous retreat and verbal taunts' – *The Salopian*, 1965). But I still caught enough of the Wang right hook to be sent crashing into the next table and to observe the patch of sawdust where I landed redden with my own blood.

When I had elevated Dave Wang to the ranks of the speaking artistes, I naturally hadn't bargained for another writer coming along and building the role up yet further by giving him a death scene – the hapless Henry Tan crushed as he fell from a ladder under the weight of a sack of stolen hearts and lungs. There was no time to explain this before the onset of hostilities. Fortunately, the scene of the violence was but a stone's throw from a real hospital, where within what must have been a mere sixteen hours I was examined and admitted for what remained of the night.

Tuesday

After a hearty NHS breakfast of cornflakes and/or orange jelly and ice cream, followed forty-five minutes later by a hearty lunch of fish fingers and more orange jelly, I was seen by another doctor, this one so senior I doubted he would see eleven again.

'So you're a writer, yeah?' he said, looking at my notes.

'I am.'

'Cool.'

'Not necessarily.'

'Really? Ben Elton does all right. And Richard Curtis. Must be great to be those guys, don't you think?'

'Absolutely – all that private health care.'

'Okay, got a bit of news, Ed,' he said. 'As well as your broken nose we also think you may have an ulcer.'

'I'm not at all surprised. I've been writing for *Holby City*.'

'Oh, that's really ironic, isn't it?'

'Yes, although it's not a word you'd catch them using.'

'Yes, it's complete poo, isn't it. Sorry is that a really rude thing to say to you?'

'Not at all. I was trying to get my agent to send them some only yesterday.'

'I hate that thing they do with the defibrillator pads,' said this very junior doctor. 'The way they bang them together before they use them. If you did that in real life the place would go up in smoke.'

'Could be a plot for *London's Burning*,' I said.

'Yeah, which is excellent, I think.'

From the entrance to the ward came a sound I had grown to loathe and dread in equal measure over the last two weeks. I hoped for a moment that I might be delirious but then I heard it again and there was no doubt it was real and getting closer –

it was Horatio's high-pitched giggle. As if the indignities of the previous fortnight had not been enough I was now to suffer the humiliation of Horatio's sympathy. Or so I thought.

'Hi Ed. Got a really really big favour to ask you.'

'Sorry, I'm signed off sick. My doctor here will give you a note – better tell him how many drafts of it you want.'

But now the doctor and Horatio were looking at each other like twins separated at birth.

'It's Horatio, isn't it?'

'Weren't you at Miles's stag weekend in Goa? Keeza, yeah?'

Dr Keeza and Horatio now assumed a strange bow-legged stance, faux rural accents and chorused a phrase which came presumably from one of the more unfunny sketch shows that pollute the airwaves. 'This weekend I am mainly eating cucumbers.' After which they collapsed into helpless laughter, Horatio's giggle penetrating enough to wake the dead. In fact, I'm fairly certain I saw two corpses rise from their trolleys in the corridor and lumber towards the lift.

'So, what are you doing now?' asked Dr Keeza, whose real name according to his lapel badge was Dr Mario Chiesa-Williams.

'I'm working on *Holby City*.'

'Oh cool. What, scripts and stuff? 'Cause I write sketches.'

'Yeah?' said Horatio, without a hint of wariness in his voice, for which I could only envy him. I had been that young once.

'Yeah, eight of us. We've got a gig tonight in the pub over the road. Come and see it. It's called *It's a Doc's Life*.'

It has long been my view that if doctors were to give up just a few of the hours they spend on being amateur comedians and concentrate instead on carrying out the essential job for which they were so expensively trained, then most of the NHS's problems could be solved at a stroke. But in a tradition reaching back centuries, probably to Hippocrates himself, it has been the inalienable right of junior medical practitioners to dress up as women, steal policemen's helmets, push one another around in wheeled baths and perform deadly shows called things like *It's a Doc's Life*.

'Oh, that is *such* a toxic title,' said Horatio politely.

'Actually, I've got to go and get into my costume,' said the good doctor. 'I've got this brilliant mask, yeah, that makes it look like the top of my head's been sawn off?'

'Oh yeah, they're great,' said Horatio, in whom I detected the first glimmerings of the professional's disdain for the amateur, 'I wore one at the *Holby* Christmas party.'

Dr Chiesa-Williams pulled a grotesque face and, assuming the voice of a mental defective, said, 'Ooo, my brain's gone bye-byes.' He chuckled at the elegance of his own wit and before heading off, probably for the hospital's wardrobe and make-up department, he turned kindly to me and said, 'You get plenty of rest now, Ed.'

'And you break a leg now,' I replied sunnily, 'in several places.'

Now that Horatio had me to himself he opened a brown envelope and held the contents in front of me. 'ESCAPE FROM THE BAMBOO NOOSE. By Ed Reardon. Tenth Draft. 2/10/1981.'

'That's my *Tenko* script,' I said in astonishment.

'It's *my Tenko* script now. I got it on eBay – really cheap.'

'Really?' So depressed had I been by the lack of bidding interest that I had handed over administration of the sale to Ping about a week ago. It sounded as if, true to her agently caste, she had got my money down even lower than if I'd done the deal myself – one and a half euros was my guess.

'Yeah, twelve hundred quid,' said Horatio with a giggle of triumph. 'Complete bargain. Look, I know you probably hate me but I wonder if you'd mind signing it.'

'My dear fellow,' I said, taking the script, 'you've just made an old writer very happy. And a lot drier too.' I inscribed it with a suitable message, signed and returned it. He held it gently, beaming like a parent seeing their new-born child for the first time. But the smile soon began to fade and I became aware that something truly terrible was taking place. Horatio was thinking.

'"To Horatio, thanks for the new roof,"' he read flatly.

'Well?' I said, trying to sound as forbidding as possible.

'It's great. Just, er . . . I don't know.'

'What's wrong with it?'

'Well, would "Cheers for the roof" get there a bit quicker? I dunno. Maybe it needs another tweak. Perhaps we could lose the roof altogether. Or . . . Ow! Oh God!'

It was completely childish, I know, but the urge to 'go medieval' on his stupid face was simply too strong to resist. Continuing the cycle of violence begun by Dave Wang in Dudgeon's, I laid Horatio out on the floor of Henry Cooper Ward with a sharp jab to the nose of which I like to think Our Enery would have approved.

Doubtless I should have felt remorse, but as my erstwhile script editor lay writhing I could bring myself to do no more than draw his attention to the red button by my bed, and make a start on my orange jelly and ice-cream dinner.

4

The Old Lock-keeper

Monday

The post arrives bright and early in mid-afternoon, some of it, by the miracle of modern technology, even addressed to me. There is the usual glossy envelope containing the announcement that I'd won £60,000, printed to make it look like a personal cheque; a very welcome repeat fee for £2.55 – *Tenko* is still essential 'turn off the telephone and cancel all dinner-parties' viewing in Malawi for some reason; and two more glossy envelopes telling the hairdresser's downstairs and the chip shop next door that they, too, have definitely won £60,000. We really should think about all taking that holiday of a lifetime together. Though on reflection, having seen the type of brochures that sometimes arrive on my mat but are addressed to The Cutting Edge, Nick and Chris's choice of holiday nightlife might not altogether harmonize with Fred and Joyce's, which I sense tends towards a walk along the prom with the promise of a toffee-apple at the end of it.

But there among the dross is a possible nugget. A letter from America, promising in its Los Angeles postmark, and exciting in its contract-like thickness. Could it be an offer for the film rights to my most recent radio play, an account of the digging of the second-longest tunnel on the Grand Union Canal?

It was after all a highly commercial if unremittingly grim story that I had unearthed while spending three days in Berkhamsted Public Library two years ago while waiting for the services to be connected in my new flat (a saga involving meter readings and previously unpaid bills too dreary to rehearse all over again). Like any explorer of a hitherto-undiscovered continent I was keen to find out everything I could about my new habitat, its history and its heartbeat. Back issues of the *Herts & Bucks Advertiser* provided some of the answers, and it was in one of its 'Bygone Byways' columns that I discovered the heroic and highly dramatizable story of the Blisworth excavation, which was destined to become *A Hodful of Blood* (in the words of the *Bedfordshire Life* radio critic 'the most harrowing afternoon's ironing I can remember').

Radio – I don't know if anyone has ever said this before – always has the best pictures, and I swear if you closed your eyes you could smell the sweat of the navvies, and see the smudges on their noble downtrodden faces as they mopped their brows with red spotted kerchiefs, while on the ridge above the tunnel the bosses in their stovepipe hats checked the time on their gold fob watches, and barked cruel instructions for the men to work ever faster. The play taxed to the utmost the versatility of its cast of four, or five if you include the folk singer in a chunky-knit sweater brought in to perform my specially written contemporary song to go underneath the play's credits. To see him standing in the BBC studio at Maida Vale, a hand over his ear as he roared out 'Damn Ye, Bloody Blisworth' brought a lump to the throat and a proud feeling of Yes! This is what Ed Reardon does best. Or Ed *Deardon* if you listened to the continuity announcer, when the play was finally transmitted a year later.

But, alas, *Hodful!* – the movie's time has not yet come. Instead the letter from America is a chill harbinger of that season when icicles hang by the wall and Dick the shepherd blows his nail – in other words the first round-robin letter of Christmas.

'Dear All, Well, it's been quite a year!!!'

This statement was accompanied by three exclamation marks, lest the reader should fall into the trap of thinking that it was a rather banal assertion.

'In the course of it the Milvane family seems to have acquired not only a new table and a barbecue lamp – quite a performance to assemble!!!!!' – just the five exclamation marks there – 'But a further Emmy award for Jaz – soon he says the statuettes will outnumber the doors in need of propping open.

A good thing we bought the ranch!!' This took the exclamatory tally into double figures.

'Seriously though' – which presupposed there being something remotely funny in the first paragraph, a glance back at which proved otherwise – 'it really has been quite a year.'

Anyone unfortunate enough to receive one of these letters soon realizes that they are nothing more than an indigestible marzipan-like slab of self-advertisement whereby each tiny occurrence has to be 'bigged up', as they say on Sky News, and a positive spin put on absolutely everything not excluding terminal cancer ('We were determined to make the most of the time left and took Dad to EuroDisney').

The letter from the third – or was it the fourth – Mrs Jaz Milvane was no exception, never mind that none of the children whose achievements were being trumpeted was actually hers.

'Delilah won a prestigious basketball scholarship – and a dishy boyfriend to go with it!! – Chip, nice guy. And after getting a powerboat for his thirteenth birthday, Dimitri has hopefully put his behavioural problems behind him!!!'

By the time I reached the passage about her zucchini sculptures continuing to draw compliments, my gorge was rising faster than Jaz Milvane's salary ('8 million dollars a movie now, though as Jaz says, who's counting!!!') – a sure sign that it was time to put in a call to Ted Cartwright, fellow writer and sympathetic sounding board for anything that was irking me at any time of the day or night. Also, I might add, someone who had seen the poetry of his work similarly mangled at the hands of the egregious Milvane, his sensitive coming-of-age novel *I've*

Got Sixpence somehow mutating into the teenage splatter movie *Happy Deathday 2*.

I knew Ted would be in receipt of one of these loathsome letters and share my opinion of it, so I was looking forward to a good half-hour of concentrated bile, as my friend was a lesson to us all in being 'a bonny hater', as the late genius Mel Torme was once described.

I could barely contain my enthusiasm when the phone was picked up. 'Hello, it's me, have you got one of these nauseating Milvane excrescences? I mean, who do they think they are?'

'Hello Ed,' said Ted's wife who had answered, sounding a bit down in the dumps I thought.

'Oh hello Sally, how are you my darling? Is he there?'

'Ed, I'm sorry – Ted died on Friday.'

'Ha! You wish – where is he, down the boozer?'

'No, he's at the undertaker's – he died, Ed.'

'But I only spoke to him a couple of months ago. He was spitting tacks after Richard Curtis got his CBE. Wasn't that that killed him, was it?'

'No, it was a heart attack.'

Oh, that's awful. Oh dear.' I then said something the tiniest bit unworthy, though I'm sure Ted would have understood. 'So – what's going to happen about the column?'

Like me, Ted had not long left London for the country, for health reasons as they say – though he soon managed to find as many pubs to accommodate him in and around Leighton Buzzard as he had in Barnsbury. Unlike me, Ted had cannily turned his sitting-in-the-corner-with-a-pint persona into hard cash, and found himself a comfortable berth as the Old Lock-Keeper, cantankerous columnist of the *Herts & Bucks Echo*. In his column Ted dispensed weekly wisdom that wasn't so much salty as hydrochloric.

'Well, he won't be able to write it, obviously,' said Sally. 'Someone else had to do it last week, after they took him in.'

Neither the time nor place I sensed, but I persisted. Life and, indeed, work must go on. 'So d'you think this same person's going to carry on writing it? Not that this is the most important thing at the moment, of course it isn't, but—'

'Ed, there's someone at the door,' said Sally. 'Looks like another sodding wreath.'

'Yes, I've got to get on, too. Off you go. Look Sal, let me know if there's, you know, anything I can do.'

I really should just have let her go. 'Like what?' Sally came back at me, her voice rising in a tone I recognized all too clearly from the last knockings of my own marriage. 'You haven't got a car, you haven't got any money, you're as drunk in the afternoon as he was—'

'Righty ho,' I said. 'Look, I'll let you grieve . . . but if you happen to come across the number among his things for—'

A click at the other end, not altogether surprising I suppose in the circumstances.

'Well well – Ted Cartwright,' I said to Elgar, who walked away arching his tail. And come to think of it Ted was never one of his favourites even if they did have a first name in common, falling on top of the poor thing now and then, and even knocking his pipe out on Elgar's head once after a heavy session. Ted was a hell of a good writer though, and some of his early *Z Cars* episodes were television classics. In particular, the one where the teddy boys broke into the pub not realizing it was a police lock-in, maintained a delicate balance of drama and comedy that some of our younger scribblers with their taste for humourless serial killers would do well to study.

The other hugely admirable thing about Ted, and which set him apart from a lot of writers of that era, was that he didn't have it easy by any means, being both born in Surrey and an ex-public schoolboy. In fact, he never even went to Liverpool until he was in his forties and that was to visit the flower exhibition – yet somehow he managed to climb the greasy pole and win the hand (not to mention all the other delightful bits) of Sally, the leading lady in his searing Wednesday Play *Our Brenda's Up the Duff*.

In common with most of us, in middle years Ted found his work had fallen out of favour with the new generation of media decision makers – or twelve-year-old-ocracy as I call them. But clever Ted succeeded in changing political horses in midstream and while waiting for the tide of fashion to turn as it inevitably must, and with the simple addition of a pair of braces, a flat cap and a lock-key perched in the crook of his arm (this being the picture atop his column) he became the 'Crusty, Controversial But Never Dull' Old Lock-Keeper.

It was, perhaps, fortunate for Ted that asylum seekers, say, couldn't read English or they would have taken Ted to the

European Court of Human Rights, where they would no doubt have been awarded six-figure damages, a free house, a car and a pony for the kids . . .

As I wrote these words it was suddenly as if the hand of Ted was guiding me, and his voice saying 'Go on Ed, have a go thi'ssen, why don't you.' Quickly I reached for the latest edition of the *Herts & Bucks Echo* to see what Ted's late replacement (or rather the late Ted's replacement) had come up with. Luckily the paper was still in one piece, as normally I extract the *TV Guide* and put the rest underneath Elgar's milk bowl, feeling I can live without stories headlined 'Hedge Clippers Theft' or 'Hemel McDonald's Set To Expand'.

The picture of Ted was still there, complete with lock key. But the prose style was emphatically not his. 'Check out the new *Bridget Jones* at your multiplex this weekend. Hugh Grant is totally snoggable and the movie's a real blast. And I tell you what – the Old Lock-Keeper is *sooo* going to see *Shrek 3* this weekend.'

Trouble at t'mill there, I thought – which was a small tribute to Ted, as this was a term he often used in his column to describe anything from local protests about speed cameras, to suicide bombers in Iraq.

Tuesday

'Hi, are you Ed Beardon?' said the girl in the short skirt, the 'TONY BLIAR' T-shirt, and the spiky hair that came in three colours that I could see. I assumed she was the *Herts & Bucks Echo* editor's secretary, or a student on what is laughably known as work experience.

'Almost,' I said. 'I'm here to see Emily.'

'That's me yeah,' said the girl, who hardly looked old enough to drink, let alone have a major influence (at least when it came to buying second-hand cars) on the newspaper-reading public in two of our larger Home Counties.

'Sorry you had to wait so long yeah, but *Richard & Judy* was on and their body language now is like so weird . . .' said Emily.

This was promising – some immediate common ground. 'Personally,' I said, 'I think it was a big mistake to move them from their morning slot.'

'They were on in the morning? When was that?'

I realized I was talking about a time when Emily probably had a prior engagement at nursery school.

'Oh, a while back,' I said. 'But it bridged the gap rather agreeably between the swim and a lunchtime gargle.'

Emily's face lit up and she dug me in the ribs with a handful of blue nails. 'You see, that is exactly the kind of thing the Old Lock-Keeper would say. I tried to write the column last week . . .'

'I saw it,' I said. 'I thought it was jolly good.'

'I thought it was complete pants,' Emily said, truthfully enough if 'pants' meant what it sounded like. 'Whereas yeah, like you could write it and it'd be more kind of, erm . . .'

'Plus fours?' I said.

'Ha – that's quite funny!' said Emily. 'D'you reckon you could keep that sort of thing up for a whole 1200 words?'

'I'm happy to have a go,' I said. 'I like to think that Ted Cartwright and I had the same views on just about everything.'

'That would be such a blast,' said Emily. 'How does a hundred and fifty quid sound?'

Faced with the mouthwatering prospect of a regular income, I forced myself to leave the office without so much as inviting Emily out for a drink, thus avoiding all the humiliating fumblings and rebuffs in the car park that would inevitably ensue.

Wednesday

Mindful that as things stand I am only to be the Old Lock-Keeper for a two-week probationary period, I was determined to make a decent fist of it. So, positioning my chair by the window, laptop on knee, I sat enjoying an early morning pipe as I looked out for abuses of common sense and decency that would get the old boy's dander up, and have him brandishing that lock-key in a four-paragraph bate. There, for example, was an obese child in need of a diet and a good old-fashioned larruping for dropping her crisp packet on the pavement. And look – failing lamentably to clear up the litter was a council cleansing vehicle, idiotically labelled 'HertsLand – Here to Make Life Better'. Making life immeasurably worse was a group of four council workmen in quotation marks – was there ever a greater misnomer? Four sitting-round-a-hole-drinking-PG Tips-men might be nearer the mark . . .

Where was one to begin, with the world my oyster and so many irritants eager to produce the pearl?

The telephone rang. 'The Old Lock-Keeper bids 'ee good marnin',' I answered in character.

It was my agent, Felix, with a suggestion that required my immediate departure for London. I had barely begun to goose the prejudices of the *Herts & Bucks Echo*'s supposed hundred thousand readers and already I was obliged to leave them to seethe unguided. A shame but this was a matter of some urgency: if you get to the Connaught Grill much later than 1 p.m. at this time of year you can sometimes find that all the grouse has gone and Felix is in a filthy mood.

'So,' Felix said once the small talk was out of the way, fixing me with an expression that looked mock-serious but was in fact deadly earnest. 'A dangerous third bottle?'

'I wouldn't disagree with that at all,' I said. 'Though I wouldn't mind ordering a starter or something,' I added, remembering that I had set myself to write 500 words of canalside common sense by the end of the day. Possibly dealing with the menace to society of youthful binge-drinkers.

'Jolly good idea,' Felix said. 'When you're ready, Renato! Now listen, Ed – I really think we should do something out of the ordinary for dear old Ted Cartwright, because heaven preserve us from one of those ghastly cremations out in deepest darkest Finchley or somewhere equally hopeless.'

'Oh no, that'd be awful,' I said. 'With the failed vicar

who's never heard of him and the undertakers all smoking in the car park and everybody wishing they were out there with them.'

Felix snorted with laughter. 'You see, you put it into words so much better than I ever could. We need someone to read something out, get your jazz band to play a bit of music, tell a bloody joke for God's sake.'

'Yes, that might be a bit more like it.'

'Well, there you go again, you see,' said Felix. '*Le mot juste*, in a nutshell, every time. So look Ed, if you could have a few thoughts, sit in your study with a hot towel round your head . . .'

Aha, the reason for the lunch. A sudden unpleasant footnote to the meal, like discovering a 17½ per cent service charge.

'You want *me* to organize this?'

'Oh, would you?' said Felix. 'Well that's terribly . . . Oh no, whose is that beastly thing?'

There was the sound of a mobile phone ringing in the near vicinity. Felix surveyed the other diners with a beady eye, before realizing that the offending sound was coming from his own yellow waistcoat pocket.

The ringtone was 'There's No Business Like Show Business'. At my last lunch with Felix it had been 'We're In The Money' and the week before the Frankfurt Book Fair I remember it was Abba's 'Take A Chance On Me'. There was no chance whatsoever that it was Felix himself who had set up these humorous tunes, and I imagined Ping regularly ministering to Felix's mobile phone, changing his ringtone for him like an intensive care nurse replacing a patient's drip.

'Ed, I'm going to have to be terribly rude . . .' said Felix, stabbing at the buttons on his phone. Though not nearly as rude as he was to the other occupants of the restaurant, not to mention the art gallery next door. Felix conducted the conversation as though talking to someone 6000 miles away, not necessarily with the aid of a telephone.

'Jaz! Howdy! Are you still stateside? Still basking in the glory of your Emmy? No, you must bask – I insist you bask! Ha! Look, are you coming over for Ted's funeral? Splendid! What? I'm afraid I don't know – but there's someone here who might . . .'

'How old would you say Ted was?' Felix asked me, maintaining the volume as if I, too, were sipping a skinny latte on Rodeo Drive or somewhere similar.

'Sixty-six.'

'Clickety-click!' roared Felix down the phone. 'Clickety-*clonk* more like!! No but it's awful isn't it? Luckily there's a dear old friend of yours sitting here who's masterminding the whole she-bang . . . Ed Reardon . . . ED REARDON . . . R-E-A-R-D . . . yes, that's right, him. But Jaz, he's like some ruthless military commander organizing the whole operation like – what was that film you did about the battle at the Earth's core or wherever it was, anyway that's what he's like . . . oh well, if you've got to go you must go . . .'

Felix finished the call and there was some sarcastic clapping from a red-faced man sitting alone in the corner of the restaurant.

153

'The valet had just arrived with his car,' said Felix. 'What a client to have. Golly, baby, I'm a lucky cuss – now what song was that from?'

'"Happy Talk". *South Pacific,*' I said. 'It was your last ring-tone but three. But talking of Jaz,' I said, sensing a work opportunity, 'did you get one of those round-robin letters from his wife? I mean the sheer self-importance of it . . . but they're all the same, aren't they . . . solipsistic twaddle. And yet you know, Felix, I think there might be a book in them—'

Felix was staring hard at me. 'You're quite right, I can't think why somebody didn't do it years ago.'

Maddeningly, as I was about to follow up, Felix took out his mobile phone again and punched some numbers – literally, it was a wonder the thing didn't fly across the restaurant to where the red-faced man was now throwing his napkin down in a fury. But for all I cared he could have a coronary and collapse into his terrine – I seemed to have excited Felix's professional interest.

'Hallo, Ping?' shouted Felix. 'Can you find out when Jaz Milvane is arriving and book him a car from Heathrow? And have we got any of those hampers left over from the party in the Chelsea Physic Garden? Jolly good – take out the jar of figs in Cointreau, he hates those, parcel it up again and get it off to the airport will you?'

Ignoring this bit of news about another guest-list that I seemed to have been left off, I pressed on as soon as Felix had finished.

'Anyway, about those round-robin letters. If we collected

them all together there could be a very funny Christmas book in them.'

'Yes, there could indeed,' said Felix. 'In fact, I've got it in my briefcase. The proofs of the American edition. Huge advance. Huge! That man really is a very clever fellow – he gets everybody else to do the writing for him, d'you see.'

'I wouldn't be able to take it on anyway,' I said. 'I'm too busy with my new column.'

'Jolly good,' said Felix. 'Now where *has* Renato gone? I'm like a man dying of thirst in the Gobi Desert.'

'It's called "The Old Lock-Keeper",' I said.

'Excellent,' said Felix. 'Now, I'll tell you a round-robin letter you *could* do, Ed . . .'

Thursday

This extra chore Felix had for me was to e-mail Ted's more successful writer buddies (i.e. those with e-mail) and get them to add their names to a letter of appreciation to *The Times*, composed by Ed Reardon. And after that inform anyone else who knew him where and when the funeral was, besides organizing the running order and the entertainment for the aforementioned obsequies. In fact, it seemed I would be required to do practically everything except chop a tree down to make Ted his coffin. It was altogether a very long way, indeed, from being a free lunch.

I thought it best not to call on Sally, the widow, just yet to see if I'd forgotten anyone, bearing in mind our last conversation. 'You're as drunk in the afternoon as he was' I found particularly cutting, as for all she knew I had kept the same working hours as Keith Waterhouse: up with the lark to write for eight hours before lunch, then up *for* larks for the rest of the day. Doubtless if I were engaged full time as the Old Lock-Keeper this might be my own timetable; in the meantime the column would have to wait again until I had trawled through my dog-eared address book. A depressing task: with its crossings-out due to death or disappearance it was beginning to take on the appearance of a First World War memorial.

'I'm trying to get hold of Norman Eddison,' a typical call would start. 'Norman Eddison? He was the head writer on *Robin Hood* . . . oh, I'm so sorry I must have a wrong number . . . unless he's driving one of your minicabs now, because he didn't get an awful lot of work after that, and he did drive a tank in the war . . . hello?'

So much for the 'E's – Elgar was just about the only one left alive. The 'F's proved hardly more fruitful, and even included pencilled telephone numbers for the late E. M. Forster, both his direct line at King's College, Cambridge and the number and address of his weekend hideaway in Brighton. Many years ago I had been the runner-up in a writing competition organized by the *Children's Newspaper* and 'Morgan', as he kindly invited me to call him at the awards picnic, seemed interested in helping further a budding career. Somewhere in a not-yet-unpacked box I still have my prize, a copy of *Howard's End* with its famous epigraph 'Only Connect . . .', under which the author had written '. . . Sometime soon with Morgan – emphatically <u>not</u> a suitable case for treatment!' a film reference which at the time I did not understand. The winner of the competition, incidentally, was one Irvine Welsh, a precocious seven-year-old who had written a fanciful piece about the Loch Ness Monster's encounter with a yellow submarine.

After a lengthy telephone conversation with Michael Frayn, which moved seamlessly from arrangements for Ted's funeral to precisely how much money I would be getting for 'The Old Lock-Keeper', how much Michael thought I should ask instead, and how if I were stuck for a subject German reunification could always be relied on to bulk out the column, it was approaching lunchtime. Or Elgar's lunchtime at any rate, judging from the paw with its claws extended which suddenly appeared on my thigh.

As I searched the cupboards and under the sink for a tin of Whiskas, or even some tuna that we could both share, I set about composing a suitable elegy for my departed friend.

Dear old Ted.
Writer of *Z*
Cars, and so much else besides.
The Planemakers—

Which was as far as I got, as anything edible was as hard to come by as inspiration (the one often has a bearing upon the other, I find) and with only 80p in the money jar, desperate remedies were called for. I dug out the 'You Have Definitely Won £60,000' envelope from the other day's mail in the recycling box, and fetched the scissors.

'What do you want me to do with this?' said the 12-year old bank teller. 'Well Hanif,' I said, looking at the badge on his short-sleeved shirt, 'I'd like you to pay it into my account.'

'Sorry?'

'Or cash it, if that's easier,' I said .

'But this is just a bit of junk mail,' said Hanif, his chair starting to swivel slightly.

'No, it's a cheque for £60,000 payable to Ed Reardon – which is me, and I've got a gas bill and a Blockbuster membership to prove it,' I said, producing them both, while deftly keeping my thumb over the bit in the demand from British Gas which referred to impending legal action.

'Yeah . . .' said Hanif with a smile and a quick look around, just in case there was a camera crew hiding nearby, ready to jump out from behind the carousel of loan brochures at any moment and inform him that he'd been 'gotcha-ed', or some such non-word they use on television on Saturdays. 'Yeah, but it's signed "F. Godmother" – like in "Fairy"? And if you turn it over there's a glossy picture of a palm tree and three laughing coconuts, and a banana wearing sunglasses driving a speed-boat.'

'But you take the point, do you not, Hanif, that setting aside its gaudy decoration this is a cheque?'

'No. Apart from the figure there's nothing that resembles a banking document at all.'

'Ah, then you must be unfamiliar with the works of A. P. Herbert,' I said, aware that a queue was building up behind me, 'in which a cheque written on the side of a cow was deemed legal tender.'

'Yeah, but that was just a short story. They made us read that thing at financial college. I so hated it. And it does not comply with the European Banking Code as currently formulated. And you're holding up proper customers,' finished Hanif, looking through me to the person behind. 'Next please.'

I regained his attention by the simple expedient of moving one of those posts that obliges you to zig-zag idiotically through the bank before reaching the counter, even when there is nobody else waiting. This opened a window of opportunity for the queue, leading them in the direction of Foreign Currency, but like cattle, they just stood staring at it.

'There we are,' I said, 'that's solved that.'

Not for the first time in my life, I had the sensation of looking down on myself, as though a more compliant and I dare say responsible Ed Reardon were hovering somewhere up in the ceiling, next to the CCTV camera.

Hanif had now emphatically put the smile away in his cash drawer and locked it. 'Sir, you're wilfully changing the flow of that queue. I must ask you to replace that post, and the retractable belt in its stanchion.'

'All in good time,' I said. 'So you won't cash this at all then?'

Behind me the queue was getting restive, one of them even shouting at Hanif to give me the money, because he was wasting his lunch hour. Realizing that they were siding with the

159

underdog brought out the worst in the young *fonctionnaire*, I was happy to see.

'Look,' he said, passing the piece of paper back to me under his grille, 'the banana is clearly stating that in order to participate in this unique offer you've got to go to the Baldock Travelodge at a time that will be given to you, when you've rung this premium rate number – 0807—'

'All right, you've made your point,' I said, tearing the end off the paper and pushing it back at him. 'Just give me two tenners for this, please.'

If Hanif's face had been stony before, it was now harder and colder than the surface of the moon. 'That is a picture of a twenty pound note that was growing out of the palm tree. So no.'

'Well, how about giving me £1.25 in exchange for this?' I said, a last sporting throw of the dice before I retreated potless from the casino into the sunset over the Croisette, bow tie askew and with a rueful Gallic smile on my face.

Hanif gave it the most cursory of glances. 'That's a cat food voucher. And it says "Do not embarrass your retailer by attempting to redeem this for other goods or monies."'

'Are you embarrassed?' I said.

'No, but you should be,' said Hanif.

'On the contrary, Hanif – I am the Old Lock-Keeper of the *Herts & Bucks Echo* and you've just provided me with priceless material for a column about the sheer asininity of modern consumerism,' I said, standing back and folding my arms after retrieving the IAMS voucher.

'Just put the belt back will you, Beardie,' said Hanif, a valediction I doubt they'd taught him back at his financial alma mater. But I complied, and allowed the queue to shuffle its bovine way forward.

Describing the events at the bank for the column, adding a few of Ted's stylistic tics like 'Daft, I calls it' and 'Progress, they reckons that is', made me a little late for the writing class. This week's module was 'Conquering Fleet Street' and I was slightly bemused to find Olive holding court there, and Stan and Pearl listening with the kind of rapt attention they rarely reserve for me (downright rude, I calls it).

'And there it was, in me hand,' said Olive. 'Four crisp twenty pound notes!' This even elicited a burst of applause from the others. Rather sheepishly, Olive went to sit down when she saw me, but her audience wouldn't let her go.

'So what are you going to do with the money?' asked Stan.

'Haven't decided yet,' said Olive. 'Might have a couple of cocktails, might go to see my sister in Newark. Hello Mr Reardon – sorry, I'm taking up your teaching time.'

'We've got a bit of a celebrity in our midst,' said Pearl.

Just then I wasn't prepared to take the bait, knowing that I would find out what was going on soon enough, and it might be useful to spin out Olive's news into that always problematic second hour.

'So this week we're going to be dipping our toe into the piranha pond of journalism, and I'm going to try to give you some basic principles and guidelines on the subject of "Selling That Story".'

'You should be getting lessons off Olive,' Stan said. 'She already has.'

This I was unable to resist. 'Has what?' I asked.

'Sold that story,' said Pearl. 'To the *People's Friend*. About a family of cats at Christmas.'

'A Winter's Tail,' said Stan. 'Spelt T-A-I-L – goes two ways, does that,' he added unnecessarily.

'Oh, it wasn't anything much,' said Olive. 'Sorry Mr Reardon, go on with what you were saying.'

But the others weren't prepared to let Olive hide her light, only forty watts though it may have been, under a bushel.

'Eighty pounds is eighty pounds,' said Pearl.

'Bet it's more than he's earned this week,' added Stan, again unnecessarily.

I couldn't let that go. 'That's where you're wrong, actually, because I've just taken over from my dear old pal, Ted Cartwright, writing The Old Lock-Keeper column in the *Herts & Bucks Echo*'.

'Ah, but the *People's Friend*'s national. Goes all over the country,' said Stan, with the smirk of a pensioner on a bowling green who has just knocked an opponent's wood into the gutter.

'It's in the form of a Christmas letter, see,' said Pearl.

'What is?'

'Olive's story,' said Pearl. 'Go on dear, you tell him. You're the writer.'

Olive got to her feet again. I imagine she is one of those women who stand to attention when she is talking on the telephone in her hall.

162

'Well,' Olive said, 'I always do the Christmas newsletter for the family, and they always like it so much, and say I should do it professionally, so I thought I'd have a go. Only with cat news. Written by Britney, the youngest.'

'Britney kitten-ey,' said Stan. 'That goes two ways an' all.'

I resisted the temptation to ask Stan to write it up on the whiteboard at the end of the room, so we could all appreciate this superb piece of wordplay. Instead, I decided to turn Olive's stroke of luck with the *People's Friend* into a piece of friendly advice, for which she would surely thank me during the years of disappointment ahead.

'I guess the thing to remember about being a professional journalist is that you can't just do one piece, you've got to keep turning them out. I was talking to Michael Frayn about this just the other day . . .'

I went to the whiteboard myself and was writing up the words '1% Inspiration . . . 99% Perspiration' when I realized that I had inadvertently set them off again.

'He's the one who lost the Whitbread to his missus,' said Pearl.

'Another one who wasn't as clever as he thought he was,' said Stan.

'Anyway, Mikey and I go back a long way,' I said before they got on to what their grandchildren were doing in Canada. 'We were chewing the fat about how we approach our columns—'

'He was a friend of that Ted Cartwright, too,' said Olive.

'He was actually,' I said, surprised.

'I know he was!' said Olive. 'There was a letter from him in *The Times*.'

'Oh, has it gone in?' I said. 'I organized that – well, wrote it actually.'

'Your name wasn't on the list,' said Olive. 'There was Sir Alan Ayckbourn, Sir Tom Stoppard, Dame June Whitfield . . . no sign of you though.'

'Not famous enough,' said Stan, checking his mobile phone which was bleeping. 'Aye aye – text from Dick. The whist's finished early. He's got the Espace outside. Come on girls—'

Stan and Pearl made for the door without a backward glance. Olive hung back.

'I'm sorry – we're leaving you on your own,' she said.

'It doesn't matter, I get paid anyway,' I said, trying to free the spiral coil on my notebook that was snagged on my jacket pocket. 'And, actually, I've got some work on the column to be getting on with.'

'That's right, dear – you keep writing,' said Olive. 'You never know—'

And with that she was gone, too.

Friday

The non-appearance of Ed Reardon's name among the great and the good in my letter to *The Times* was a setback to be sure, but after due reflection I decided not to mention this in the column. There is a fine line after all between self-pity, however

justified, and the red-blooded irascibility that is the local newspaper columnist's stock in trade. But now it was high time for
the Old Lock-Keeper to unsheathe his sword of truth, and set
off on behalf of his readers in search of the elusive 'F.
Godmother' and her £60,000 cheque – and the even more
elusive 375 words I still had to write.

'And after you've all filled out your questionnaires there'll be
complimentary non-alcoholic beverages and biscuits, before we
move you through to the Nigel Mansell Suite,' said Jacqui,
whose laminated name badge was even larger than Hanif's, the
boy in the bank with the A. P. Herbert problem.

It is just about possible to appear relaxed while seated on a
velour stacking chair in the Baldock Travelodge, but I would
certainly not want to try it again without a pipe. A
meerschaum marks its owner out as a man not easily flus-
tered, but the main reason for lighting up was the teasing
aroma of unfinished breakfast wafting through from Phineas
Fogg's Brasserie next door. The thought of those metal
troughs of scrambled eggs and baked bean lakes glistening
under their halogen heating lamps was almost too much to
bear. But a pipe buys a temporary respite from the pangs of
hunger. And say what you like about sales reps' hotels they do
not lack functioning ashtrays – unlike the Marriotts and
Ramadas of the world, who fill their public spaces pointlessly
with marbles and exotic seed pods.

'Excuse me,' said a woman at one end of my row with three
plastic bags containing, as far as I could see, only more plastic
bags. 'When do we get the money?'

'After you've all filled out your questionnaires,' said Jacqui, her voice obviously operating on some sort of computer loop, 'you'll be one step closer to that £60,000, because you'll be entered in a prize draw.' She left a dramatic pause at the end of this as though expecting whoops and applause.

'Do we get the biscuits anyway?' asked a man sitting at the other end of my row, his right leg up on the two chairs between us.

'Yes,' said Jacqui, 'and then we'll be moving you through to the as I say Nigel Mansell Suite where you'll be shown some unbeatable offers.'

'Bloody time-shares again, I bet,' the man muttered to me.

'So, time to tick those boxes!' said Jacqui. 'And we would obviously ask you to return your pens with the questionnaires.'

'Stingy buggers,' said the man. 'Right, I'm having that bottle of lime juice then.'

In every conference suite in every Travelodge or Moat House on every bypass outside every town there is a blond-wood table and on that table sits a tin tray and on the tray you will see half-a-dozen dusty glasses and a bottle of Rose's Lime Juice (or increasingly, in this gimcrack society, Somerfield's or some other adjacent hypermarket's own brand).

As I jotted down these thoughts I became aware that they might be a tad subtle for the Old Lock-Keeper, whose horny-handed appearances in conference suites were probably limited to the AGM of the British Waterways Board, so instead I decided to quiz the man with his leg up, seemingly a veteran of these events.

'Do you do a lot of this?'

'I just sit in the lobby and see what's on,' said the man, shifting his leg companionably so I could move closer. 'Sometimes you have to listen to a lot of talk about bus lane proposals and wind farms but there's usually something at the end of it.'

'Does it happen every day?' I asked, making a surreptitious note because Jacqui was prowling round the room with her painted-on smile. In fact, I had a little time on my hands after rapidly ticking the 'Yes' box in every category.

'Well I don't come Wednesdays because that's my hospital appointment – ever since the accident with the miracle peeler. It was a good promotion, though. We all got document wallets straight off, and a fruit compote. Some of us got silver scooters. I don't have much use for a silver scooter as you can see but I was hooked by then.'

All of this was gold dust, a sick consumer society summed up in a couple of sentences and oven-ready, as they say, to be shoehorned into the column.

'Well, it's been very useful talking to you – George,' I said, reading the name stuck to his chest. Unlike the lucky laminated few, we guinea pigs had to make do with a piece of gummed paper with our name scrawled on it. I had resisted putting one on, preferring to work incognito like a restaurant critic. George chuckled.

'Garn, you don't think that's my real name, do you? Put that on the form it's like opening the gates of hell.'

This was timely advice, as by now Jacqui was circulating and collecting up questionnaires, and more particularly the pens. I scribbled down a name and address and then she was on me.

'Thank you . . . Jay, is that?' she said, peering at the questionnaire.

'Jaz,' I said.

'Right everybody,' said Jacqui, 'now it's time to relax in the Nigel Mansell Suite where you'll be able to feast your eyes on some unbelievable holiday opportunities!'

'Told you,' said the man calling himself George.

Tuesday

The day of Ted Cartwright's funeral. In honour of his memory I spent the morning honing my first Old Lock-Keeper column, and such was the level of coruscation achieved therein that I failed to notice the time slipping by and barely made the scheduled start of the service by the skin of my teeth.

My experience at the Travelodge was the rock round which the bilious river eddied and flowed. 'George' may have been right in his supposition that this was nothing more than a scheme to sell time-shares, but he was incorrect in describing it as a descent into hell. The Nigel Mansell Suite turned out to be a level of purgatory, from which there was only one escape – by signing away one's – or thankfully in my case, someone else's – soul. Once on the other side of that chipboard door I imagine anyone less resilient than myself would have been eternally consigned to the flames.

'And you're happy for all further correspondence to be sent to this address?' said Jacqui, after what seemed like five hours of interrogation masquerading as banter ('I don't think our friend here is interested in having the holiday of a lifetime for ten days every third year').

'Yes,' I panted, giving a pretty good impression of a man whose spirit had been broken on the property-sharing wheel.

'And you'd have no objection to offers you might be interested in from other responsible companies being sent to the same address?' said Miss Whiplash's satanic sidekick, or 'Darren' to give him the name of the human body he was occupying.

'No, I'd positively welcome them,' I said. 'Am I free to go now?'

''Course you are!' sang Jacqui, another shrunken skull swinging from her belt.

'And we look forward to doing business with you, Mr Milvane,' said Darren, standing up and turning his chair back the right way round.

'Please, call me Jaz.'

'Excellent stuff. Turn the anglepoise off, Jacqui, and unlock the door of the Nigel Mansell Suite, if you'd be so good.'

Jacqui pressed a button underneath the table and there was the sound of an electronic lock clicking back and, I could swear, the faint moaning of thousands of Dante's damned as they realized one lucky perisher was about to fly forth freely from their midst.

'There we are,' said Jacqui. 'And a safe journey back to LA, Jaz!'

In fact, it was the arrival of the real Milvane in North

169

Finchley that delayed the start of Ted's funeral. As it turned out there had been some kerfuffle at customs over Jaz's wretched welcome hamper from the agency and the threat of its being impounded for containing suspicious substances in syrup. But we mourners weren't to know that and I volunteered to take over trumpet as well as jug-blowing duties in 'Medley For A Mischievous Talent', the Bayou Boys' musical tribute that I had arranged. Not that my selflessness cut any ice at the band rehearsal in the vestry.

'Whoa, whoa whoa!' said Cliff, our vocalist. I thought for a moment he was segueing from 'My Very Good Friend The Milkman' to 'Horsey Keep Your Tail Up' but in fact he was criticizing my performance. 'I hope to God a trumpeter turns up this afternoon because I've heard better sounds come out of a radiator.'

'It's like a dirge, Ed,' said Frank.

'Well, it is a funeral,' I pointed out. 'It's not my fault Jaz isn't here.'

'You did tell him it was today, didn't you, Ed?'

This prompted another wearisome burst of jealousy. You might think that any glimmer of success among a group of failed fifty-five-year-olds would be smiled upon by the others, but you would be wrong.

'Too busy doing his column, Frank.'

'Has he got a column, Cliff? It completely slipped my mind – he hasn't mentioned it for at least fifteen seconds.'

'Just because you haven't got one,' I said, trying to rise above the level of schoolyard abuse. 'We'll give Jaz as long as we can. We'll start with me doing my bit. Then we'll have the

12-year-old vicar who's never heard of Ted say something inappropriate, then Sally's going to read a bit of Auden.'

Mention of Ted's widow brought an immediate reaction from the rest of the band, turning them as it were into naughty choirboys whose snowy vestments hung on a nearby rail.

'Phwwooar,' said Cliff, 'reckon she'll do it in the nuddy?'

'Still does it for me, that girl,' said Frank, the steam on his spectacles in danger of melting the masking tape. Ray played a snatch of 'The Stripper' on the trombone. Needless to say, I had been similarly smitten with Sally's appearances in the buff in such widely differing productions as *I, Claudius* and later, as work proved harder to come by, *Adventures of a Plumber's Mate*. But that was many years ago now, and these days Sally was only ever seen in public fully dressed and with a scarf round her throat.

'Then we'll play the coffin out with "Tiger Rag," I said, 'unless Jaz still hasn't turned up in which case we'll have to do "My Very Good Friend The Milkman" again.'

'Will the vicar allow that?' said Frank.

'Probably have to be the "Red Flag", or the theme from *Friends* these days,' said Ray.

'If you're trying to get a job on *Grumpy Old Men*,' said Cliff, 'you're twenty-five years too old for it, son.'

'No I'm not,' said Ray. 'And anyway,' he went on, gamely clambering on to his hobbyhorse despite still being a little breathless from his last exertions on the trombone, 'they're not old and they're not grumpy. *Mild-Mannered Children* they should call it.'

I saw an opening. 'Well, you just wait till you see what the Old Lock-Keeper has to say'.

This produced another groan. 'Excuse me,' said Frank. 'What possible relevance does that have to what we were talking about?'

'Come on,' said Cliff. 'Let's have another blow then it's time for a bijou drinkette.'

I would have joined them across the road but I was instructed to stay in the vestry until I was at least within spitting distance of the right opening notes, an unfortunate reminder of my Curio, Gentleman Attending Upon Orsino, in the Shrewsbury school production of *Twelfth Night* ('E. F. Reardon's attempt to play the lute during the famous first "If music be the food of love" speech left no one in any doubt that this was meant to be a comedy').

If proof were needed of the depressing fact that everything is in thrall to the celebrity industry these days, one need look no further than the officiating vicar, whose patter was as callow as the peach fuzz on his chin. He had clearly been working strenuously on his 'links', as if expecting there to be a talent scout in the congregation who would pluck him from his Gothic revival fastness and find him a presenter's job on *Songs of Praise*, or more probably one of the cookery or antique programmes either side of it.

'And now I'd like to "hand back", as they say in the media that Ted chose as his calling, to someone who knew him. Edwin Reardon.'

I stepped up to the pulpit, careful not to reveal my prepared text before I opened my mouth. I find that an audience in this kind of situation will greet anything that looks to be more than two pages stapled together (as this was, much more) with immediate restlessness and an intake of disappointed breath, which can knock one off one's stride straightaway.

'Well I've written a poem for Ted,' I said. 'It goes like this:

'Dear old Ted,
Writer of *Z* . . .
Cars and so much else besides.
The Planemakers, *The Onedin Line*, couple of *Doctor
Finlay's Casebooks*, And then he sadly d—'

'Jaz! My dear fellow!' hollered Felix from the front row of seats, for all the world as if he were on his mobile phone again to California.

But no, here came Milvane himself, trotting down the aisle and acknowledging the crowd, the practised gesture of a man about to go up on stage and collect an Emmy and an air kiss from a daytime TV starlet with an envelope bigger than her dress. The organ meanwhile had struck up 'Simply The Best,' possibly after some pre-arranged signal, which I wouldn't have put past him.

'Sorry I'm late everybody,' said Jaz. 'Ed, would you mind taking it from the top again? That sounded good.'

But I sensed I had lost them, and though I struggled through to the tenth stanza, which incidentally dealt in a neat rhyme scheme with the advent of colour, I cut short the rest and handed over (as they say in the media, which the vicar wished he had chosen as his calling) to Sally, the widow, who performed Auden's 'Stop all the Clocks', a little overemotionally for my taste. 'Stop all the time between the lines for a look up at the rafters and a little sob' would have been nearer the mark. But 'Hey, this thing isn't about me,' as Jaz put it afterwards in the upstairs room in the pub across the road. Although to judge by his baroque performance of 'Tiger Rag' to round off the formal proceedings one could never have guessed it. He all but climbed up on the coffin for the final bars.

'You know what, Ed, that man was worth more than the whole lot of us put together,' said Jaz, putting his flushed face into Extreme Close-Up about an inch from mine, and generating as much heat as the pub's log-effect fire behind me.

The thing I have learnt about parties after funerals is that, like family gatherings on New Year's Eve, one can give vent to one's true feelings and they will be ascribed to the emotion of the moment, and forgotten about in the next day's general hangover. This works even better if one has the strength of character to get through the proceedings without imbibing, while all around are falling down drunk. Power without responsibility: the prerogative of the harlot and the sober party guest.

'Well, he was worth several of you, Jaz.'

'Exactly,' said Jaz, or to be more accurate, 'Ezzhahe.' 'He had more talent in his—'

But I had him now, and followed up the rapier thrust with a poniard plunged into the heart. 'Especially after that toe-curling letter your wife sent round. What on earth possessed you to marry her?'

'God knows. They come and go. Anyway. How *are* you?' said Jaz, thrusting his face even closer than I thought possible.

'Oh, still churning it out. Bit of radio. And I've got a column now – "The Old Lock-Keeper"—'

'Ah-ah-ah,' said Jaz, wagging his finger like a metronome. 'This is Ted's day.'

'That's all right,' I said, 'it used to be his column. Actually Jaz, talking of canals, did you get the tape of my radio play, *A Hodful of Blood?*'

'I did,' said Jaz, nodding judiciously. 'It was *excellent*. Fabulous title.'

'I'm not sure the actors got it quite right,' I said. 'But it would make a great movie.'

'Remind me what it was about again?' said Jaz, still nodding. 'Thank you sweetheart,' he said to a girl who was going round topping up glasses. This was an important moment so I put my hand over mine, but she had gone anyway.

'The digging of the Blisworth Tunnel. I suppose there might be a problem with it all being set in the dark.'

'Great for radio though, have you considered that?' said Jaz.

So there it was. Jaz had never even listened to the tape of the play (which I'd been obliged to record on a cassette of rare Billie Holiday tracks) much less heard of the Blisworth Tunnel. I resented the calculated insult to all the navvies who had died, I resented my own wasted effort sticking Sellotape over the little hole on the back of the cassette, most of all I resented the loss of at least three large glasses of Côte du Rhône at a time when the Dr Jekyll of free drink was about to metamorphose horribly into the Mr Hyde of the cash bar.

I was determined Jaz would pay for his insouciance. 'Then again, that last movie you did,' I said, waving at the girl with the bottles, now down to their dregs, 'that was set in darkness at the earth's core – yet they were still walking around in bright light. The crew got out of the ship thing – they were so lucky there was air to breathe down there – had the battle with the monkeys—'

Jaz was now leaning back, looking at me as though weighing up my game plan. 'I thought the monkeys were good – they gave it a Conradian feel.'

'Really?' I said. 'I thought they gave it a straight-through-to-video feel.'

Jaz carefully put his glass down on a round table. 'You looking for a fat lip, matey?'

'Oh yes? You and whose army? Commander Zargon's of the Zod Fleet?'

'That was Christopher Plummer, I'll have you know,' said Jaz.

I felt sure he was about to invite me to take further discussion of his oeuvre out into the car park, but at this moment Ted's widow Sally interposed herself between us, no doubt seeing the way the wind was blowing. Ted himself had been a past master of post-funeral fisticuffs, most recently after we took our leave of another *Z Cars* veteran, and Ted and Alan Plater had wound up rolling among the floral tributes at Golders Green Crematorium, demolishing a large wreath of red roses spelling out 'Ta-ra Wack' from Alan Bleasdale who couldn't be present. This altercation had started over whose episodes had been chosen for the DVD of *When the Boat Comes In*. Ted's hadn't as I recall, and his boat remained firmly wedged out on Tynemouth Sands.

'Ooh Plummer,' said Sally. 'I was very rude with him once. Or was it Christopher Biggins?'

'Definitely the former, I'd have thought,' I said.

'Now then,' said Sally. 'He was a bit of a sexpot as Nero in *I, Claudius.*'

'Ah yes, Clavdivs,' said Jaz, using its familiar television insiders' name as if he somehow had even the remotest connection with the programme, instead of directing episodes of *It Shouldn't Happen to a Vet* 300 miles further north. 'The golden age of broadcasting. Anyway, look Sal,' he said, putting an arm round her and automatically resting his hand on her bra strap, 'it's so good to see the old gang gathered together again. And even though this is such a sad occasion, it's been worth every cent.'

'I really am very grateful, Jaz,' said Sally.

'Shhhh,' said Jaz, putting a finger to her lips. 'Now I have to go talk to Felix.'

He lurched off and Sally pulled a face at Jaz's back – gratifying enough, though I would have preferred her to go the whole hog and rub frantically at her mouth to expunge all traces of his attentions.

'He always has to let you know he's paying,' said Sally. 'Even if it was a cup of BBC coffee in 1975.'

'Yes, I'm afraid he's gone well and truly Hollywood.'

'But you haven't, Eddie,' said Sally, tugging at my beard in what I'm sure she intended as affection, but which all but drew blood. 'Sorry I was such a cow on the phone when you offered to help.'

'No no you weren't,' I said. 'Well, maybe just a touch of Guernsey.'

'But actually, Ed, there is something you could do for me.'

'Name it, Sal,' I said, resting my reassuring hand on her back where Jaz's unwelcome one had been only moments before. 'Anything – take the unwanted food off your hands . . . knee-trembler out the back—'

'No, it's not that,' said Sally.

'Is it the other one then?' I said. In truth I would have been happy with either.

'No – it's a rather special piece of writing you could help me out with.'

Wednesday

'Dear All, Well, what a year it's been chez Cartwright*!!*' Two exclamation marks seemed about right there, I thought, upbeat and offering the promise of more to come. 'Ted passed away, which was sad.' No, none there, let the facts speak for them-selves. 'But undaunted, I'm learning German, and miraculously the dwarf wall I erected in March is still standing!!!!' Four exclamation marks there, that particular titbit of dreary infor-mation needed all the help it could get.

Wednesday

Sally's task had nothing to do with writing the preface to Ted's collected works, and everything to do with taking the burden of writing her annual round-robin newsletter off her hands. The biter bit, indeed.

'So a Happy Christmas to all' I typed before the thought occurred that she, in her girlish, minidress-and-suede-boots-in-the-Kings-Road way, would still call it 'Crimble'. With a flower over the 'i'. With an effort I put yearning memory aside and added a PS. 'For anyone worried about the fate of Ted's Old Lock-Keeper column, fear not, it's in good hands!!!'

I felt confident in asserting this after ascertaining from Emily, the editor of the *Herts & Bucks Echo*, that my e-mailed column had arrived safely on her desk, crusty sentiments all present and correct. What's more, she had invited me to the office that afternoon to discuss the future. Perhaps before too long there would be a Sally substitute for me to conjure up at lonely moments.

Nevertheless, I hedged my bets by including a jokey invoice with the draft newsletter I posted off to Sal on my way to the newspaper office. 'To Ghosting Round Robin out of the goodness of my heart, One Tongue Sandwich plus VAT.'

'I'm sorry Ed,' said Emily, 'this is just not right.'

For a fleeting fragment of a second, I entertained the hope that my editor might be referring to the arrangement of shells and sequins attached to the bright pink flip-flop that sat on the desk in front of her. She snipped at a loose thread with a pair of office scissors and tutted impatiently. But I knew in my heart that the chief object of her displeasure was not her dainty footwear but the four double-spaced pages of Lock-Keeper copy that lay underneath it, lightly pressed yet at the same time fatally crushed.

'But it's a piece of investigative journalism,' I said.

'That's not what the Old Lock-Keeper does. He moans about wind farms and travellers and stuff.'

'Well, this week he's moaning about time-share scams which are just as offensive to the great British public.'

Emily held up a folded copy of the most recent issue. 'Look Ed, what's the first thing you see when you pick up the *Herts & Bucks Echo*?'

'You mean after I see the fifteen pieces of junk falling out of the paper and on to the floor and wasting my valuable time picking them up and putting them in the bin?.

'Those pieces of junk, or flyers as we call them, are worth fifty grand a year to us. Without the advertising from those time-share guys – who you call – where is it . . .'

'The Spanish Holiday Inquisition, I was rather pleased with that.'

'Without the money they bring in we wouldn't be able to publish, yeah?' said Emily.

'So the Old Lock-Keeper's being gagged, is he?' I said, then realized I had better try to be a good sport if I wanted another shot at it next week. 'That bain't be what I was a-expecting of to hear, m'dear.'

Emily stared at me. 'Whatever, we're just putting a different spin on him. Look, I'm really really sorry it hasn't worked out Ed, but now I've got someone waiting to see me,' she said.

Clearly someone who caused her some trepidation, as she looked round her desk, refitted the flip-flop to her foot and hastily scooped a large India rubber shaped like a penis into a drawer. The door opened and in walked Olive.

At first I didn't recognize her, as one doesn't seeing a familiar face out of context. But then the penny dropped. As well as my professional life being at the mercy of twelve-year-olds I now had 112-year-olds snapping at my heels.

'I'm ever so sorry about this, Mr Reardon,' said Olive. 'But like you always tell us in class, it's all about being in the right place at the right time.'

'Yeah, Olive sent us in some brilliant stuff,' said Emily. 'Really quirky.'

'So I take it you're going to be the Old Lock-Keeper's Cat, are you?' I said to Olive.

'Oh thanks, Ed,' said Emily. 'That is such a good idea – we can use the same masthead only with a paw-print on it.'

'Oooh, masthead!' said Olive. 'Proper Fleet Street!'

At which point I made an excuse and left.

Thursday

Luckily, my disappointment over not receiving a regular weekly income for the first time since assisting with the traffic census for the M25 was assuaged by a message from my esteemed agent's assistant, Ping, inviting me to lunch 'to discuss a proposition thingy with Felix and Jaz'.

'Bring us two more bottles, Renato, save your feet,' said Felix. 'And what is it you're drinking, Jaz?'

'Canarino,' said Jaz.

'Come again?'

'It's hot water and lemon.'

'Er, come again?'

Luckily, it was a term with which the sommelier was familiar, for I was bursting to get to the meat of the proposition thingy.

'So let's cut to the chase, as I think you say in your neck of the woods, Jaz,' I said.

'No,' said Jaz, 'I've never heard anyone say that.'

'Ha!' guffawed Felix. 'Reason for luncheon – well, no reason except that it's bloody good fun getting sloshed with your chums – main reason is Jaz and I very much wanted to run something past you.'

'Correct me if I'm wrong,' I said, 'but would this have anything to do with the digging of the Blisworth Tunnel?'

'Yes – you are wrong,' said Jaz.

'Jaz has just had some remarkably good luck,' said Felix. 'He's just won – well, you tell him, Jaz, I want to concentrate on these little buggers,' he said, attacking a plate of assorted molluscs and plankton.

'I seem to have won sixty grand, just out of the blue like that,' said Jaz. 'It was one of those so-called prize draws you don't pay any attention to because they're scams and nobody ever wins.'

'Oh, one of them,' I said, a yawning gap opening up in the pit of my stomach that felt bigger than Blisworth itself. 'And it was your name on the prize, was it? And your address?'

'Yeah, proper cheque and everything.'

'And you didn't have to do anything or go anywhere like the Baldock Travelodge to get it?'

Jaz shrugged. 'Nope. Complete mystery. Sixty grand – not much but I figure I might be able to do a bit of good with it over here.'

'Now, isn't that just typical of Jaz,' said Felix, dabbing at his chin then refixing the napkin into his collar. 'Eight million a picture but he never forgets the struggling writer.'

I hardly dared hope what might be coming next. Though to be strictly fair, the £60,000 was technically mine anyway and what's more I had gone to considerable time, trouble and humiliation to earn it.

'But this is wonderful,' I said.

'Well, you gotta put a bit back, don't you,' said Jaz.

'A scholarship for promising young writers,' said Felix. 'The Jaz Milvane Award.'

'Whatever,' said Jaz. 'Milvane or Jaz Milvane – either.'

'*Young* writers?' I said, feeling the gap opening up again.

'We've already had an overwhelming response,' said Felix. 'Literally thousands.'

'But you still think I'd have a chance of winning?' I said.

'You? Of course not,' laughed Felix. 'You'll be too busy reading all the scripts.'

'What?'

'Well, someone's got to do it and I'm too busy,' said Jaz. 'And you're on about how I wouldn't recognize a good script if it bit me in the arse. And anyway, you're too old, mate.'

'Come on, Ed, eat up,' said Felix as I stared at my Scallop and John Dory Concerto. 'Fish *is* supposed to be very good for the eyesight – because some of these scripts aren't even typed, you know – lazy so-and-sos.'

He gestured behind him and for the first time I noticed half-a-dozen Harrods bags, bulging with manuscripts of all shapes and sizes but with one thing in common – they were all massively thick.

'By the way, Jaz,' said Felix, 'Did you get that letter from Ted's widow, Sally?'

'God, yes,' said Jaz. 'Happy *Crimble??*'

'And wasn't it deadly dull,' said Felix. 'Yet she's so gorgeous – what a shame she's such a bore on paper. Now then, Jaz, I refuse to let you drink that muck,' he said as Jaz's hot water and lemon arrived. 'Let me give you a proper drink. Not you, Ed – you need your wits about you for all those scripts.'

And Felix took my empty glass and put it out of reach on the next table. Three exclamation marks there, I thought.

5

The Winona Defence

Monday

What should I call her? My muse? My inspiration? I did know
her name actually. It was on a business card, but I folded it up
and put it under a wonky table leg in the pub. So I shall just call
her the Girl – like in Daphne du Maurier's novel *Rebecca*.
Though I realize that somebody my age should really have his
fancy tickled by a Mrs Danvers figure with all that she might
have to offer in the way of sewing, cooking, keeping the curtains
clean, etc. But was it only Friday morning that it all began,
with a chance remark in my agent's office?

'Well, chick lit's still very big, Ed,' Ping had said. 'You could
try your hand at that.' This was in response to my light-hearted

suggestion that she and Felix might like to have a bash at doing what agents are traditionally supposed to do for their 10 per cent, and that is to seek employment for their clients. My jocular tone failed to mask an underlying desperation that Ping and Felix recognized all too easily, hence the unhelpful proposal that I work speculatively and for nothing. I cheerfully dismissed chick lit as altogether too gynaecological a genre for my hard-boiled prose style, adding that I didn't think I'd be up to it anyway – which was an odd thing for me to have done given my finger-gnawing need for a job.

'Why don't you do an illustrated history of Snetterton race-track?' suggested Felix, as if he'd only just thought of it. He hadn't, of course; it was a project he'd been urging me to undertake for the best part of ten years. 'Now *there* was a circuit,' he said, for what must have been the thirtieth time. 'It tested the driver's skills to the full.' It also would have tested the author's skills to the full to live on the meagre royalties the book was likely to earn.

Felix's success as a literary agent is founded on a deep respect for the stupidity and narrow-mindedness of the book-buying public. Never let it be forgotten that this is the man who secured a six-figure advance for *The Farter's Dictionary*, 1998's Christmas publishing sensation. Felix has handled so many Princess Diana conspiracy-theory books you could build a cathedral out of them (the Beatified One could lie in its crypt alongside her secret lovers Elvis Presley, Osama bin Laden and Harold Shipman). Whenever a round-the-world yachtsperson goes bonkers and eats their plimsolls in mid-Pacific Felix is there to secure the serialization rights to the tragic story even before the rescue services have arrived. The current bestselling book of mobile phone photos taken by witnesses of the London tube bombings shows Felix Jeffrey to be a literary agent at the very peak of his powers. But like all great men Felix has a dangerous weakness which occasionally clouds his judgement. Just as Churchill was overfond of the bottle and Hitler's brains turned to strudel at the sight of an Alsatian puppy, Felix has a sentimental attachment to Formula 1 motor racing which does not translate into successful sales figures. *The Brand's Hatch Story* (1997) and *The Love Poetry of Nigel Mansell* (1999), in both of which I had a hand, were dismal sellers although the latter contained a couplet I still feel deserved a far wider readership than it reached:

My heart beats just like when I get a
Problem with my carburettor.

Felix's predilection for F1 has been the bane of Ping's life since she joined the agency from Oxford a year ago. She has tried with variable success to get him away from the subject, while taking care not to trample on his dreams.

'If you look at the figures though, Felix,' she said, trying to appeal to his innate greed, 'rom-com's the leader of the pack right now.'

'No, it's Ferrari, isn't it?' said Felix, who knew exactly what she meant and also that she was right but he had decided to retreat into baffled-old-poppet mode. 'Mind you, it's a Lotus you need to get round Snetterton – don't you think, Ed? Or are you more of a BRM man?'

'I can't drive so—'

'Hagh! Neither could Luigi Musso, but he still won the Argentine Grand Prix in 1956.'

I had lost track of the argument that this appeared to clinch but Ping persevered. 'Felix, nobody'd buy a book like that.'

'I would. I'd buy two – one for the bedside table and another for the dining room for when Fiona's on the phone. Or doing that texting thing they do.' He raised his bushy eyebrows and assumed a gormless, wobbly-jowled expression, 'I'm texting . . . have you texted yet?'

None of this was getting me any closer to solvency so, in order that the day shouldn't be a complete waste of an evaded rail fare, I gave in and threw myself on Ping's tender mercies.

'All right then, Ping, tell me about "rom-com" – it's basically Mills and Boon, isn't it?'

'It's more like Mills and Boon meets Richard Curtis for a latte in Siena or somewhere funky.'

'Drives me absolutely insane,' continued Felix, still inside his existential bubble. 'Beep beep beepety beep.'

Meanwhile, Ping went through the salient elements of the rom-com genre. A pink and lime-green cover seemed to be fairly essential, with a punning title in big yellow letters. *Bad Heir Day* and *Last Chance Salon* were quoted as prime exemplars. The form requires the story to treat of a scatty thirty-two-year-old's adventures as she knocks about London and the Home Counties in search of a husband and, crucially it seems, a particular brand of Italian handbag whose name I didn't catch.

'Obviously, she's got to get a husband in the end 'cause she can't be a total dog,' said Ping. 'You might want her to meet Mr Right at her best mate's wedding or it could be at Wimbledon like in *32-Love*, that's up to you, but the main thing is the shoes and the bags and the where-she-goes-for-the-weekendy-type bollocks.'

'Presumably,' I said, tugging pensively on the meerschaum, 'I could look these shops up in *Thomson's Directory*?'

'What's wrong with a postcard, for God's sake?' said Felix. 'Or a telegram if it's *that* bloody important?'

'Oh, yeah, and Mr Right drives a Porsche.'

'It's not a Porsche,' said Felix, correcting her pronunciation. 'It's a Porsch-a. Did they teach you nothing at Balliol?'

'No.'

'Clearly not.'

'Well, yeah, actually, they taught us not to worry about stuff, 'cause what my tutor reckoned was, like, there'll always be people who *didn't* go to Oxford who can sort it for you.'

'Very well,' I said, 'by the sound of it, I should be able to get something to you by the middle of next week. Or Friday, if I have to come up with an author's pseudonym.'

'Good idea,' said Ping. 'That means you can really lower your standards. Oh-oh-oh, don't forget, vital story element – at the wedding, yeah, she must get her skirt caught in the back of her knickers.'

'Why not? It worked for Tolstoy.'

'And Chardonnay – she drinks it by the gallon.'

'Good God,' said Felix, 'the Barbarians have breached the gates. Porsches . . . Chardonnay. This is a respectable literary agency – you're fired, Ping!'

'Cool.'

'AAAAAA Locks, Chains and Burglar Alarms' was the first entry in the phone book on which my eye alighted when I sat down to work yesterday afternoon, but somehow I couldn't quite see Charlotte shopping there. Unless she'd had to buy a bicycle to get to her best friend's wedding. But that would have given her far too much character and probably frightened off Mr Riley or whatever the chinless Porsche-driving man's name was.

Anyone who has read *Who Would Fardels Bear?* knows that Ed Reardon is not a writer to shrink from tackling the mysterious power of sexual attraction. The scene between Vince and Barbara in the back of the Mini Countryman was as explicit as anything else that appeared in 1975. 'Would that the windows had steamed up in the lay-by sparing us the sordid details of this loveless coupling,' quailed the *Listener*'s reviewer. But that was thirty years ago and with the passage of time my interest in and experience of the subject has dwindled to a level of papal indifference. At the first sign of on-screen canoodling I either hit fast-forward or get up to put the kettle on. It has the same effect on me as the song in the *Morecambe and Wise Show* in that it stimulates nothing so much as a desire for a cup of tea. Or a sip of milk in Elgar's case because, strangely enough, I have observed the selfsame lack of interest in his body language when love is in the air. Elgar, however, has an excuse in that he was neutered. Or is it spayed? I know it cost forty quid. Me, I'm just neutered by nature. That's the Ed Reardon default setting. Or so I thought.

I had just completed my maiden rom-com sentence: 'Charlotte Spade bought a large glass of Chardonnay from a shop (details to follow)' when a splintering of wood and a tumble to the floor of a strictly non-amorous nature confirmed that my typing chair had disintegrated – possibly in protest at the kind of work I was forced to undertake. Anyway, it necessitated a visit to the Berkhamsted Back Shop.

An electronic beep sounded as I crossed the threshold of the shop first thing this morning. And there she was.

'Hello, can I help you?' She pronounced 'you' as 'ye' thus dating herself as a good twenty years younger than me and for once I found myself objecting to neither. Nor to the bright yellow Doc Martens and rainbow-coloured hair braids.

'Yes, I need, rather urgently, because I'm a writer, one of your orthopaedic typing chairs or stool things.'

The girl clasped her hands in a parody of a servile shop assistant and said in a voice familiar from a hundred *Monty Python* sketches, 'I'm sorry, Sir, this is a cheese shop.' It foxed me a bit, although I, too, sometimes like to amuse myself in pointless ways. About a year ago I went through a phase of answering the phone and saying, in what was – though I say it myself – an uncannily accurate impression of weatherman, John Kettley, 'Looks like another mixed bag this weekend so you can't put that umbrella away just yet, I'm afraid.' If anything, the bafflement of my callers only encouraged me to do it more often, so I admired the Girl's perversity.

'What kind of writer are you?' she asked.

'Does that make a difference as to what kind of chair I buy?'

'No, I'm just interested.'

'Well, I'm currently writing a novel.'

'You'll need plenty of lower back support for a long-term project like that.'

'It's not that long-term – but you're right, I'll need to sit down to do it.'

'So what's your name?'

'Well, I was thinking of Deirdre Sawbridgeworth. Though that might be a bit long given the attention span of my readers. But normally I write under the name Ed Reardon.'

'You wrote um . . .'

This was the start of an all too familiar ignominy which any author, however celebrated, will instantly recognize. The humiliation normally continues along the lines of 'You wrote that thing um, oh what was it? . . . erm', followed by a long silence which it seems bigheaded to break and agony to prolong. But if you are so foolish as to supply a book or play title you are likely to be frozen out as if you'd made an indecent proposal – 'No, never heard of that' is the most common response, and sometimes 'Maybe I'm thinking of someone else.' If you try to change the subject they come back at you very hard indeed, belabouring you with the achievements of Nick Hornby, Ben Elton and the like. 'Bet you wish you'd written *Fever Pitch*, etc.

etc.' So I braced myself to be scolded for my anonymity, unfavourably compared with Jeanette Winterson, asked if I'd ever considered writing for films and heaven knows what other indignities.

'You wrote *Who Would Fardels Bear?*,' said the Girl. 'That's one of my favourite books.'

'Really? Is it?'

'That and *To Kill a Mockingbird*. It's quite odd, actually, because they turned your book into one of my most unfavourite films.'

'They did, didn't they.'

'And it was twenty minutes too long.'

'At least. I can't believe you know this. People your age don't know anything. I'm sorry, that's rude.'

'Yes. But, actually, it's a reasonable assumption. We're living in a culture where everything's reduced to the lowest common denominator, and it's all run by twelve-year-olds who if I'd had my way would have been drowned at birth in a bucket of raw sewage.'

Had this been a rom-com film by Sir Richard Curtis, based on a novel by His Grace the Duke of Highbury, the voice of some rebarbative chanteuse would have soared to a schmaltzy climax at this point. And although there's no obvious similarity between Hugh Grant and myself – except that we both look irredeemably guilty in a police mugshot – the next thing I knew I was bumping into things in the back shop and offering to give the Girl a signed copy of *Who Would Fardels Bear?*

Which presented a bit of a poser, because when I got home

I found that I only had a solitary remaining copy – a first edition. And much as I liked the Girl, especially the cast of her mind and turn of phrase with particular regard to raw sewage, there are some sacrifices a writer can never make. However pleasing she might be. And I confess it was hard to get the legs out of my mind – or at least those bits that were visible through the slashes in her jeans worn underneath a vintage pink cocktail dress. As I say, a poser.

Tuesday

I began my search for a copy of *Fardels* in what the popular press still quaintly refers to as London's West End. By midday I was standing in Foyles bookshop among the lurid covers of my fellow chick-literati. An entire wall was stacked with copies of *At the Drop of a Chateau* and elsewhere dump bins overflowed with similar masterpieces such as *Auvergne Ready* and *Advantage Lucy*. I sneaked a look at a random page of one just to get the feel of the competition. It contained two examples of the old line-space trick. The line-space trick is used when the author has run out of steam on a particular subject or reached a narrative cul-de-sac. He or she simply presses the carriage return key three times and starts again on a new topic or bit of story. It can save hours of tortuous linking and every writer in the business resorts to it from time to time. But only one author in my experience would have the brass neck to sneak it past an editor twice on the same page and that's old Cyril Rogers. It was comforting to know that *Game, Set and Matricciana* and for all I knew *Catch Him if You Cannes* could well be Cyril's work. He was a real pro, was Cyril. If memory serves he once ghosted three books in a single year (1974, I think): Jimmy Osmond, Rab Butler and Arkle plus thirty-five episodes of *Bagpuss* and a *Colditz* (the one where they all went barking mad and tried to eat the fence). It was reassuring to know he might still be around and I begrudged him not a penny of his success as I pushed my way through quite a crowd in search of a copy of *Who Would Fardels Bear?*

'Would you mind joining the queue, please,' said a snotty woman of the kind most other bookshops phased out years ago. She had a severe grey bob and at her neck a big chunky agate whose sole purpose was, like a Yardie's lump of gold, to intimidate.

'I'm just trying to buy a book.'

'So is everybody here. If you want Mr Milvane to sign it, there's a twenty-minute wait at least.'

I'd inadvertently stumbled into a melée not of chick-lit consumers but a subspecies even more intellectually impoverished clamouring for copies of Jaz Milvane's memoirs. I vaguely remembered him telling me about it but once it was clear that I wasn't going to be the lucky hack offered £50,000 to ghost it for him I'd put it out of my mind. He'd called it, with typical, self-effacing modesty, *Making it Big in Hollywood*. Whereas, as the Girl had so rightly pointed out, it should have been more accurately entitled *Making a Big Pile of Poo out of Someone Else's Carefully Crafted Rites-of-Passage Novel in Hollywood*.

195

I saw it as my duty as a friend to discomfit him as he sat behind the signing table facing a queue of admirers. So I pushed past Mrs Snotty and approached him.

'Whose idea was that title, then?'

'Terrible, isn't it. I wanted to call it *Huge in Hollywood*.' He finished signing a copy and returned it to a spotty teenage punter, adding with a repulsive oily smile on his face, 'Thank you so much.'

'I'd just like to say thanks, Jaz,' said a twitchy, middle-aged man in a tie and denim jacket. 'Your movies have changed my life.'

'He was perfectly normal before,' I whispered to Jaz as he signed the misfit's book. 'Look what you've done to him.'

'Thank you so much.'

'You just spelt thanks with an "X",' I said.

'Well, there's a lot of them to get through. Can't hang about – and if you're just going to stand there criticizing . . . Are you here to buy my book or not?'

'Certainly not, I'm here to buy *my* book. I'm not buying *your* book. You didn't even write it. And if you had you'd only have made a dog's breakfast of it like you did with my book.'

'Why are you buying your own book?'

'I have to get a copy for someone.'

'What's her name?'

'I don't know. Who says it's a she?'

'So it is then.'

A soft-faced man wearing a short-sleeved shirt and a lapel badge saying 'Keith' had been standing on the other side of the table fiddling with his tie and trying not to overhear. Jaz directed the oily smile towards him and said 'Hello' in a way that would have been arrestable if addressed to a minor.

'Er, yes. Please can you put "To Mary, I know nothing will make up for Tuesday but this might help – Keith".'

'Not much point in getting him to write that, Keith,' I said. 'You could've done it yourself and saved half an hour's queuing.'

Jaz stopped writing and looked at me. 'So where did you meet her, then?'

'We both work at British Home Stores,' said Keith.

The snotty woman had been struggling with a dilemma for some time: to leave us alone or to have me thrown out. Either might risk Jaz's displeasure. On the other hand any contact with Huge of Hollywood was better than none.

'Is everything all right, Mr Milvane?' she said, flicking her eyes meaningfully towards me then back to him.

'Wouldn't mind a ten-minute break, Georgia.'

'Of course, would you like to come to the office? There's some coffee on the go and a day bed if you want to rest.'

'No thanks,' said Jaz, grabbing me. 'Come on, you. We need to get to the bottom of this.'

'No, we don't,' I said as we moved away from the table, leaving Mrs Snotty, not for the first time, I suspect, alone and seething in her earth-toned linen.

Punters waiting for Jaz's autograph voiced a disappointment bordering on despair. A few with initiative broke ranks and followed us. But hell hath no fury like a snotty Foyles woman scorned.

'Everybody stay in their places,' she snapped. And they did.

'But he's only halfway through my dedication,' pleaded Keith.

'Quiet! And feet behind the line.'

Finding a copy of *Who Would Fardels Bear?* was straightforward enough, but I had to suffer the embarrassment of Jaz failing to bully the cashier into giving it to me for nothing, accompanied by the equally bullying tactics used to elicit information about the Girl.

'No, I haven't "done the deed" yet. For heaven's sake, Jaz.'

'Well, how far have you got with her?'

'I'm contemplating buying an orthopaedic chair from her.'

'Oooo! You dirty dog. Is she mad?'

'No, I don't think so.'

'Because if she is, just stop right now. Draw a line under it. Move if you have to.'

Jaz's deadly seriousness on this last point hinted at an exotic personal history of suede jackets doused with bleach and of phones ringing at five-minute intervals through the night, of favoured sunglasses crushed under car wheels and shoes buried in the garden. When I told him she just seemed like a nice girl who was keen on my work, he looked away considering whether or not to deliver a five-minute lecture on the art of avoiding mad women, but after a moment's thought he settled for a patronizing pat on the shoulder.

'Always remember, Ed, if you can make them laugh you've got them halfway into bed.'

'You've never made anyone laugh and you've had about seven wives—'

'Four.'

'Not one of whom, so far as I know, has ever cracked a smile.'

'No, but I'm rich. A woman doesn't bother smiling if she's got a rich husband. The question is, what are we going to do about this situation of yours?'

'We're going to leave me to get on with it, thank you very much.'

'No we aren't. You've got to bring her along to the gig on Sunday. We'll have a look at her, see if she's mad. In the meantime I'd better sign this book of yours. That'll give you a head start. Right. "To ——" better leave that blank till you get a bit further in the relationship.'

Before I could stop him he had written 'Thanx for liking my movie – Jaz.'

'That should do the trick,' he said, and handed it over.

Wednesday

Yesterday's trip to London was exhausting and far from cheap. At the end of it I was left with a book that was all but useless as a nosegay from a potential swain. It was becoming apparent that I was not suited to the Casanova lifestyle. Besides, I had neglected my rom-com duties. Charlotte had not had a sniff of Chardonnay for days and my feisty heroine was a very long way indeed from getting her skirt caught in the back of her knickers. But the besetting dilemma of the life literary is always whether to invest one's time and energies in a project which might realize royalties two years down the line or, if you and your cat need to eat a bit sooner than that, to nip down to the police station and pick up a quick tenner for standing in line at an identity parade.

'Don't forget to leave your e-mail addresses when you collect your money from the desk,' said the officer in charge of today's more than usually time-consuming line-up. The kid's mother had come back for a fourth look at all of us, especially me and my fellow regular, Doug, whose graphic design business hit the buffers a year or two back.

'Any chance of another one next week?' asked Brian, a former ITV documentary producer.

'Can't say at this stage, Brian,' said the officer. 'But there's a steam weekend coming up at Knebworth. That usually flushes out a few wrong 'uns, so fingers crossed.'

'Fingers crossed, indeed,' said Warren who used to fly Tridents for British Caledonian and could be paralysingly boring on the subject. I hung back as the three redundant fifty-somethings headed up to the canteen to take advantage of some of the most competitively priced jacket potatoes in the Hertfordshire area. I would normally have joined them but I felt my place was at home with Charlotte Spade – I was having the devil's own job getting her to Isabella and Miles's engagement party with the right accessories. Possibly I had made a rod for my own back by trying to route her past some of the shops whose websites I had managed to plunder for material, but that was all the more reason to get back to her.

'Top of your game this morning, Mr Reardon,' said the

officer. 'You get better and better if you don't mind my saying so. Really had me worried about allowing my *own* nippers out on the streets.'

'Good job I didn't shave the beard off.'

'Oh, doesn't bear thinking about. Cheerio then.'

I turned to leave and as I did so she came through the swing doors.

'Hello.'

The yellow Doc Martens, the pink cocktail dress, belted with a big buckle over slashed jeans – the outfit that had featured so much in my thoughts that its components had become even more confused and ill-matched than they were in real life, rather in the way that a cloud changes shape the longer you stare at it. Over the last twenty-four hours the boots had changed colour in my imagination while the cocktail dress had mutated into a sort of pinafore. Her features had shifted around as I tried to fix them in my mind's eye and, strange as it seems for one so smitten, I would have been hard put to describe her face. But there was no mistaking the real thing.

'Hello again,' I said, hoping my skills as a wordsmith would come to my aid before too long.

'I've got the averages for you, Norman,' she said to the officer. 'D'you want to put them up on the board?'

'You're a treasure. Don't know what the lads'd do without you.'

'Yeah, right. What are you doing here, Ed?'

'Um – I was about to ask you the same thing.'

'I'm the scorer for the "F" Division cricket team.'

'You do the scoring for a team of cricketing policemen?'

'Only the Sunday games. I don't do the league matches, I'm not that sad. And you haven't answered my question – what are you doing here?'

'Oh, I'm just doing a bit of research.'

'Ah, "research" – that's the Winona Ryder Defence.'

'The what?'

'That was what she said when she got caught nicking stuff. It's what all celebrity shoplifters do. That and go on *Comic Relief* to get themselves filmed standing by a well in Malawi. Makes me want to vomit.'

'Oh me, too. And hardly any of the money gets to where it should, you know. The whole thing should really be called Richard Curtis's KnighthoodAid.'

'You still haven't answered my question.'

'Well . . .' The *Comic Relief* digression had given me a little time to think but what came out next was still far from plausible. 'I'm a writer as you know and as a way of understanding the criminal mind I find it helpful to come here and . . . inhabit the character of the er . . . miscreant by—'

'Excuse me, Mr Reardon, sorry to interrupt,' said the officer. 'But when we asked you all to take your glasses off, you left yours on the ledge.'

I thought about denying they were my spectacles but reckoned, correctly, that I'd been rumbled by now anyway. 'Thank you,' I said, and took them. She smiled.

'How much do you get for pretending to be a flasher?'

'Ten pounds an hour.'

'Wow!' she said. Then she saw the poster on the wall and read out the line at the bottom that had caught my eye a few months ago. '"If you get picked out by mistake – NOTHING HAPPENS". Well, that's a bonus.'

'To be honest, love,' said the officer, pinning up the batting averages, 'we could give him *twelve* quid an hour and he wouldn't be overpaid. And by the way the canteen's closing in a few minutes.'

'Don't suppose you fancy a subsidized cup of tea and a chocolate biscuit?' I said.

'Always up for a cheeky Wagon Wheel,' she said.

I had forgotten how a striking-looking woman elevates one's status in the world. Not that there was ever going to be much difficulty getting a table at the police canteen but it was noticeable that ours was wiped clean immediately (by Beauty-Clarice Otienayah, according to her laminated labelling) while my fellow freelancers had to clear space for their jacket potatoes among plates, discarded crisp packets and uncompleted *Daily Express* crosswords. I was pleasantly aware of their glances as the Girl and I talked of books and music and films. Before long we had discovered a mutual loathing for Mike Leigh, the plays of David Hare and that new announcer on Radio 4 who can't pronounce the letter 'R.' I spoke briefly about the drudgery of my own work and the time flew. When the canteen's serving hatch rattled open again, after an hour's break in which Beauty-Clarice and her colleagues gorged on staff-price jacket potatoes, it was four o'clock. We shared a second Wagon Wheel and I decided it was time to move things on a stage.

'Look, I don't know if this is the sort of thing I should be saying to you, but . . .'

'Try me.'

'Because I just don't think I'm very good at it.'

'Come on.'

'Well – my heroine Charlotte has been to four handbag shops already and she's got drunk in all of them – I even had her getting drunk in a ship chandler's but I had to delete that because there aren't any trains that go to Ascot via Gosport, I checked, so that was ten pages lost, and then I had her going from a jeweller's in Hatton Garden to Bond Street via Harrods which was ridiculous – and there's still a hundred pages to go before she gets to the wedding and I'm desperate, I'm absolutely desperate.'

'Can I just ask you something, Ed?'

'I know what you're going to say and I agree, how does she buy wine in a handbag shop? If she works in publishing she'd have a briefcase and the directions to the engagement party would have been texted to her anyway so—'

'No, listen. If you're so broke you have to do police identity parades, and what you're doing makes you this miserable, and you're not getting paid for it anyway, I suppose my question would be – why do it?'

'Because it's what I do.'

'You don't have to do *this*. If you're going to suffer, you might as well suffer for something good. Something useful.'

'Maybe I should be writing that illustrated history of Snetterton instead.'

'No, write something like your novel which you promised me a signed copy of which I still haven't got – even though I read it when I was fourteen and it inspired me to go to university and drink cider for three years. And watch *Countdown*.'

'But that was then. Now I'm the one watching daytime television and drinking whatever's on three-for-two offer at Threshers.'

'You see this is what you writers do, you sell out when you've got a bit of success and start working for agents and publishers. They're just leeches and spongers, Ed – the dregs of society! '

I would like to say she looked magnificent excoriating the shabbiness of Grub Street, but actually her voice became somewhat shrill and she allowed her roll-up to go out.

'I'd round 'em all up, every single one of them, stick 'em up against a wall and machine gun the—'

'Would you mind keeping your voice down?' said a woman police officer almost apologetically. 'I agree with you, love, but we've been ticked off about canteen culture so we all have to toe the line now.'

I must admit that it's not totally unpleasant to have a conscience again – I thought I'd left it behind with my LP collection in Camden when my ex-wife threw me out after the barley wine in the Wendy house episode. Especially, it has to be said, a conscience as easy on the eye as this one. But what the Girl doesn't seem to realize, with her innocent idealism and fat £150 weekly pay-cheque from the Berkhamsted Back Shop – plus presumably her free tea and cakes at all those cricket matches – is that experienced writers simply do not have the freedom to write what they want. At least, to get to the point where they *can* write what they want, they have to show they can write what other people want, or what other people tell you that other people want, which, of course, might not be what they want at all. And the trouble is that by the time you have acquired sufficient status to be able to write what you want, you've completely forgotten what it was you wanted to write about in the first place.

Regrettably I have to conclude that what I really want is the Girl.

Thursday

I spent today experimenting with different strategies to put her out of my mind. At one point I tuned into the shipping forecast only to find a cricket commentator talking about batting averages. But by doing the hoovering, brushing Elgar's coat and, as a last desperate resort, working on Charlotte's heart-to-heart with Henrietta about Ben's recent moodiness I managed to get through to six o'clock. For the first time in many weeks I was glad to be able to set off to the Sports Centre to face my writing class.

'This week we're going to be tackling the part of the job that every writer dreads, but it has to be done.'

'VAT?' asked Pearl.

'No, you have to earn 60,000 for that,' said Stan. 'He would-n't be registered.'

'No, we're going to address the thorny issue of writing romantic love scenes.'

This news was met with groans from my students who, being loyal readers of the tabloids, interpreted the word 'love' as being on a par with 'dating' and 'romping' as a euphemism for unbridled licentiousness and perversion of the kind that assails us from every orifice of the media.

'It's everywhere,' wailed Olive. 'You can't turn the TV on without someone waving their great BTM at you.'

'It was bad enough in the Olympics,' said Pearl. 'Those chaps adjusting their tuck-boxes or whatever they call them now.'

'Are we to write about full frontal nudity?' asked Stan, man of the world. 'Pants off and everything?'

'You can write about what you like as long as you're sincere and follow the golden rule – never be cynical. Right, let us suppose we've got a heroine – Charlotte's as good a name as any. As an exercise why don't we try to get her to meet the man of her dreams at someone else's wedding? How might we engineer that?'

It was a trick I'd tried before with limited success. Three of Jane Seymour's household hints came from Olive, though I'm ashamed to say she wasn't listed among those to whom the author was 'eternally grateful' in her charming preface. Olive had, in fact, supplied a fourth hint but the editor felt that 'Make that brawn last a day longer by wrapping it in greaseproof paper' wasn't quite Jane.

And as a resource for Brand's Hatch folklore the class had

been worse than useless, apart from an admittedly interesting half-hour where we discussed which racing driver policemen might have cited to admonish speeding motorists, before Stirling Moss became a household name. 'Who do you think you are – Fangio?' didn't have quite the same ring.

'What's Charlotte's back story?' asked Olive. 'We don't know anything about her, do we.'

'Well, she likes shopping and Chardonnay.'

'Sounds a bit superficial,' said Pearl.

'That's what all girls are like in books and on telly,' said Olive. 'Falling over drunk. You can watch for a week and not see a single one clothed and upright. Specially nurses and teachers.'

Much as I was enjoying the notion of Olive going head to head with Germaine Greer on the *Late Review* it wasn't helping my cause much, so I changed tack.

'Well, why don't we say she went to university, dropped out and now works in, oh I don't know – a shop catering for people with bad backs.'

'That's a bit more believable,' said Stan. 'Is she a stunna?'

I had to think about this. 'Yes . . . I suppose . . . she is, absolutely. What happens if we get her in a romantic situation with Mr Right. How would he . . . what's the best way for him to—'

'Is he nude, too?'

'Not so far. Far from it. In fact, I think he's in two minds about whether he wants to get into this situation at all. I mean he's got responsibilities – maybe a cat, he could be a bit set in his ways. Possibly.'

'Sounds a bit like you,' said Pearl.

'I suppose we're all writing about ourselves to some extent,' I said, aware that for the first time in two years I had their undivided attention.

'So is he going to go out on a date with her, then?' asked Pearl with a sympathetic tone I hadn't noticed in her before.

'I don't know. Maybe he should.'

Sunday

So I took the plunge and asked her to today's Bayou Boys gig at a pub by the Uxbridge roundabout on the A40. Rather to my surprise she arrived with perfect timing towards the end of the first set, just as Jaz was embarked on a particularly self-regarding trumpet solo interruption to 'When the Saints Go Marching In'. The rainbow braids were slightly repositioned and the jeans and vintage dress had been swapped for a miniskirt and purple leggings. The band had been scanning the pub for likely Reardon ladyfriends for some time. The clever money was on a fat woman in her fifties chain-smoking and reading the *Sunday Telegraph* but there was also interest in a tracksuited dog owner drinking pints of lager. Consequently the Girl's entrance went unnoticed.

'Settle an argument, Ed,' said Frank, leaning over his drum kit. But fortunately Jaz's irrelevant solo had ended and my turn had come to shine on the jug. I blew like a Force II (Violent Storm) gale, oxblood brogues thumping the floor and raising dust as I tore through my dirtiest repertoire. Amazing how the presence of a woman inspires one to unimagined heights of artistry.

'Fiver says it's the dog woman, ' I heard Cliff say to Frank.

'You're on. Turnip-tits and Sunday papers, I reckon. Fiver.'

The Bayou Boys came together for the final eight like a musical version of a bus queue trying to pile on to the last E2 from Greenford to Perivale and we reached journey's end roughly together and on schedule, give or take a few seconds. There was a bit of clapping from the jazz punters if not from the regulars who remained morose and unmoved, and the Girl came over to speak to me.

'Well done, Ed. That was great.'

'Bloody hell,' said Cliff.

'Let me buy you a drink, sweetheart, you won't get one off him,' said Frank.

'Better not, thanks. I'm driving.'

'Got a car too. You don't want to let this one go, Ed,' said Ray.

'Maybe a St Clement's?' Frank persisted.

'Come on Noël Coward, the lasagne's solidifying,' said Cliff, heading for the Butler's Servery.

Jaz approached and delivered what I believed to be his most oleaginous 'hello' ever, virtually five syllables. 'I'm Jaz. I've been hearing a lot about you.'

'No, he hasn't,' I said. 'I've been very discreet.'

'If I closed my eyes I could have been listening to Humphrey Lyttelton there,' she said.

'Thanks. If that's good.'

'Well, I still think the definitive version was Louis Armstrong in 1924.'

'1924 eh? What label was that then?'

'Vectraphone, I think.'

'She's right,' I said, noticing that Jaz was scrutinizing her carefully.

'So, do you like looking round second-hand shops for 78s?' he asked casually.

'Yes, I do actually.'

'Hmm. Can I have a word, Ed?'

'I'm not mad, you know.'

'Course you aren't.'

'Sorry,' I said, 'Jaz is a bit uncomfortable around women unless they've got a fur coat and a facelift.'

'You wouldn't get the price of a lipstick out of him,' countered Jaz. 'Did he give you the book I signed?'

'What book?'

I did, indeed, have the Foyles copy of *Fardels* with me. This morning I had been about to scissor out the blank page that Jaz had signed when Frank arrived outside the flat honking his horn, so I only had time to put it in a Morrisons' bag before leaving. I handed it to the Girl, keeping the bag tightly folded hoping she wouldn't open it. But, of course, she did.

'Oh, Ed, thank you. That's so—' Her face fell and she looked at Jaz. 'Why have *you* signed it?'

'Well, because movies are a collaborative process.'

'But this is Ed's novel. And you've spelt thanks with an "x" – on top of everything else.'

211

'On top of what everything else?'

Barking from a nearby table attracted the attention of Cliff and Ray.

'Wer hey. Frank's pulled,' said Ray.

'Good boy!' said Frank, tossing a Hula Hoop to the Alsatian.

Grateful for a diversion, I called out, 'Careful Frank, that's your washboard hand', which drew appreciative laughter from the band. Say what you like about the Bayou Boys, they do enjoy a laugh at each other's expense. I perceived the first signs of a sense of humour failure in the Girl and sure enough her features soon assumed the killjoy's wince as she said 'Ed, we'll have to leave in about half-an-hour if we're going to get to Amersham in time for the game.'

I dimly remembered the plan for the day had involved a policemen's cricket match but had assumed that, like most normal people, once she'd found herself in an agreeable pub she wouldn't want to go anywhere else for rest of the afternoon.

'You can miss the first hour or two, can't you?'

'Of course not – I'm the scorer.'

'Wooo, are you, love?' said Cliff ribaldly. 'Play your cards right you can have a nibble of my lasagne.'

'It was going a bit curly the last time I looked, Cliff,' I said, trying to lighten the atmosphere. It worked as far as the band was concerned. They laughed heartily as people often do when a man with a pretty girl makes a joke, but I could see that it wasn't working for her. 'We've got another set to play,' I explained.

'Okay, fine,' she said. 'See you.'

And off she went leaving the book and the Morrisons' bag on the table.

'Yup, told you,' said Jaz. 'Complete fruitcake.'

Monday

Woke up this morning alone – and pretty relieved about it, I have to admit, after coming within a hair's breadth of couple-dom. And although it's never flattering to the self-esteem to have a woman walk out on you in a pub – the frivolous remark on the night of Princess Diana's funeral comes to mind, not to mention the misconstrued tongue sandwich with Ray's new wife after Jonny Wilkinson's drop-kick – it did at least mean that I was once again a free man whose weekends could be spent at home or in the pub rather than in IKEA. Nor would the chilling 'B' word besmirch the pages of my social calendar – discussing house prices at a barbecue in someone's wet back garden is no way for a sentient human being to live, especially not one who has 15,000 words of bubbly rom-com to write by dawn.

Tuesday

Which I'm proud to say, with the help of a bottle of scotch and a pouchful of baccy, I achieved. I e-mailed it to Ping, showered, breakfasted on a tin of sardines and waited. By lunchtime I'd heard nothing so I phoned the office.

'Yeah, it came through fine,' said Ping.

'And?'

'It's just not there yet, Ed.'

'It's over a hundred pages, what more do you want ? I suppose I could bring the margins in, that'd get it up to 130 or so.'

'No – it's the heroine and hero, they just aren't connecting.'

'But I've got him running to the airport at the end and shouting, "I love you Charlotte Spade."'

'The name, Ed, is great – it's just everything else about her.'

'Such as?'

'Well, like when she stands on the table at the wedding and goes on about the decline in public service broadcasting and how – what is it? "These days pig-ignorance is celebrated in the way that Victorians revered chastity".'

'Well, she has got her skirt tucked in the back of her knickers.'

'Doesn't matter. That's not Charlotte talking, Ed – that's you!'

'It isn't, actually. So what are you suggesting I should do, Ping?'

'For a start come up with something that modern women travelling to work on the tube respect and aspire to.'

'Like a car?'

'There's one that's walking off the shelves at Sainsbury's at the moment, yeah, called *Rescue Moi*, where Charlotte's working as a PA on *Comic Relief* and she falls for this really hunky doctor from Médecins sans Frontieres. Literally, right, because she falls into this like really polluted well in Malawi and he rescues her.'

'Really? And you don't think that's the sort of thing to make right-thinking people vomit?'

'Ed, there's major wonga to be made here if you behave yourself.'

'Right, shouldn't take me five minutes to tweak that.'

'Listen, listen – why don't I get you to meet some publishers, see the sort of thing they're after?'

'By all means.'

'There's still a few who haven't had their summer parties yet.'

'How fortuitous.'

'I'll get you some invites, as long as you promise not to talk like that.'

'You have my word as an underrated author.'

'Or that.'

The electronic beep sounded a little more harshly than usual, I sensed, as I crossed the threshold of the Berkhamsted Back Shop this afternoon. From her position behind a table the Girl must have seen me coming, but as I approached her eyes remained steadily focused on the *Spectator* crossword.

'Hello.'

'Oh, hi. Problem with the typing stool?'

'No, just the typist.'

'That sounded like an apology.'

'It wasn't meant to be.'

'Good, because I wasn't expecting one.'

'Oh. Right then.'

She looked back down at the crossword and the embarrassing silence resumed. I noticed she hadn't yet cracked the tricky six-letter clue in the top right-hand corner of the grid, without which many of the others were unsolvable. I'd got it this morning while waiting for Ping to call but I hesitated to supply the answer lest I be thought 'patronizing'. Then I remembered I had gone almost three years without patronizing a woman and it might be a very long time indeed before I got another chance – in fact, I wasn't at all sure that I could still do it. There was only one way to find out.

'Faeces,' I said, and almost immediately I could see, as it were, the penny drop. There was a minuscule twitch of her right hand as she restrained herself from filling in the squares. She was patronized all right.

I stood in front of her for a while longer but she neither moved nor spoke. So I turned to go.

'Bye,' she said, just before the electronic beep marked my exit.

The beep sounded again ten seconds later when I walked back into the shop. This time she looked up.

'I just wondered if you wanted to come to a barbecue at the weekend,' I said.

'I hate barbecues,' she said and I noticed her hand slowly moving to cover the top right-hand corner of the crossword.

'So do I. But it's a publisher's do. There might be some people there you can insult.'

'Oh, which day?' she said, softening.

'Sunday.'

'I can't, I've got to be in Pershore all afternoon.'

'Ah yes, sharpening your scoring pencils.'

'Actually I use different colour felt-tips. What are you doing tonight?'

'I should be working really.'

'On your *rom-com?*' she said with a curl of her devastating upper lip.

'Yes, I've been asked to give it a bit of social relevance.'

'So it'll be more of a *docu*-rom-com?'

'Yes, with a dram-edy spin. But I suppose I could let it marinate for an evening.'

Now I appreciate an obscure fact or piece of arcane knowledge as much as the next man who lives alone. I feel better for knowing that the guns of HMS *Belfast* are trained on Scratchwood Services on the M1. I can name the nine muses, the capital of Burkino Faso and the actor who was the first full-frontal nude on British television (Christopher something – I've forgotten his surname). But as soon as general knowledge becomes competitive I completely lose interest. And so, fond as I am of trivia, beer, crisps and smoking, I have always been indifferent to the allure of the pub quiz. But when the Girl invited me to join her team (Herts Minds) for the quarter-final round of the Mr Porky Scratchings Trophy this evening I confess I was quite excited at the prospect. There was no pressure on me as I was only filling in for someone who'd had to drop out at the last minute, owing to a *Red Dwarf* convention taking place at Watford. And after my success with 'faeces' my confidence was high. I was, as the sportsmen say, 'well up for it'.

Alas, faeces proved to be something of a flash in the pan. I hadn't realized quite how much the importance of the occasion would unsettle me. And as we walked home from the pub after our hundred-point mauling at the hands of the Tring Stingers there were recriminations.

'Cuthbert, Dibble, Bill Brewer, Jan Stewer!' she said with a mixture of disbelief and contempt. 'Honestly!'

'Well I got Pugh, Pugh, Barney McGrubb right.'

'It's McGrew, you idiot. The firemen's names in *Trumpton* are one of the first things you learn when you do a pub quiz!'

'Well, as I said, it's the one personality disorder I haven't managed to acquire.'

'And as for saying that H. Rider Haggard wrote *The Yeomen of the Guard* – that was just embarrassing me in front of all my friends.'

'So those are your friends, are they?'

'They are, yes.'

'Including the one who ate two biros and got ink all down his cagoule?'

'Especially him. There's nothing Matthew doesn't know about *Doctor Who* and *Blake's 7*. I'm pretty good but he's just awesome.'

'I'm sure they all are.'

'Anyway, what about that bunch of deadbeats you hang out with?'

'Fair point. Though one of them does command 8 million dollars a movie.'

'Yes, for making rubbish and ruining your book. And yet you

still play in a band with him. I think that makes eating biros look pretty normal.'

'Another perfectly valid observation.'

We had now reached my front door and the hardest question of the evening so far was looming. We were not entirely alone as the chip shop queue had spilled out on to the pavement. Once again the presence of an audience rendered me somewhat inde-cisive.

'Um, would you care for some chips?'

'Not really.'

'No. Inadvisable, perhaps, after all those complimentary pork scratchings. Um . . .' I swallowed, coughed and went for broke. 'Are you coming in?'

'Yes,' she said, then looking at the door. 'No.'

'I know – it's a tricky one. I'm not at all sure either.'

'I mean – no, you've got a cat flap. I'm allergic to them.'

'Oh dear.'

'Yes.'

She gave me a sympathetic peck on the cheek. And sneezed three times.

'It's in your clothes.' She sneezed again. 'And your beard.' Another convulsion.

'Bless you.'

'This isn't going to work, Ed. Aaaaa-choo.'

'No. Bless you.'

'Sorry. Chooo!'

'Bless you.'

'Sorry. Chooo.'

The Winona Defence

With most of the chip shop queue echoing her sneezes she walked off into the night and out of my life.

On my return, Elgar's piteous miaow for Whiskas Senior in jelly was met with a mask of cold indifference from his significant other. But eventually I mellowed and he and I made it up, rather like the scene in the third act of Jaz's Oscar-nominated weepie where the dolphin plays softball with the blind girl who thinks it's her estranged father. Sort of a dol-rom really, I suppose.

But I was grateful to the Girl for helping me – with my research, as Winona Ryder would say. And to prove it I posted her my irreplaceable copy of *Who Would Fardels Bear?*, signed with a correctly spelt 'thanks'. Because she was right about so many things – not just *Trumpton* and the 1925 FA Cup losing finalists, but the direction in which Ed Reardon's career should be going.

It was now nearly midnight but I knew I had to put a call through to the agency before my courage deserted me.

'You're through to Felix Jeffrey Management,' said his voice mail, each word carefully enunciated by the man himself as if he was making the first ever radio broadcast. 'There's nobody in the office right now – but if you're a burglar there are a lot of ferocious dogs here . . . Ruff ruff – grrr. Down Caesar! Down I say! Ha! But you can leave a message, though I've absolutely no idea how to retrieve it. Please speak after the beep.'

Which I did. 'Felix, Ping, it's Ed. I'm very sorry but I don't think I should be doing rom-com – I haven't really got it in me.

As someone said, if you've got a good chair, you shouldn't have to write bad stuff . . . So from now on I'm going to be looking to do the kind of work that brought me to the agency in the first place—'

Aware that the tape was about to run out, and that I wouldn't dare be able to say all this again, I hastened to my peroration.

'But while I'm working out what I really want to do, there's absolutely no reason why we shouldn't have lunch and talk about the illustrated history of Snetterton . . .'

6

King of the Road

Monday

'And that's yer weather! Coming up after yer news and yer
travel, yer texts and e-mails on the latest housemate evictions.
Do you think Sharon was out of order in the shower with Lee?
We wanna know what you guys thinks!'

I wrote down these words (though most of them really
shouldn't be dignified with the term) verbatim as they came out
of the radio. If Ed Reardon's diaries were ever to be buried in a
time capsule, they would surely give a more accurate picture of
what it is like to exist in the dumbed-down celebritocracy that
is New Labour Britain than the usual contents of such artefacts
awaiting discovery in 250,000 years like mobile phones, pot

noodles and Nick Hornby novels – the last two both offering instant gratification but no lasting nutritional value.

I am penning these idle ruminations as a displacement activity for what I really should be doing, which is a thousand words for my old school magazine, the very same *Salopian* that shunned my poetry forty years ago because it had the barefaced audacity to rhyme. Never one to bear a grudge, however, I have agreed to give them the benefit of my experience on the subject of 'The Writer's Life For Me' ('Hi diddly dee – not the sniff of a fee').

This came as a result of adding my name and career details to the old boys' website in a weak moment, at the thin end of a bottle of £2.99 Bulgarian Cab-Sauv – with which there was nothing wrong at all I might say. So I find myself committed to giving advice to the lads in the sixth form – who, I suppose, now they are pushing seventeen represent the grey constituency and are almost on the scrapheap. Still, at least I have been asked, unlike I suspect the editor of the magazine at the time who rejected my poetry and who might find it difficult persuading anybody to follow in his footsteps (I note from the website) to Saskatchewan and a life lustily spent classifying mosses.

'One of the great joys of the life literary,' I began, 'is the freedom to work whatever hours you choose and be beholden to nobody. You don't have to work in an office, or stand outside it if you fancy a smoke. You don't even have to wear a suit and tie, you can sit and work naked but for your bathers before a mid-morning swim if you like. Take it from me, boys . . .'

I paused in mid-rhapsody to my profession as some sparks

from my pipe seemed in imminent danger of drifting down on to my polyester swimming togs, which could have caused a fire rendering the preceding paragraph not only ironic but tragically redundant. Batting the sparks away with an unopened red final reminder from BT, I knocked over the anglepoise lamp which in turn caused my tumbler of Scotch to slide off the desk and into the wastepaper basket, soaking the earlier drafts of my *Salopian* piece but happily not breaking the glass. A sad waste of whisky but, still, I could have been frittering my life away in an office.

The telephone rang just as I was (ignominiously, I will admit) sucking one of the pieces of paper from the wastepaper basket to see if any nutritional value still remained therein.

'Dad? It's Jake.'

Ah yes. My son, from whom I hadn't heard since the arrival of that offensive (and offensively late) copy of Lynne Truss's wretched bestseller for my birthday. Though on reflection an anonymous gift of £250 had miraculously appeared in my bank account just before the first day of the Cheltenham racing festival – a more honest endeavour for all its thieves and cutpurses than its abominable literary namesake – and had somewhat less miraculously disappeared from it again almost immediately.

'Are you okay?' said Jake. 'It's just that none of us have heard from you—'

'*Has* heard from you, I think you mean, Jake,' I said.

'What? Look, did you get the £250 I transferred into your account?'

'Yes, I did. Thank you very much – money is so convenient

sometimes. I know I should have written a note of thanks, but quite frankly I've been so busy the moment passed.'

'That's great,' said Jake. 'So, Dad, what are you up to?'

'Oh, scribbling away. This latest piece I'm working on is autobiographical. But don't worry, none of you lot are in it. But Jake, how are *you*? How's college? Are you still doing Media Studies? Of course, that's compulsory these days isn't it, like Chaucer used to be. Module 1 – *Thunderbirds* . . .'

I sensed Jake was letting me run out of steam or witty put-downs, whichever came first. A habit I had always found infuriating.

'Actually, Dad,' said Jake after a pause, 'I'm putting together a series of guest lectures at the uni here and I was wondering if you could help.'

This was typical of my son. Another favour for no money. Well, I'm afraid *The Salopian* had used up my ration of the milk of human kindness for one week.

'We've got a proper budget for this one,' said Jake, my silence speaking for itself.

'Oh well, right you are then – the old man's your man! What do you want me to do?'

'I was wondering if you could get me a contact number for Jaz Milvane.'

Yes, of course, to be sure, happy to oblige and after that I would go round and paint Martin Amis's house. And clean out Julian Barnes's toilet. Though I imagine he is so fastidious that this would not be such an arduous task, just a matter of freshening the potpourri.

'Because I've tried Miramax . . . his agents won't help . . . sorry Dad, are you really offended?'

'No,' I said, hoping that simple negative conveyed something of Lear's toweringly raging resentment about serpent's teeth and thankless children.

'Hang on, I'm just crossing the road,' said Jake. 'Look Dad, thinking on my feet here, how about if we got you involved too, doing the interview or whatever 'cos you're such old mates—'

This was more promising. 'When you say "a proper budget".'

'Oh yeah, there'd be a fee and expenses.'

'And we wouldn't have to share a room, would we? It may come as a disappointment to the crowds gathered behind the barriers in Leicester Square or outside Grauman's Chinese Theater, but Jaz is both a snorer and a farter.'

'Actually, I've got to where I'm meant to be now, I'd better go. I take it that's okay then, so could you just leave his number on my voice mail? And Dad, it's *Mann's* Chinese Theater now – keep up!'

'I'll try,' I said. 'How's your mother—?'

But Jake had gone, to where he was meant to be. I stopped trying to eke out the last drops of spilt Scotch from the crumpled wad of paper and looked up the most recent number I had for Jaz in Los Angeles. Then I resumed giving career advice to the young gentlemen who had no need of it because, like Jake, they would soon effortlessly inherit the earth.

Tuesday

'So Ed,' said Ping, handing me a satisfyingly thick envelope, with little strings trailing from it. 'Here's your train ticket, your Go-Eat refreshment vouchers, your taxi fare to the lecture hall, your executive luggage tags and a print-out of your hotel reservation, okay?'

Money, transport, a bed for the night and possibly food. I just needed to be sure that there were no concealed mantraps in Jake's package of goodies before I permitted myself a little mental jig of delight.

'"Go-Eat" – what's all that about?'

'It means you can't go into the restaurant car but you do get the At-Seat trolley service. There you go – have a nice awayday, okay, Ed?'

'Thank you for sorting this out for me, Ping,' I said. 'If I'd dealt with my son directly he'd only have shafted me. He's done it before.'

'A bit of a tearaway teen, yeah?'

'I wouldn't know about that – I haven't seen much of him since he was eight.'

Ping knitted her lovely brow, as she might when forgetting in which Hickstead car park she'd left her Punto. 'Right – so that's when he shafted you?'

It may have been over ten years ago, but it still smarted. 'Bloody little tea leaf,' I said. 'It was a school trip to Whipsnade Zoo – he told me it was Switzerland, and I had to give him two hundred quid. Cost me half my *Eldorado* script fee.'

'But it's so good that you've still got a relationship with him, isn't it,' said Ping.

'Really? I just don't know what he's going to do with himself.'

'He seems to be doing okay at uni. And he's got the lecture thing well sussed.' Ping seemed to be regressing to her days at Balliol before my eyes. The next thing I knew she'd be getting her scout to boil up a Vesta curry in a bag.

'Yes, Ping, but what happens when he leaves?'

I hadn't meant to sound quite like such a concerned parent, but it brought out the maternal instinct in Ping.

'Ed, the problem is not Jake. It's what we're going to do about you.'

Oh dear. Once again it was that time in the tax year when I was obliged to justify my existence. Luckily, on this occasion, I had come prepared.

'Well, I think for my next project what I'd like to do, bearing in mind the pitiful state of our national culture, is a contemporary anatomy of Britain based on my forthcoming trip to Northumbria – a sort of *English Journey* or *Road to Wigan Pier*, following in the footsteps of Priestley and Orwell—' I stopped as I realized I had lost Ping some way back on the journey.

'You want to just run those names past me again?'

'Priestley and Orw— All right, Harry Secombe – have you ever heard of him?'

Again the blank look, which turned into one of alarm as I essayed some of the winsome Welshman's career highlights.

'I'm the famous Eccles! Hoo hoo hee hee. "If I ruled the

world . . ." Anyway,' I said quickly as Ping seemed about to pull a mace spray out of her bag to keep this capering ninny at bay, 'he went around the country in a vintage car – but I won't be doing that, or singing hymns.'

'Somebody mention vintage cars?' said Felix, coming in wearing a big smile and carrying a rolled-up glossy magazine which he thwacked every so often against his other hand, probably to get the circulation going again after lunch.

'I was thinking of writing a modern *English Journey*, Felix,' I said.

'Why not, everybody else is – David Dimbleby, Alan Titchmarsh, Ricky Gervais – he must have done one by now. You'll have to save all your bus tickets and apple stickers and what-have-you so the publishers can put photos of them in it, that's what you have to have in a book nowadays. Lots of piccies, not much text. Books for bears of very little brain.'

Felix seemed genuinely concerned about the state of the industry for a moment, but then his attention wandered and he unrolled his magazine. 'Wonderful photography in here, have you seen this? Look at that, two Type 35 Bugattis.'

'Anyway, Ping,' I said as Felix subsided into his *Vintage Car Monthly* gatefold, making little noises to himself which could well have been 'Poop Poop!', 'I thought I could write about things that disappoint not just me but I think all of us deep down.'

'Like what, Ed?'

'Well – so-called customer-friendly jargon . . . bogus heritage . . . all those new street names on new housing estates –

Dean's Croft, Monk's Meadow – I mean, who thinks those God-awful things up?'

At last Ping was nodding excitedly. 'Yeah, Richard Stilgoe did a very very funny song about them – I'll burn you the CD, Ed – you can play it on your lappy-toppy while you do your journey thingy.'

'By the way, Ed,' said Felix, 'I'm awfully impressed with your boy. Pushy – I like that. He's at one of those places that calls itself a university but isn't really.'

'Northumbria,' I said. 'God knows what he's going to do when he leaves.'

'Well, d'you know what?' said Felix. 'I've a good mind to offer him a summer job here.'

'Yes . . . but then there's the autumn,' I said. 'What on earth's he going to do then?'

'Oh, Ed,' said Ping, and for the life of me I still have no idea why.

Wednesday

William Cobbett never visited Hell during his celebrated *Rural Rides*, so Ed Reardon finds himself filling the void. Mired in the misery of modern rail travel I was about to experience what the incomprehensible announcement would call 'our first station stop,' followed by a fatuous reminder about luggage, as a way of deflecting one's attention from the unconscionable lateness of this so-called service. To compound the agony I found myself invited to savour the dubious delights of Go-Eat's At-Seat trolley service.

'Excuse me, sir,' said the twelve-year-old in an elaborate catering company uniform that wouldn't have disgraced the Swiss Guard. 'Would you care for—'

'Yes, I know,' I said. 'I have been here before. "Teas, coffees, powdered cappuccino . . . a range of not very hot and very frozen snacks . . ."'

'Actually, we'd greatly value your opinion on our chef's new light meals,' said the boy. 'And, of course, there'll be no charge as this is in the way of an experiment—'

'Yes, I'm sure. No doubt a tottering pile of brie and mandarin oranges drizzled with olive oil. I think I won't if it's all the same to you, Eric,' I said, reading his badge. Yet another underling whose employers denied him a surname in the interests of 'customer-friendly service'. I went through an entire week once dealing on the telephone with a string of such people working for banks, gas and electricity companies and the council, and not one of them was in possession of a second name – except perhaps for Vivaldi, whose ubiquitous *Four Seasons* I must have heard in its entirety at least eight times while being kept 'on hold,' the length of the wait being in inverse proportion to the alleged importance of my call to them.

'Actually the chef's very keen on traditional fillings,' persevered Eric. 'As long as it's the best of whatever's fresh. So why not see if there's anything here that takes your fancy, Sir? And meanwhile can I offer you a complimentary glass of red or white wine?'

'Red, please – though I doubt if I'll be amused by its undrinkability.'

'Actually it's a new Sicilian, Sir – very lively. If you'll just bear with me while we're slowing down.'

'Good afternoon ladies and gentlemen,' said a voice above my head. 'We will shortly be arriving at Peterborough station, twelve minutes ahead of schedule . . .'

There was something wrong with this scene, from the mellifluousness of the man on the public address system to the polite affability of the trolley boy. I must have unwittingly strayed on to a train populated by aliens or robots – next stop Midwich, final destination Stepford.

'If you are disembarking at Peterborough why not visit the Cathedral, first built in AD 655 and the burial place of Catherine of Aragon,' said the voice on the PA. 'A figure of real importance, unlike what passes for celebrity on television these days . . .' Now it seemed I was in a scene from *Invasion of the Body Snatchers* – my mind at any rate had been appropriated and its innermost workings broadcast for all in the carriage to hear.

'Are you by any chance a writer, sir?' said Eric as he filled my glass.

'Yes,' I said. I might have added that at this moment I was an extremely thwarted writer and, if I was being truthful, unable to use hardly anything that I'd noted down for my coruscating critique of society since we left King's Cross. I pressed the Delete button and for the first time a frown crossed Eric's face.

'Sir, if you wouldn't mind turning down the speakers on your laptop just a little?' he said. 'As you see from the signs on

233

the window by your head and on the table in front of you, this is a Quiet Carriage.'

'Is this man causing trouble again?' came a familiar not to say irritating voice behind me.

'Oh, hello Jaz. I didn't see you on the platform.'

'I was in the restaurant car. A very acceptable steak-and-kidney pud.'

Confronted by a person he had most likely seen preening or pontificating on television, the trolley boy went into a strange crouch – half-genuflection, half-trying to stand upright against a strong wind.

'Yes, you probably don't get that sort of thing in Hollywood, do you Mr Milvane?'

'Only when I have it flown in,' said Jaz. 'What are you doing here, Reardon?'

'The same thing as you.'

'What, talking to the students?' said Jaz, sitting down oppo-site me. Eric hovered with his choice of lively wines. 'They're good people aren't they – ticket arrives, cash for the cab, restau-rant car vouchers – facing the direction of travel, even. There was a very bright boy who talked me into it. You want to keep in with him in case you meet him on the way down – or are you on the way up? I never know which way you're going.'

'That's my son, Jake, actually.'

'Is it? Oh yes, I remember him,' said Jaz. 'Vividly, actually – because he once got a tenner out of you to do a sponsored walk.'

This was one of my rosier memories of family life, when an angel-faced seven-year-old came running tearfully into my study, saying he'd been watching *Blue Peter* on the television and could he do something, anything, Daddy, to help the starving in Africa?

'He was always getting involved in charity things in those days. I must have done something right,' I said.

'As I remember he gave that tenner to me to put on the Tories to win the 92 election,' said Jaz. 'He made forty quid out of that. Didn't he give you a cut?'

Only the one when I heard that, but it was to the quick. Jaz's mobile phone bleeped loudly, destroying the peace of the Quiet Carriage. I gestured to the signs on the window and the table before Eric had a chance.

'Whoops! Sorry everybody,' Jaz called to the carriage. 'Should have turned that off.'

'That's all right Mr Milvane – we'll forgive you this time,' simpered Eric.

'Thank you. Leave both bottles would you, please?'

'Of course. And if you want to shout "Action" or "That's a wrap", that's fine, too.'

'Thank you very much,' said Jaz, studying his phone. 'Ah – it's your boy wanting to know if I want still or sparkling water on stage. He thinks of everything.' He began text messaging his reply as I decided to try the white. 'You don't know who's going to be asking the questions do you?' said Jaz. 'Probably some deadbeat local hack who's only read the back of the DVD box the night before, it usually is.'

'It's me, actually,' I said. 'And I don't have a DVD player so I'll be relying on my own knowledge and perceptions.'

'Ah', said Jaz. 'Sparkling in that case, I think . . .'

Wednesday Night

Or is it? In a featureless anonymous hotel like this it could be any time, anywhere in the world. Though if I am intending to write my *English Journey* it would be better to restrict these *aperçus* to this country. But the fact remains that were it not for the TV screen displaying the message 'Welcome Ed Rear' I would be so discombobulated by the surrounding blandness that I wouldn't even know who *I* was. Small wonder that after a few weeks on tour, staying at hotels such as this, a band of rock musicians feels the need to go berserk and throw the trouser press out of the window and take the mint from the pillow and flush it down the WC like so many crazed Visigoths.

I was just checking Google to see that there wasn't already a band playing under this name, when the phone rang. It was Jake, inviting me out to dinner. I would have pleaded work as an excuse, wanting to get my notes (and the few surprises I had up my sleeve) prepared for the interview with Jaz tomorrow, but Jake was already waiting at reception.

I picked up my keys and my wallet from the bed, made sure I had stowed the credit-card-style door key safely in my wallet (it being the only card in there made it somewhat easy to spot), put a clean handkerchief in my top pocket, checked my appearance in the long hotel mirror, sighed at my sagging tum, and on the way to the door looked around the room again to make sure I hadn't inadvertently left the key behind and found it was still in my wallet. Why was I so nervous? I was going out to dinner with my son, not my father.

'Just order whatever you want,' said Jake.

I decided on lasagne, the most expensive thing on the menu although that was only £3.95. Clowns was clearly a restaurant popular with students, though most of the posters decorating the walls were of comedians (W. C. Fields, Tommy Cooper, Sid James and half of the Carry On Team) who had laughed their last before most of them were born.

'So, Dad, how's it going? Plenty of work? Plenty of girls, I'll bet, if you're a Reardon!'

'Actually, I'm a Rear here. Oh, you know,' I said, really not wanting to get into ten minutes of brittle banter. What I was actually interested in was the situation regarding Jake's mother. But he wasn't prepared to let my love life or lack of it alone.

'So, nobody special on the scene?'

'Not really. There might have been one, but she was allergic to cats.'

'So, playing the field, then,' said Jake, raising his eyebrows comically like Fernandel or M. Hulot or whoever the unfunny French fellow was whose poster was next to the contraceptive machine in the corner.

'Look, can I get a drink?' I said.

'Of course, the wine list's on the other side of the menu.'

It was a little on the limited side, this list, though easy to wipe clean I would imagine. I studied it for much longer than was necessary, humming along to the jaunty Andy Williams track coming out of the CD player next to the plate of carrot cake on the counter.

'Eye to eye, they solemnly convene to make the scene . . .'

'Now come on, Dad,' said Jake, finally meeting me eye to eye. 'Tell me how work's going.'

'Oh, there are one or two things in the pipeline. There's – well, this job I'm doing for you tomorrow. And, well, there's this *English Journey* project . . .'

'Sounds interesting,' said Jake, bless him. Because it didn't really, not even to me.

'Well, I'll feel I'll have done my job if it exposes the shallowness of our culture, how everything's rotten basically...it's going to be pretty hard-hitting, far too hot to handle for most publishers. In fact, I expect they won't dare to print it.'

'Well, in that case,' said Jake, fishing out a piece of lemon from his Diet Coke and sucking it, 'there's no point in going to all the trouble of writing it really, is there, Dad?'

As I was trying to think of a sensible comeback to this, which didn't immediately spring to mind, I was luckily diverted by a youth in an apron who took my drinks order. Which was a bottle of plonk. In fact, that was its name, the label illustrated with a smiley face with crossed eyes and its tongue lolling out.

'It seems to me, Dad,' resumed Jake, now biting down on a piece of ice, 'that you should be thinking of writing something that people want to read, or see on television, or even rent from the video shop. Yes?' he said, lowering his head slightly and looking out at me from under his spiky gelled hair.

I sighed. I had no answer, apart from the one guaranteed to cause only further trouble. *Whatever*, as most of the other occupants of the tables in Clowns had said to each other at least once since we sat down. 'So how's your mother? How's that toyboy of hers?'

Jake gave me an old-fashioned look, in other words one that would not have been out of place in a Renaissance painting of a curia of particularly sanctimonious cardinals. 'He's only six months younger than you are, Dad. And he's about to be ordained.'

'Typical.'

'But she'd say just the same, you know, about your career, or lack of it.'

'Thank you very much. I seem to recall sending you each a copy of my last book, *Pet Peeves*.'

'Oh, yeah,' said Jake. 'I got through it on three trips to the toilet. Did it make any money?'

'Well, they don't let you in on that sort of thing for years. But look, this – what do you call it? – Cinema Seminar I'm doing with Jaz tomorrow . . .'

'Yeah, it's going to be fab,' said Jake. 'A complete sellout. We could have filled the place three times over.'

'Well, maybe I could do some more of this sort of thing,' I said. 'In my own way I am a bit of a movie buff. I know I'm bit hazy on the development of the art form after the *American Pie* series, but . . .'

'Well, let's just see how this one goes, shall we?' said Jake.

But now I had the bit between my teeth, *faute de mieux* – how long could it take to microwave a piece of Bird's Eye lasagne? 'I could introduce you to all sorts of other people in the business, and then interview them – or I could do one myself, if you like. "An Evening with Ed Reardon" or "Ed Reardon and Friends". We could get on to the college lecture circuit – if we took it to the States we could make an absolute stack over there. You could film them, get them on BBC4, like that series on the Performance Channel where that creep in a beard brown-noses famous actresses. I could be that creep, Jake! I've been on camera before – d'you remember when they made that *Aquarius* film about me in 1978? I know it was before you were born and we only had a copy on that big Betamax tape, but it was very well received. Jake, I think we should definitely go for it. Seriously.'

I sat back, spent. If this had been the States, even that impossibly saccharine version of it represented by Jaz Milvane's movies, the whole of Clowns restaurant would have risen to their feet to applaud, and carried me shoulder high up the steps of Capitol Hill and thence to the White House. But this was England, where the energy expended on finding reasons *not* to create something, be it a film, television or radio programme, far outweighs what it would take to make the thing itself. Jake was looking at me dubiously.

'Let's not run before we can walk, okay, Dad?'

'Why do you always have to do this?' I said.

'Do what?'

'Be so boring and sensible all the time? It makes me want to puke.'

I sat back with my arms folded, sulking until the drink arrived. Jake grinned and called me Kevin the teenager, a reference which I neither understood nor, indeed, wished to.

Thursday

I have no idea what the technical term for sexual relations with a fish is, some conflation of piscatorial and bestiality, I imagine. Suffice it to say that the ending of Jaz Milvane's movie *Dermot* skated perilously close to deep waters indeed until the unlovely possibility was rendered null and void by a typical Hollywood ending, which I must say I found even less attractive.

'And even though the cards were stacked against us . . .' began the voice-over to a scene which showed the unlikely hero and heroine romping together, but fortunately not in the tabloid newspaper sense, in the surf, '. . . me a blind Jewish girl for God's sake and Dermot a dolphin, yet in a funny kind of way that game of softball taught us that somehow, sometime we'd pull through. Maybe not in this life but whenever . . .'

Close-up of dolphin smiling as it ran its rubbery snout over the girl's unseeing and weeping eyes. Cue music crescendo. Cue snort of incredulous laughter, at least over on my side of the stage in the auditorium. A healthy reaction which I was alarmed to find was not shared in the least by the large student audience overflowing and sitting in the aisles, many of whom were openly dabbing at their own eyes, even though they had presumably all been able to see the ridiculous farrago unfolding before them.

The applause was tumultuous. I realized I would have to temper even the pretence of honest criticism if I hoped to get out of there alive.

'A very powerful ending, Jaz,' I said into my microphone. 'And interesting that you thought you could get away with it.'

'Yeah,' said Jaz. 'That's why I insisted on putting that voice-over – what we call a VO – in. It's a tricky subject but I wanted to go for the truth of the situation. Otherwise, there'd be a danger of – well, as the producer said, "She gonna make out with the fish or not?"'

'And anyway,' said Jaz, after milking the knowing laughter and applause for a good three minutes, 'the Academy seemed to agree that I wasn't too far wrong.'

This produced an actual standing ovation. It was high time the worm turned.

'Difficult family relationships are something of a running theme in your work, Jaz. It goes back to – well, to our first collaboration.'

'Oh yes,' said Jaz, adding for the benefit of those who might not be aware of my own career, '*Sister Mom*.'

Damn me if they weren't all up on their feet again. Say what you like about our education system, the sheep it produces are second to none. 'An adaptation of my novel,' I said, raising my voice above all the baaing and bleating. 'I think it's sufficiently far in the past for me to 'fess up and admit I always absolutely loathed that title they gave it.'

The applause died as if shot in the head. The undergraduate audience, many of them open-mouthed, sank back into their seats with looks of complete bewilderment on their friable faces.

Jaz had the audacity to wink at them. 'So, what, you think we should have stuck with *Who Would Fardels Bear?*, do you? That's gonna pack out the multiplexes, isn't it?'

A gale of relieved laughter rocked the room. So Jaz, in his

own parlance, wanted to play hardball, did he. Well, if so, he'd come to the wrong lecture theatre. Or the Jimmy Nail Centre for Culture and the Arts to give it its full title.

'Film is often referred to as a director's medium,' I said, 'and I suppose it is in the sense that writers tend to be disgracefully badly treated and ill-used. Is there any hope that this might change, Jaz?'

'Well, it would if they delivered the rewrite on time instead of getting drunk and having a tantrum every time we wanted to change a comma,' said Jaz, talking to me while looking out at the audience in the manner perfected by Richie Benaud. 'Then trying to get off with Sally Field when she needed to concentrate on her difficult abortion scene.'

There was hesitant applause at this, because a private argument was apparently unfolding on stage. And they didn't like the cut of my jib at all. Which suited me down to the ground. I was used to this, and what's more I was getting paid for it.

'The abortion scene wasn't in the book, of course, was it?' I said. 'But Jaz,' I continued quickly as he opened his mouth, for all the world like his precious Oscar-nominated Dermot, 'talking of multiplex or mainstream cinema, and I think it's fair to say that despite your early promise that's where you are now . . .'

'I guess the box office speaks for itself. Not that that should be the yardstick of course, but hey, who wants to see a movie that nobody else wants to see?'

Not only was the fish's ugly mouth open, it had swallowed the bait.

'So bearing that in mind, Jaz, I wonder how you react to criticism of your recent work . . .'

'Such as?' said Jaz, clearly thinking that any snowballs I might lob at him across the stage would soon melt under the hot lights.

'I've got a cutting here,' I said, detaching it from my clipboard.

'Thought you might have.'

'Yes. It says, "In every Warner Village you will find a Warner Village Idiot, happily watching the movies of Jaz Milvane as he tries to find his mouth with his junk food. Question his taste",' I said, putting on my thickest accent, as if my previous incarnation the Old Lock-Keeper was now a resident of Ambridge, "and he'd say, 'Oooo, Oi loikes they Jaz Milvane fillums—'"

'Where was this?' said Jaz, as urbanely as his buffeted self-esteem would allow.

I read on. "'Oi could watch they all day – 'coz Oi be the lowest common denominator, be Oi".'

Jaz literally ran across the stage and seized the cutting from me. 'You've just written that in!' he shouted. 'It's your writing.' This was no less than the truth.

'Fair point though, isn't it,' I said, now on my feet, too, and addressing the audience Benaud-like.

'You're just a sad frustrated failure, that's your trouble,' shouted Jaz. 'Isn't he, everybody?' This rabble-rousing was unworthy even of him, and happily not altogether successful. Although there were a few youngsters who shouted their agreement, yea-sayers that one finds in any crowd, the majority

seemed eagerly but quietly to be anticipating what manufac-
tured mayhem would happen next, evidence I would say of
their viewing habits being bounded by soap operas and Jerry
Springer.

They weren't to be disappointed. I barely had time to get the
words 'And you're a disgrace to your profession' out before Jaz
was upon me with a snarl of 'You've asked for it now, matey, oh
yes!'

Writers' Guild guidelines state that in the event of a director
physically attacking a writer, the former has automatically con-
ceded the moral high ground, and any verbal points that the
writer can score while trying to avoid blows to the head will
count in any subsequent arbitration. I was more than up to this
and, indeed, got my first laugh of the day by ducking easily
away from Jaz's flailing arms and telling the audience, 'He's a
big man but he's in bad shape', a canny reference to the movie
Get Carter which still resonated in those parts. Then Jaz was
chasing me round the stage while I taunted him further in my
Warner Village Idiot persona.

'Ooo don't be angry with Oi – the loikes of Oi pays for ee's
speedboat in Malibu. And ee's Viagara and stupid hair dye . . .'

The entire audience was on their feet roaring us both on by
the time we rolled off the stage, almost all of them holding up
mobile phones to record the proceedings. And the story was
even taken up by that night's local news programme, *North by
North-East*.

'Now,' said the pretty girl presenter, the pretty male presenter sat alongside her smiling at the camera as he waited his turn.

'Do you think of lecture theatres as stuffy old places where nothing exciting ever happens? I know I do . . .'

This was no doubt quite true. In my long experience of watching the local news, wherever I happened to be living at the time and weary after a day at my writer's lathe, I soon realized that these autocue-reading dolts plucked from the typing pool or wherever were obliged to make a virtue of appearing stupid – the school of 'If like me you think rain is wet, well you'd be wrong' – because stupid was exactly what they were.

'But in a violent scene reminiscent of one of his movies,' said the pretty male presenter, taking up the story in a classic case of BBC overmanning, 'Hollywood movie director, Jaz Milvane, traded some punches today. Except this time the fight wasn't at the earth's core but in a lecture theatre at the university . . .'

The screen cut to a murky scene of two apparently middle-aged drunks not so much fighting as holding on to each other in slow-motion, accompanied by the legend 'Amateur Footage.'

'. . . And his assailant wasn't a monkey but one Ed Reardon, described as a writer. The celebrity lecture went disastrously wrong when—'

At this the hotel television was turned off by the remote control, which Jake had miraculously cajoled into working. If he was that dextrous with hotel technology he could have a crack at the button on the bath taps which failed to operate the shower head, or the shaving point which didn't work, or the toilet seat which shot one across the room whenever one tried to sit on it.

But somehow I sensed these complaints were now irrelevant, as I doubted I would be staying another night.

As my son stared at me, I tried to ease the atmosphere of the approaching storm. 'Don't turn it off, Jake. That's where he falls off the stage and cuts his head!'

'And this is the sort of thing you want to take to America, is it?' said Jake

'Well, we could,' I said. 'A kind of thinking man's World Wrestling Foundation. I wouldn't mind taking a swing at that woman who made *The Piano* – or Richard Curtis, he's been asking for it for about five films now.'

'Dad,' said Jake, 'I've just lost my promoter's licence because of that.'

'Oh, I'm sure something else'll come along. You'll find another way of making money,' I said, trying to make it sound like beating pensioners over the head and running off with their handbags. 'Help yourself to your new stepfather's collection plate, start an airline or something . . .'

'If you're just going to treat this as some kind of joke then I wash my hands of you,' said Jake, forgetting not for the first time exactly who was who in this relationship. But I'd had enough. I wanted to get home and see my cat and be able to sit on a toilet in safety.

'All right, Jake,' I said. 'Just give me my hundred quid and my ticket back and I'll see you in another ten years.'

'What??' said Jake, laughing for the first time that day, albeit mirthlessly.

Friday

Apparently there was a clause in the small print of my contract – to which Ping had failed to draw my attention, no doubt thinking that at least I couldn't bugger this one up – that the fee and with it the return half of the ticket, At-Seat meal vouchers, etc. would only be payable on completion of the engagement to the satisfaction of my employer – i.e. my son – and 'any future employers yet to be discovered wheresoever in the solar system'.

Luckily, I was able to draw Jake's attention to the past, and claw back some of the monies fraudulently acquired from his non-existent charity walk in 1992. Which meant I had a tenner to get back home. The gravy train had suddenly become the somewhat thinner gruel of the National Express coach and I was dropped off when my ticket expired at Lincoln by the diligent driver, who pointed me in the direction of the ticket office, and reminded me that it would cost another £17.50 to get to Berkhamsted.

Such casual unhelpfulness from strangers restores one's lack of faith in the innate goodness of humanity. It made me think bitterly of the kindly sea captain who comes to the aid of Gulliver in Jonathan Swift's masterpiece. And thinking of this made me resolve to turn today's setback to advantage. I decided to regard my predicament as one of those gifts that comes so rarely to a writer out of the blue. For here I was, marooned in middle England armed only with my native wits and a laptop and a mission to record the sights and sounds of now, this moment in time as the fashionable tautology has it.

Suddenly having no money granted me the freedom of the open road, and access to real people living a visceral existence at the sharp end.

'Now look – you've spilt it all over that man's computer!'

Having a mewling and puking infant trying to clamber over me in the cafeteria was bad enough – potentially disastrous was the blue Slush Puppy that even now was draining away between the keys of my laptop and into its innards, seizing up its brain with God-knows-what additives. I wiped away what I could and prayed I had saved my recent musings.

'Real people rooted to the land, as opposed to the dismal denizens of our dumbed-down celebrity-obsessed media . . .' Thankfully I had, as I would never have got the precise plangency of that sentence back again.

'You've got to buy something if you want to sit there, mate,' said what I presumed was the cafeteria owner, coming over with a handful of Scooby-Doo tissues to mop up the mess.

'Sorry? Oh yes, buy something. Where would I . . . ?'

'Over there,' said the man. My reduced circumstances necessitated my getting up and going in the opposite direction to the array of brightly packaged junk, but I was still able to hear the conversation as I hung around outside deciding on what to do next.

'See, he had no intention of buying anything,' said the man.

'I'm sure I've seen him on TV,' said the mother of the toddler, who was now eating the tissues. Hearing this came as a surprise, as I was fairly sure my most recent appearance on the small screen, giving Jaz Milvane a long overdue what-for, would not have made it out of the area covered by the *North by North-East* programme. Unless, of course, it had made its way into one of the pervasive melanges of out-takes and bloopers that would otherwise consist entirely of former stand-up comedians promoted to actors uttering the f-word when they haven't been professional enough to learn their lines properly.

'He's probably a writer,' said the café owner. 'We get a lot of them in here. Ever since they found out that J. K. Rowling used to write in caffs . . .'

'My dear boy, how are you?' said Felix, when I finally got through to him on a payphone. It was raining and I was hungry and still at the bus station and enthusiasm for my *English Journey* was starting to ebb away very slightly.

'Felix, I'm actually in a spot of bother.'

'Sounds like jolly good material for your literary peregrinations,' said Felix, echoing my thoughts of three hours ago. 'Where are you now?'

'I'm in Lincoln.'

'Got yourself in prison again have you?' said Felix. 'Ha! Well done! Jonathan Aitken's career went from strength to strength after a spell in chokey– I've just done a very good deal on his novelization of the Bible.'

'Felix, all I want to do is to get home and feed my cat. So could you send me a bike with some money? Or just a bike and I can get a lift on the back of it?'

'Tut-tut,' said Felix, the only person I knew who tutted by actually saying the words. 'You're supposed to be doing a modern *English Journey*, tramping the King's Highway! You don't think Jack Kerouac called his agent, do you, bleating for money and saying, "Please Hiram, I'm only on Route 65 and I need a lift the rest of the way"? No he didn't, he stuck his thumb out, had a reefer and got on with it!'

'I'm sorry,' I said, 'but I refuse to hitchhike. I don't want to have to listen to lorry drivers telling me how they thought they could do a bit of writing if they had the time.'

'Just a minute, Ed,' said Felix. 'Ping's here and she wants to say something.'

Like Felix, Ping sounded warm and cosy and well-fed, and not far off opening a decent bottle that a grateful client had brought in. 'Ed, this sounds really exciting! You could be a highwayman to get some wonga – you could be like "Your money or your life", yeah? Or, or, or, or – you could sell your body!'

'Well, it's very kind of you to think that might be an option, Ping . . . but I fear it wouldn't get me much further than Baldock . . . and I've got a writing class to teach, so—'

At which point my last 30p ran out, but not before I had heard the unmistakable sound in Felix's office of a cork being pulled. I lifted my laptop down from the top of the payphone and studied it.

I doubt that Computer Planet, with its futuristic lower-case lettering and light-bulbs illuminating the two letter 't's from the bottom up, was the most modern computer shop in the world, or come to that in Lincoln. For instance, there were several posters inside extolling the virtues of something called 'The

251

Information Super-Highway'. But any port in a storm, and by now it was bucketing down and I had to pray that the rain didn't get into my laptop as I ran down the road holding it over my head.

'Well, normally I'd say fifty quid,' said the man behind the counter, who wore a humorous tie depicting a computer mouse with whiskers, ears and a long tail. A play on the word 'mouse,' I would guess.

'It did cost six hundred,' I said, a little disappointed at this depreciation.

'Yeah, but it's got all this stuff on it.'

'Oh, that was just some toddler who spilt its wretched Slush Puppy on it. Saving him from heart disease in the nick of time, no doubt.'

'No, I mean all this rubbish on the hard drive,' said the man.

I tried a foray into what I hoped wouldn't too obviously be techno-babble. 'Couldn't I just, ah, burn that on to a CD?'

'Yeah, we can do that,' said the man. 'That would come out at sixty-five quid plus VAT. So it's all a question of what you want to do, my friend.'

'I see,' I said. 'Say you dumped the lot, how many quid would I get then?'

'Forty exactly, Sir. Cash.'

'Right. Let's do it,' I said. My *English Journey*, not to mention notes for a sequel to *Pet Peeves*, would have to bite the dust, but what does a writer have if not an indomitable spirit that is able to bounce back whatever the reverses? Was it not Dylan Thomas who left his only draft of *Under Milk Wood* in a taxi following an afternoon's drinking in Fitzrovia? And it hardly held him back, he just picked up where he left off. I gather he did some more writing, too.

'You sure about this?' said the man. 'Pity to lose the screen-saver. Nice-looking cat.'

'Yes, but I'll be seeing the real thing soon enough, I hope. So yes – go ahead.'

The man performed some intricate hand gestures on the keyboard, like Russ Conway playing 'Sidesaddle' on the *Billy Cotton Band Show*, there was a sound which I would describe as meltdown and my laptop was mine no more. 'There – gone,' said the man. 'By the way, haven't I seen you somewhere before?'

The following is being typed up from my account, written per-force in longhand, of the events of the next few days. I have preserved the chronology but regrettably not the form in which it was written: a florid italic script in the style of a seventeenth-century literary journal with authentic Jacobean spelling, rococo frills and trills, and a feast of wicked but always reverential ref-erences to the onliest Samuel (Pepys of that ilk) – a delight for all lovers of the diary form, one would have thought. Well, not so according to my publishers Messrs Simon & Schuster for whom these parodic *petit fours* are 'a bit indulgent'. For some reason, indulgence is only considered a vice in authors seated at their desks and not in bloated editors troughing in Soho restau-rants on the proceeds of their wholly undeserved monthly pay cheques. But in the interests of maintaining cordial relations with these mindless Morlocks I have chosen to concede the point. The story therefore continues in bowdlerized form.

Monday

After my brush with the sewage-pipe blockage – the characterless, homogeneous, noxious slime otherwise known as contemporary Britain – it was a relief to return home to my creature comforts and, indeed, to my creature, Elgar. Who needs a screensaver when one has the real thing? It took me a while to adjust to the nonconformist atmosphere of my flat – no piped music, no live Bloomberg channel on my TV and, strangest of all, milk poured into tea or coffee from a jug rather than squirted over oneself from miniature plastic pots called Dairy Fayre.

Moreover, the lack of a laptop has given me a useful insight into the working methods of my illustrious predecessors, Cobbett, Daniel Defoe and George Orwell – though he probably worked on an early Amstrad, or possibly an Enigma machine. Unable as I am to check this last fact on Google, it will have to stand as inspired speculation.

Walking from the flat to my teaching engagement this evening at the Sports Centre ('Berkhamfted Fportf Fentre' as my censored caprice originally had it), I was hooted at a zebra crossing by the driver of a white van. My first thought was that it must be a plain-clothes police unit come to arrest me for contravening Mr Blair's new laws on the compulsory watching of *Celebrity Pop Idol*. Possibly, I was being picked up on suspicion of having a volume of Thomas Hardy in my loo instead of a Sudoko puzzle book as the local bylaws require. But somewhat mystifyingly the shaven-headed driver merely leant out of his window and called out, 'Have you sat down today yet, mate?' and laughed hideously. His lumpen grin lingered in my mind long after he had driven off and it was still with me as I stood to address my class ('addreff my claff' was so much more felicitous).

This evening's topic – the literary journey from Pausanius to Bill Bryson – rendered my students uncharacteristically silent. As I staggered through my opening remarks I began to panic at the lack of insulting interruptions on which I had come to depend as a way of prolonging matters until the official finish at 10 p.m. In practice, we seldom go beyond 9.30 or we'd all be asleep but by 7.04 this evening I was sweating and reaching inside my briefcase for the video of my *Tenko* episode.

'Research,' I blathered, 'is of primary importance. So . . . Er – do stop me if there's anything you want to ask me – you're very quiet this evening.'

Silence from the third agers. I stumbled on.

'For example, in my own recent work, I made it my business to find out that the ticket office at Lincoln bus station is adjacent to Bay 21. It is only when you have facts like that at your fingertips, to give the work the extra flavour of authenticity – only then can you sit down to work with confidence.'

All three of them laughed as I had never known them to do before in response to anything I said. Olive waved her arms in the air and Pearl slapped the table with her hand, rings gouging chunks out of the surface.

'It is him!' said Olive. 'He said it. I told you it was him!'

'I'm still not convinced,' said Stan.

'It *is* you, isn't it?' said Pearl.

'It's me what?' I asked.

'In that new piles commercial. Haemorrex.'

'Absolutely not.'

'Don't knock it, it's good stuff,' said Olive.

'It's one of those postmodern ads,' explained Pearl, 'where they use a bit of old film, and it's you in the old film.'

'Can you say it again, please?' asked Stan.

'Say what again?

All three then chorused the phrase with which I was to become so horribly familiar over the coming days, a phrase that will probably haunt me to my grave and beyond: 'Now I can sit down to work with confidence.' Out of innocent curiosity I did as Stan asked and repeated it, 'Now I can sit down to work with confidence.' It produced an even more voluble response than before.

'Put the TV on, Stan,' said Pearl. 'It's on Channel 5 every ten minutes, we won't have to wait long.'

Stan did as he was told while I fought to make sense of it all. 'I'm sorry to disappoint you,' I said, 'but I have never suffered from piles, never appeared in a commercial and nor do I have the slightest intention of becoming some celebrity product endorser.'

'Too late. You are one,' said Pearl.

Monday

'You've got big sideboards and an engine-driver's hat on,' said Olive, 'and you sit down in an egg-shaped chair.'

This last remark struck a chord of terrible recognition. My ex-wife had, indeed, bought me a white, egg-shaped chair from Habitat in the seventies. It was part of a spending spree that we only recently finished paying for, and it had been brought on by the prospect of a Thames TV film crew coming to the house to make a programme about my writing life. Mention of the chair, which I remember was called simply 'Ovum', stirred fond memories of the post-*Fardels* success. But as Pearl had predicted the Haemorrex commercial soon popped up on the classroom television and my salad days were held up to ridicule.

A brash seventies soundtrack played as I approached the Ovum in thick glasses and wild hair. I sat down and lit my pipe while an Austin Powers-type voice-over yelled, 'This looks like one cool cat out back – waddya say, baby?'

My 26-year-old self turned to the camera. 'Now I can sit down to work with confidence,' I said and sat in the Ovum.

'Haemorrex and Haemorrex Spray!' said the voice-over. 'Sock it to me, baby! Yeah!'

Stan flicked the remote to turn the television off. 'I had sideboards like those,' he said. 'I had the lot – dolly bird and an E-type. People thought I was Jason King. Used to turn my ankles over on those cuban heels, though. I tell you, I welcomed the advent of the deck shoe with open arms.'

'So what were you up to, love?' asked Pearl. I explained that it was a clip from an edition of the arts series, *Aquarius*, and truth to tell it was probably not the most embarrassing moment of the programme. I remember with a shudder the sequence of me getting drunk at the Chelsea Arts Club, putting on a false Frenchman's moustache and abusing Albert Finney.

'Still, at least you're back on telly again,' said Olive kindly, 'Cause it's been a while since *Tenko*, hasn't it.'

On my return home I found further evidence that the situation was getting out of control. Three messages blinked on the answering machine. The first was from Cliff.

'Just ringing to check you're on for the gig at the Lamb on Sunday. We'll get you a chair so you can – sit down to work with confidence.' At which point laughter overcame Cliff and all those in the room with him. Message number two was from Jeremy Hunter, editor of the *Old Salopian* magazine, informing me that they were holding back my piece, 'A Writer's Life', until such time as I had become a little less notorious. 'I hope,' he said, collapsing into giggles, 'I hope you're *comfortable* with that.'

Next up, Frank and Cliff singing to the tune of 'Oh When The Saints Go Marching In', 'Oh Haemorrex, that is the one!/ That Ed shoves up his bum.' This was followed by a flatulent trombone riff and more puerile laughter.

It was as sure as egg-shaped chairs is egg-shaped chairs that my fame was going to last a good deal longer than fifteen minutes. So much for Andy Warhol or whoever it was who coined this wildly inaccurate prediction – Michael Fish, probably. To make matters worse I received a late-night phone call

from Ping summoning me to the agency at my earliest convenience. Felix Jeffrey Associates must have been looking for
some time for a reason to end our relationship and here it was
at last.

Tuesday

'What's this?' I said, looking at a folded piece of paper that
Felix had placed on the desk in front of me. 'Some sort of sev-
erance agreement?'

'A cheque for ten grand,' said Ping.

'And you should prepare yourself to receive several more of
these,' said Felix.

It seems that the advertising agency who had made the piles
commercial had failed to clear permission to use the clip and
had, therefore, breached some sort of copyright law.

'When we realized it was you in that extraordinary hair and
chair,' said Felix, 'Ping went burrowing down into the cellar and
found the old Thames TV contract.'

'We had them over a barrel, yeah,' said Ping.

'By the time I finished with them,' said Felix, 'they were in
sore need of an immediate application of their own product.'

I had expected the interview to be a brief one but I never
thought it would be me who cut it short, still less that I would
do so in order to get to a bank and pay in a large cheque before
Nemesis could start to strut her customary stuff. But Felix was
having none of it.

'No, no. We'll get someone to do that for you, you're going to be far too busy,' he said.

'We gotta go through your diary,' said Ping, ''cause there's a shedload of offers coming in. There's *Pop Idol* – they want you to be one of the judges.'

'Absolutely not,' I said. 'Under no circumstances whatsoever.'

'But you can say what you like about twelve-year-olds – to an audience of millions instead of just me,' she said, which I had to concede was a legitimate point. 'That's after you've got back from series six of *I'm a Celebrity Get Me Out of Here*.'

Swapping the mean streets of Berkhamsted for the Australian jungle was one concession to popular culture too far. No amount of money was worth the stigma of being seen discussing star signs with a game show panellist. The diet of lizards and witchetty grubs would certainly be an improvement on some recent meals that Elgar and I have shared, but what if I were to be bitten by a poisonous spider? Oh, the indignity of an obituary that reads 'Piles Man Dies'.

'Don't knock it, Ed,' said Ping. 'They're talking about using another bit from your film where you say, "I can't sit down without it".'

'But I was talking about my pipe. I'm a novelist – or I was at the time.'

'Exactly, dear boy,' said Felix, 'and that's why we're going to get you on the Booker Prize panel.'

'Congratulations, Ed,' said Ping, hugging me in a way I had often imagined her doing as I returned from the stage clutching my Oscar, 'you've made it to the C-list!!'

Tuesday

Felix picked up a small handbell from the side of his desk, rang it, and called out 'Boy' in a creepy high-pitched tone, a bit like an ordained housemaster in need of toast and goodness knows what else. The door opened almost immediately and in walked my son, Jake.

'Run along and pay this cheque in, there's a good fellow. We're going to lunch for the rest of the day.'

'Yes, Sir,' said Jake. 'Oh, hi, Dad.' Then he looked at me, no doubt considering some suitably pompous reproof for his father's sellout.

'Hey,' he said. 'Respect.'

'Thank you,' I replied. 'I wish I could say the same.'

Gaining the long-overdue respect of my son by becoming a 'cult figure' was a moment of satirical irony that the Master himself, Voltaire, would have regarded as irresistibly exquisite. Though, mindful of the fact that there will be other Pings at my new publishers, casting uncomprehending eyes over these journals, I feel I had better replace 'Voltaire' with 'Stephen Fry' to be on the safe side.

The epithet 'celebrity' is one of Ed Reardon's most frequently used terms of opprobrium, or so I see from the word search function on my bright and shiny new laptop. And, while joining their deceptively welcoming ranks will bring temporary respite from duns at the door and the pleadings of a hungry cat, the nagging thought occurs: will I ever again be able to – in the buzz-phrase seemingly on the lips of every twelve-year-old in the media – 'sit down and work with confidence'?